WILD RIVER

Patricia Stinson

Copyright © 2024 **P.S. Read LLC**

All rights reserved. No part of this publication may be reproduced, distributed, or transmitted in any form or by any means, including photocopying, recording, or other electronic or mechanical methods, without the prior written permission of the publisher, except in the case of brief quotations embodied in critical reviews and certain other noncommercial uses permitted by copyright law. For permission requests, write to the publisher, addressed "Attention: Book Rights and Permission," at the address below.

Published in the United States of America

ISBN 978-1-963379-37-2 (SC)

P.S. Read LLC
222 West 6th Street
Suite 400, San Pedro, CA, 90731
https://www.patriciaStinsonwriter.com

Order Information and Rights Permission:

Quantity sales. Special discounts might be available on quantity purchases by corporations, associations, and others. For details, contact the publisher at the address above.

For Book Rights Adaptation and other Rights Permission.
Call us at toll-free 1-888-945-8513 or send us an email at
admin@stellarliterary.com.

Acknowledgments

A huge thank you to Pam Knotz for her valuable input, and the wonderful editors: Dr. Hensley and Kat Marusk.

Also, to the reader, I express my thanks for reading my work of fiction. There are some historical figures portrayed, but the dialogue they engage in is fiction.

The incident at Dragoon Springs did happen but I fictionalized it. I changed the names of all the characters. I used the incident to illustrate the reason some characters had for their prejudice against Mexicans.

Colonel Kit Carson led the army in the fight against the Navahos. I portrayed him as my research led me, but this is a work of fiction.

This book is the property of P.S.Read, LLC

To contact the author, go to pstinson23@comcast.net Her blog is http:s//gogoreadgo.blogspot.com

Website is https://www.patriciastinsonwriter.com

Praise God for all His blessings.

Wild River Journal

Chapter One

The old man crouched low in the saddle and whispered in his horse's ear, "Rascal, stay as quiet as all get-out." His body froze except for his fingers as he stroked the horse's withers. He peered under his slouched hat brim at the five riders carrying rifles, crossing the rocky terrain twenty yards from his position in the bull muhly grass and the stand of willows. Two riders had a feather twined into their hair as they rode bareback with their moccasin-clad feet dangling against the sides of their appaloosas. Three adolescent boys each rode a bay, buckskin, or a black as they followed the leader. The second rider with a feather brought up the rear. The riders passed by in single file at an easy lope.

When they were out of sight over a rise in the terrain a half-mile away, the old man straightened up. He spat out the tobacco juice locked tight in his mouth. "Them Navahos are sure riled with us settlers right now. Don't want to run into them unless I got to. They ain't wearin' war paint, so they must be out huntin' for dinner, same as me." He edged his horse out of hiding and rode toward the river. "Reckon we'll head upriver, Rascal, the opposite of where the huntin' party was goin'. Critters should be wanderin' toward water about now."

Rascal's head bobbed in time with his pace as if he nodded in agreement. Ten minutes later, they stood on land sloping into a deep gully. Water swirled down the riverbed. The rider glanced at the signs on the rocky cliffs bordering the banks; they showed the current had flowed three feet higher in recent days. Lifting the reins as he tightened his abdominal and backside muscles, he urged his mount forward. Rascal slid on his haunches as he dislodged the rocks and pebbles going down the embankment. At the bottom of the ravine, the gelding was knee-deep in water. The old man could feel the swift current's tug against the horse.

Rascal fidgeted and balked.

"There must have been a whale of a storm in the mountains to send all this water cascadin' down this way. It ain't called Wild River for nothin', that's for blame sure. We best climb out to higher ground." He neck-reined to the right and touched his right heel against the horse's belly. Rascal moved his hind legs away from the pressure and turned his head to the right. He splashed his way to the narrow, rocky bank.

"What in tarnation?" When the old man sat deep in the saddle, Rascal stopped. Taking off his worn hat, he combed his fingers through his dirty gray hair and spat tobacco juice into the dirt. "I ain't never heard a critter sound like that a'fore. It sounds sorta like a coyote pup and sorta like an injured goat." He pulled his Brunswick from its scabbard and put in the powder charge and ball.

"Well, Rascal, whatever it is, Wilma will know how to cook it for supper." He moved the reins forward as he tightened his calf and thigh muscles. The horse walked forward, picking its way through sandy soil, rocks, and cold water.

The man twisted in his saddle to listen for the wail. It pierced the air above the water's roaring torrent. "Bless my soul. I know that sound. I ain't heered it for fifty years." He jerked his head and the reins as he urged the horse upstream and around the bend. A large cottonwood tree lay across the river, partially damming the flow. The river gushed into and out of a wooden flour barrel wedged in the tree's fork as the branches lay half submerged in the stream. The screaming came from the cask.

He removed the ball from his rifle and jammed his weapon back into its scabbard. Rascal fought and balked as the man urged him to move into the middle of the torrent. The man sucked in air as the cold water flowed over his boot tops. Rascal's hindquarters rippled as he switched his weight back and forth, fighting the old man's commands. In desperation, the rider edged the horse back to the narrow, rocky, flat riverbank. He uncoiled his lariat, tied one end to his waist and one to the saddle horn. Upon dismounting, he stood knee-deep in water. He tied the reins to tree roots. Holding onto the tree trunk, he took out his Bowie knife.

A grunt of air forced its way out of his lungs as he sank the blade deep into the bark. He moved along the cottonwood, holding the knife handle with one hand and tree branches with the other. The water swirled around his thighs. He sawed the knife back and forth until it released its hold on the tree, and he stabbed it again into the trunk farther out in the river's flow. The numbing water came up to his chest as he neared the fork in the tree at the middle of the turbulent river. He felt the water yank at his feet, trying to pull them out from under him. He clung to the knife and, heaving his shoulders up, grabbed a tree branch sticking up on the top. His muscles straining and his lungs gasping, he pulled his body onto the trunk. He rested for a moment, filling his lungs with air. Swinging a leg over, he straddled the tree as he scooted up to the flour barrel. He pushed aside the wet branches and leaves.

"Tarnation, Lord, what have you gone and done?" Wrapped in a water-soaked quilt, a baby stared up at him. A scream burst from gaping lips. The water swirled through the barrel, and a trickle went into the infant's mouth.

The old man's work-hardened hands pulled and snapped the smaller branches where they held the cask in the tree limbs' grip. Soon blood ran from his hands and mixed into the icy river as the branches tore at his knuckles and palms. Taking his knife, he hacked at a thick, stubborn limb. The wood finally dislodged, and he yanked the barrel-shaped cradle from the tree. The wood was splintered, but it held together. Water poured out of the cradle as he lifted it from the icy stream. He hefted it to his shoulders and looped his rope around it to hold it in place. He inched down the tree as far as he could; then, balancing the cradle, he edged back into the water. Using the lariat, he pulled the cask and himself to the bank. The baby wailed.

Rascal shied away from the noisy object. The man put the cradle down on the ground. Untying the reins, he sidled up to his horse, talking to him in soft tones. He reached for the saddle horn and mounted, surprising himself with his agility and speed. He bent down and pulled up the waterlogged barrel. When he urged his horse back up the river, Rascal clambered up a sloping bank.

On the ravine's rim, the man wiped water from his face with his soggy, waist-length, gray beard as he slumped in the saddle and looked at the howling infant. "Don't know why you're alive. You were close to drowning, and would have, too, if I hadn't come along. Didn't aim to come this far, but I sighted the Navahos' hunting party."

The old man smiled, showing brown teeth and tobacco juice saliva. "Didn't know'd holdin' a babe was so cheerful-like. Last time I held a little one was when my fifth brother was born. Or was I the fifth and him the sixth?" He looked over the terrain, wary of seeing the hunting party returning to investigate the cause of the noise. "It was a long time ago, so I don't 'member it good. Wonder if any of them are still living, or my two sisters, for that matter. From all the racket you be makin', you are going to be one ornery cuss.

"Rascal, you gettin' as tired as I am with this bellowin'? Take us home 'fore unwanted visitors show up." He turned the horse in the direction of his ranch, bent his right knee, and drew his leg up and back until the heel of his boot touched the horse's side. It moved forward into a canter. The man lowered his leg and tightened his calf muscles. Rascal entered into a gallop. When the old man leaned forward in the stirrups, keeping his heels down, the horse ran flat-out.

❈ ❈ ❈

A gray-haired woman in an ankle-length, faded, tattered dress put down two buckets of whiskey in the ranch yard. She moved the rifle she carried under one arm up to her face and squinted as she sighted it toward the galloping horse's hoof beats. She lowered the barrel when she saw Rascal run through the fence gate and stop at the barn. Its sides heaved and sweat streaked its hide.

Wilma charged up to the rider, yelling, "Eli, what's the matter? Did you run into Indians? You know better than to run a horse like that over rough ground. And what's all that caterwaulin'?"

"It's this here." Eli handed the cradle to his wife. "Wilma, we got us a baby."

"Consarn, it is! Where did you git it?"

"Down at Wild River. Hung up in a tree washed down from someplace up stream."

The woman put the cradle on the ground as Eli dismounted. She picked up the baby and pulled off the wet blanket. "It's a boy. Wonder where his folks are? He sure is noisy. What are we goin' to do with it?"

"Thought you'd know. You're a woman."

"I ain't never had a baby. You know that. Just cuz I'm a woman don't mean I know'd about them. They're a whole different critter than grown folks." Her eyes glowed with warmth as she watched the screaming child. "We got to get help. Hitch up the wagon. We need to go to town." As she cradled the child, a smile spread over her wrinkled face and tears filled her sparkling eyes. "I ain't held a baby in seventy years or more." A gentle sigh escaped her lips.

❈ ❈ ❈

"Hortensia, come quick. I think the devil is riding into town!" a man's voice yelled into the wood-frame house.

A middle-aged woman opened the door and stepped onto a board porch. She could see the entire town from the side porch, as the house was on a small rise on the only street. At the other end was a wooden barn that functioned as the livery and blacksmith. Between the two ends of the road was the wood-frame saloon, a tent for the general store, and another tent almost attached to the first, with a sign saying, "Baths, Ten Cents for a Bucket of Hot Water, Soap Extra", run by the general store owner. Next to the bath tent was a small tent stretched over a wood-frame gunsmith shop, another building that served as a stage depot, freight office, and post office--except there was seldom any mail sent from or brought to the town followed by a three-sided wheelwright shop with a burlap canvas roof next to a tanner's store. The tanner did cobbling and harness making. His shop had a wood frame with tanned hides for the walls and roof. Between the stores were several tents used for the town residents' accommodations. A tinker's wagon that came and went on a circuit route was now behind the saloon, as the owner was "socializing."

"Clem, what's happening?" Hortensia asked her husband.

He grabbed her hand, and they ran down the steps and followed the dirt road to the middle of town.

Dirt, whipped up by thundering horses' hooves and careening wagon wheels, swirled in mini tornadoes, adding to the dust devils of sand the dry wind pulled into town. Eli stood in the wagon seat, his hat dangling around his neck by its chin strap, his waist-length beard and his hair blowing wildly as he pulled back on the reins to stop the racing horses. Wilma bounced on the seat, holding the crying baby with one hand and the wagon seat with the other. The wagon jolted to a halt in front of the saloon.

Hortensia, Clement, and the town's other residents, including the saloon owner Buster Buttwill, the general store proprietor and his wife John and Sabilla Platt, the livery owner Sam and his five- year-old son Kenny, were drawn to the commotion. They gathered around Eli and Wilma. The town folks yelled and jabbered above the baby's screams as the horses tossed their heads, pawed the ground, and snorted.

Eli shouted, "Did anyone lose a baby? I found a baby!"

"Where? Eli, where?" Voices mingled and shouted.

"Snagged in a tree in Wild River."

"I haven't heard of a baby around here. It must be from travelers, but none been by here in a month or more," Clement said.

"Then somebody tell us how to care for it." Eli's wide eyes scanned the gathering.

"You can't keep it," Sabilla, the wife of the general store and bathhouse owner, said. She looked to her husband for agreement. He nodded his head while his eyes stared in disbelief and his jaw hung open.

Eli dropped the reins. One hand took his Bowie knife, and one hand went to his pistol. "It belongs to Wilma and me. Nobody claims it as theirs, so it belongs to us. It's from the Lord. A blessing from God Almighty, and we ain't about to tell him no. Just like Moses, the child was drawn from the river." Eli's defiant voice showed his determination.

Wilma's weathered, wrinkled face smiled at her husband. The glow in her eyes deepened.

"You gonna call it Moses?" the saloon owner asked in a mocking tone.

"Of course not, Buttwill. Wouldn't be proper, as he weren't found in Pharaoh's land. No, the boy's name will be Jason, after Wilma's pa, if she likes." Eli turned to his wife.

Wilma grinned, showing tobacco juice and brown teeth. "That would be right fine. My pa was a good man back in the Ozarks. He took Eli in when he needed a home, and he gave him my hand in marriage when I was thirteen. He taught us good whiskey-making'. Jason it is. Jason Wilcox."

"Eli, how are you and Wilma going to protect the little one from a Navaho raid? You're so far from town, we wouldn't know'd if you be in trouble." John Platt spoke up after his wife nudged him in the ribs.

"Me and Wilma been defendin' our place from Navahos, Apaches, and thieving Mexs most of our lives. Reckon it's you folks in this bitty town of yours without a good shot amongst youse that need to look out more than Wilma and me." Eli spat tobacco juice.

"The army comes by once in a while. This is 1849, you know. Colonel John Pennington is trying to get the Navaho head men to sign a peace agreement. He even got old Nabona to agree to meet with him next month or so. The Navaho respect the old chief. If he signs, they'll abide by it. The whole New Mexico Territory will be safer after that, that be darn sure," Buster Buttwill stated as he removed his hat and wiped his forehead with his shirt sleeve. "This town will grow, you watch and see. This will be a good place to raise a babe."

"I don't care what year it be or who be Nabona or Pennington. The treaty ain't signed yet, and even if it were, I ain't trustin' no Indian while he lives. Wilma and me can handle them all. The boy belongs to us." Eli stood straight and puffed out his chest as he glared at the growing crowd. "Now, with that settled, Wilma, you go talk with the ladies to see what needs to be done while I talk to the gents. We're going to put in wood flooring in our digs. My boy isn't going to be crawling in the dirt. And while we're at it, a one-room shack ain't good enough. We're going to add two more rooms, one for the boy and one for us."

"Eli, I ain't never had a wood floor or more than a one-room house."

"Can't see why we can't have it. We're as good as most folks." Hortensia reached up and took the baby while Wilma climbed down from the wagon seat. The men gathered around and made plans with Eli to redesign the house.

Wilma took the infant from Hortensia. "Hortensia, Sabilla, you got to teach me what to do to feed and care for this young'un." The ladies walked off to the tent where Sabilla and her husband sold dry goods.

Hours later, Clem and Hortensia sat on their porch as they watched Eli drive the wagon with his new family back to their ranch. "I feel right sorry for that baby, being raised by them two old-timers. Bet they're nigh on to eighty. I don't see how the mite will survive. But we would have had to kill both Wilma and Eli to get that little one away from them." Clem tapped tobacco into his pipe.

"I'm glad we lent them our milk cow. We have an excuse to go to their place to get butter and check on things. But, Lord, have mercy on that child." Hortensia shook her head.

"Amen to that." Clement lit his pipe.

Chapter Two

"Abigail. Abigail, come in here, and bring the eggs." A woman in her thirties brushed a strand of hair back into her snood as she stood in the small kitchen, looking out the back door. Closing the door, she turned and picked up the butter mold from the cupboard.

A girl in pigtails and a flushed face dashed through the door to set a basket of eggs on the kitchen table. "Here they are, ma. Seven." Ma held the mold as she put her hands on her hips. "Abigail, you ran into the house, and your face is red. Have you been running outside? How many times do I have to tell you not to run? Young ladies do not run. Do you hear me? And what took you so long to gather a few eggs? Have you been playing and wasting time again?"

"Ma, I saw the prettiest butterfly, and I just had to chase after it. I wanted to bring it in to show it to you. But I couldn't catch it." The girl sighed as she looked down at the eggs.

"Did you want to kill it?"

"No, of course not. I just wanted to catch it."

Ma scraped butter from the churn, put it on the table, scooped salt into it, and worked it with her hands until it was the right consistency. She patted it into a roll. "If you touch a butterfly's wings, it will die. God made them beautiful for us to look at, not kill."

"Then I'm glad I didn't catch it."

"Candle the eggs to be sure they are fresh, and mind you, don't hold the egg too close to the flame. We're going into town, and we can see if Mrs. Harper at the mercantile wants to buy our eggs so she can sell them, but having soot-stained shells brings down the price. And hurry. I'm going to the hotel stable to bring your father his lunch." Ma wiped her buttery hands with a smile of satisfaction.

"How come Pa is working there?" Abigail leaned against the table as she stood on one leg and swung the other back and forth, brushing her bare feet against the floor.

"This part of Minnesota was in a drought last year so the crops weren't good, and so far this year looks bad. He took this job to tide us over. Still, 1858 is going to be a good year for us. We got statehood. That is bound to be good for everyone." Ma's smile widened as she studied the three rolls of butter on the table.

"Is Jack coming, too?"

"No, your brother has his chores to do as well as some of your father's. Now, scat, and candle the eggs."

"Why are you making so much butter? We won't use all that this winter, will we?"

"Abigail, honestly, the questions you think up when I'm busy. Here, now that the butter is salted and, in a roll, lift the lid to that cask by the pie safe." Ma's hand indicated the cupboard. "And bring me the jug of brine. It's by the stove. Be careful. The stove is hot."

Abigail fetched the brine and lifted the lid to the barrel as her mother put the fresh rolls on top of the other layers of butter. The eight-year-old girl handed the jug to her mother and watched as she poured the brine over the rolls until they were covered. After her mother weighted the butter down so it could not float up, Abigail placed the lid on the cask.

"When the barrel is full, your father will seal it tight, and the butter will keep as fresh as the day it was made. Then, when winter comes and the cows don't give milk and we can't make butter, we will have more than enough for ourselves and plenty to sell. When butter is scarce, it fetches a good price." The woman put her hands on her hips and considered Abigail. "You look good enough to go to town. I'm going to clean up the churn and freshen myself up a bit. And by then, young lady, those eggs should be clean and candled and put into the basket. You hear me?"

"Yes Ma." Abigail picked up the basket. "Do I need to wear shoes to go into town?"

"No. Just watch where you step. I don't want you smelling of horse manure while we are in the store."

"Thanks, Ma." She shoved open the kitchen door and ran through it toward the well. The door fell back with a bang.

"Abigail Lester! How many times have you been told not to run, especially in the house? Never in the house!"

Chapter Three

"Hey, Pa. Someone's ridin' up." Jason ran to the barn.

Eli put down the feed sack and picked up his Brunswick musket before hurrying to the barn door. "Jase, you go back to the house. Tell your ma, if 'en she don't know already, and stay there with her."

"It's a white man, Pa."

"Don't make no difference. He's a stranger. Now, git, and do as you're told."

The boy ran as fast as his short legs could move. He bounded up onto a small wooden porch with a sagging roof and charged through the door.

"I see'd him, boy," Wilma greeted Jason as he entered the door. "You get the pistol by my bed. I'll cover your pa from here with my rifle. You use the pistol if needed." She closed the inside shutter and pointed her rifle out a small hole cut into the wood, sighting down the Brunswick barrel.

Jase entered the bedroom and fetched the single-shot pistol on the floor by his parents' bed. He pointed the muzzle down as he entered the main room.

"Boy, you cover the other window gun hole. I got this here one. See, Jase. It were smart of your pa and me not to waste money buying fan-dangled glass panes for windows." The powder horn, a metal ball, and a grease patch lay on the table within arm's reach.

Jason dragged a backless four-legged chair to the window on the other side of the door. He knelt on it and sighted the pistol through the gun port.

"You skeered, boy?"

Jason kept his eyes on his pa and the stranger. "No, Ma. The fella looks to have a reaping rifle, but it's in its scabbard, and the six-shooter is in his holster. We got single-shot muskets and pistols, but there be three of us to his one. Besides, he ain't no Injun or thieving Mex. And you're here, and Pa's here."

Wilma's tobacco-stained lips curved up to smile at Jason. "Right proud of you, son."

Jason squared his shoulders. "You skeered, Ma?"

"No need to be. You're here, and so is your pa." Jason also smiled.

Eli walked toward the rider coming in the gate. The horse trotted to the cabin porch, and the rider held his hands high, away from his weapons.

"Howdy. I'm lookin for an Eli Wilcox. I was told he lived about here."

"That be me. You want to buy a jug?"

"No. I'm your brother, Charlie Wilcox--or might be, that is. Was your pa Gar Wilcox, and was your ma Ebba?"

"Yup. That be my kin. But I don't recollect no brother named Charlie."

"I was born after you left home. Least, so I'm told."

"Might as well get down and rest a bit on the porch. Wilma, Jase, it be all right. Come out and meet some likely kin and bring a jug of our best."

Charlie Wilcox tied his horse by the water trough under the shade of the lone tree in the yard before joining the other Wilcox family members.

Wilma and Jason came out of the cabin and stood in the shade of the porch roof.

"This be Wilma and our boy, Jason. This here fella says he be my brother, Charlie." Eli put his rifle down on the porch as he said, "Sit." Charlie stood on the step, took off his Stetson, and wiped his forehead with a red bandana. He looked at Jason. "No disrespect, brother and sister, but you seem a bit old to have a boy so young. Is he your grandson?"

"Nope. He's our boy. We found him in a river just like Moses was found. He is ours, finders keepers. Been so about eight or nine years, do you think, Wilma?"

"Must be. He can read and write, too. A lady in Wild River, name of Hortensia Pluckhaus, taught him real good. He's a smart one, he is. Right proud of him." Wilma laid her boney, callused hand in a caress on Jase's head.

Jason sat quietly at the edge of the adults, staring at the stranger.

"Now, you say you be my brother, Charlie Wilcox. Talk about that."

"Pa talked about you, seeing as how you left home before I was born," Charlie said as he sat on the porch's top step.

"Yeah, Ma had eight to look after, so I left--oh, maybe I was about twelve, or thirteen and went to the valley where Wilma's family lived. Worked for them 'til Wilma and I married and set out on our own."

All but Jase passed the jug as they talked.

"Ma had eight more kids after you left. Some lived. I was next to the last. I tell folks I'm fifty-four, but Ma couldn't keep track of all the birthdates, so I may be older."

"Yeah, for me, too. I 'spect she and Pa are dead."

"Yup. Ma died when I was a young'un. Pa lived a couple years longer. But, they had time to teach those of us that lived how to survive."

"Yeah, Pa was a ring-tailed roarer, for sure. He could out-fight, out- kick, out-bite, out-scratch, out-throttle, and out-gouge anyone who had the gall to take him on."

Charlie laughed. "You're right about that. He was a good provider of meat for the family, too. Course, most men were, with the game so plentiful, but it ain't that way now. Times have changed."

"That's for sure. Back home, Indians were shot anytime the folks saw one. Indians were there for the killin'. Things are changing out here. Now, we're 'posed to live in peace with them and kill them only when we got to. Pa and his time were right, but today's folk are soft." Jason listened to the grownups talking as he stared at his new Uncle Charlie. He picked up a piece of wood lying in the dirt, took out his knife from the sheath attached to his belt, and began whittling. The boy hoped keeping his hands busy would prevent him from interrupting the elders' talking. When he stayed with Hortensia and Clement and they taught him to read and write, they used the Bible and a McGuffy Reader. He had learned all the sayings, including,

"Children should be seen but not heard." Hortensia said that meant children should be quiet when grown folks were talkin', so he whittled and listened.

Charlie handed the jug to Eli.

"Now, tell us what you're doing." Eli moved his tobacco chaw into his left cheek and took a big swig before he handed the jug to Wilma.

"I'm working for the Overland Stage Company. They bought out the Jackass Company and are setting up stage and freight routes. The stations will be about twenty miles apart, and I'm in the crew that will be rebuilding an abandoned Jackass place at Sara Flats."

"That's about sixty miles from here, near the Apache Stronghold," said Eli.

"Yup. We got a crew of five whites and three Mexicans to get the Dragoon Springs station up and running by mid-September. The boss man is Mervale Cooper."

"You watch out for the Apaches, them being close to the station, and those Mexs working for you. You know what they did at the Alamo and Goliad," warned Eli. "You can't trust the lot of them, that's for dang sure."

"The Mexs on the crew are okay, I reckon. They been pullin' their weight and not causing trouble. Anyway, I talked to the boss man and asked if I could come ahead and see if I could look up my brother, as I heered you'd moved out this way."

"Right glad you did. Can you stay for a while?"

"Reckon I can spend a day, and then I'll meet up with the crew just before they get to the station."

"Humdinger! Wilma, we got to fix a feast tonight. We got kin!"

Chapter Four

T he thin, round-shouldered woman sat down at the wood plank table near the lit kerosene lamp. "Boys, you got your nightshirts on?" Two voices sounded from a small room off the kitchen: "Yes, Ma."

"Then come here. I'll read the letter I wrote to my sister, your Aunt Alvina, and her family in Minnesota."

"Martha, the boys need to get to bed. We got plenty of work to do tomorrow," said the lanky man who sat across from his wife, whittling on a short piece of oak, fashioning it into a spigot for a barrel bung.

Two boys walked past their father in their bare feet and went to the table. They swung their legs over the bench next to their mother.

"Please, Lemuel? It won't take long, and they should know about their family."

"Why? It ain't your kin's business to know about us. I don't see why the boys need to know about people in Minnesota when we're in New Mexico Territory. It ain't likely they'll ever meet. I reckon you've wasted good money writin' all them letters. Reckon it's been four or five letters in the past twelve years."

"Please, Lem? They write back, and it helps me. It gives me joy to hear from my family."

"Guess I better agree to it or you'll go around mopin' for days. Be quick about your readin', and you boys better get up first time you're called in the mornin'."

The two boys glanced at their father and looked down as they answered in unison, "Yes, Pa."

Martha hugged the boys. "Now, I know you ain't never seen your Aunt Alvina as your pa and I came to Wild River the year we were married, and…." She stopped for a moment and smiled, remembering. "your aunt and uncle married the same day your pa and me were married. A double wedding! Do you remember my talking about it?"

"Yes, Ma."

"Silas, you were born two years after their first child, Jack, was born, but in the same year their daughter, Abigail, was born. So you are both eight years old, and she is your cousin."

Silas snuggled closer to his mother. "Uh-huh."

"What about me, Ma?" piped up the younger boy.

"Otis, you are seven, so you are one year younger than your cousin Abigail and three years younger than Jack." She hugged him.

"Hurry up with your readin', Martha."

"Yes, Lemuel." Martha wiped the ink pen nib on the ink bottle's edge. She put down her pen before capping the ink bottle with a small cork. Picking up the paper, she cleared her throat and read, "Dear Sister Alvina and Brother-in-Law John, we are doing fine here and hope the same for you in this year of our Lord eighteen fifty-eight." Martha stopped reading and nodded at the boys before she continued.

"As I wrote before, Lemuel and I lived in our wagon and a tent for ten years as he worked on building our fine barn and starting our herd of mules and horses. We are raising the best mules in the whole Territory. Everyone says so. They are good for plowing, hauling, and wagon-pulling, and not only good for farm work in general but also ranchers and the army buy from Lemuel."

Martha glanced at her husband and raised her voice a notch to be sure he heard.

"Lemuel is a hard worker and provides for his family. These last three years he has built us a fine wood-frame house to live in, with a wood floor. I have a real kitchen with a cook stove, and near it I put the pie safe Pa made for me as a wedding gift. I'm sure you enjoy the one he gave you. I often look at it, and it brings back so many happy memories of our ma and pa.

"Otis, my youngest, as you remember, and Silas have their very own beds, bunk beds, in their own room next to the main bedroom. Our main room is joined with the kitchen, of course. And we now have actual glass window panes in this room and the kitchen. It is so nice to be able to see outside in the day and to let in the glorious light. We have strong wooden shutters to cover the glass in bad weather or if Indians, such as the Navaho, are about, or the many Mexican thieves that cross the border on raiding sprees. I don't know if you heard back in Minnesota about Dragoon Springs here in the New Mexico Territory, where three Mexicans attacked and killed Overland Stage workers without provocation last year. Lemuel says Mexicans and Indians can't be trusted. So, he taught the boys and me to be good shots with a rifle if the need arises. Lemuel is a good husband, father, and provider." Martha glanced at Lemuel for a moment as he sat at the head of the table. He did not look at her. His face reflected his concentration on carving a spigot. He gave no sign of hearing his wife's praises.

"The town of Wild River is growing a bit. More tent stores are becoming wood buildings. There is even talk of having a boardwalk someday and perhaps a hotel.

"I know it would be difficult for you to leave your farm to come for a visit, but if ever you can come, please consider you are welcome. I would love to see all of you, and it would be great if the cousins could meet."

"Humph. How can we do our ranch work if we have to loll around with visiting kin and farmers to boot?" Lemuel scowled at his wife.

"I don't expect they will ever come, Lem. They can't leave their farm no more than we can leave the ranch, but it's polite to invite them just the same."

"Humph! That letter is gittin' too long. Finish up."

"That's it. Except the last part, 'I put down this pen with sincere respect and affection. Your sister, Martha.'"

"Now, boys, off to bed, and sleep tight. Give me a kiss before you go."

The two boys kissed their mother on her cheek and scurried to their room and closed the door without a glance at their father.

Chapter Five

"Abigail, Jack, come quick. Your father brought home a letter from your aunt Martha. I'm going to read it." Mrs. Lester shouted out the front door to her daughter swinging on the gate and to Jack pumping water at the well. She entered the kitchen and sat at the table next to her husband.

Mr. Lester sat on the straight-back chair and stretched his legs out next to the table and cook stove. He smiled at his wife when he saw her hands shaking with excitement as she held the letter and opened it with care so it wouldn't tear when she broke the seal.

Abigail banged open the front door and dashed into the kitchen. Both her father and mother said, "Abigail"

Before they could finish, their daughter caught her bare toe against her father's foot. She sprawled forward, catching her other foot in the hem of her dress. She raised her arms and hit the pan of boiling water on the stove, sending it down on her while she slid against the hot side of the stove.

Her parents gasped and jumped up, shouting, "Abigail!"

Abigail did not hear their voices. Her screams of pain pierced the air. Her brain, her body, knew nothing but searing, scorching, indescribable pain.

❊ ❊ ❊

The doctor straightened up after bending over Abigail, who lay on her left side on her parents' bed. He faced Mr. and Mrs. Lester. "I must tell you, this is the worst case of burns I have ever seen."

"Will she be all right? Will she live?" Mr. Lester had his arm around his wife to give her support as they stood next to the bed. Tears were running down both faces. Mrs. Lester was sobbing.

"I can't say for sure. I really don't know. It's a blessing she is unconscious. When she wakes, give her a few drops of laudanum. But only when the pain is unbearable. Fortunately, the burns are on one side of her body. She will be able to lie on the other side." He sighed as he said, "It will take a long time for her to heal, if she does. I will need to come at least twice a day to apply equal parts of limewater, olive oil, and glycerin on lint. In some areas that aren't as bad, I'll use lint with clean tar."

"Come as much as you need to. Do whatever you need to do. We will pay you whatever is needed," Mr. Lester choked out.

"If the healing progresses, you will be able to do most of the care she will need. One thing you must do, when the wounds are not so deep, is to purify hog's lard. Boil the lard in water until the salt and impurities settle, then set it aside and cool until the lard solidifies and floats. Put it in a bowl and set the bowl in hot water. Keep the water hot until all the water in the lard has evaporated. This won't be needed, I would judge, for several days, perhaps even weeks." He shook his head. "She will have horrible scars for the rest of her life. I'm so very sorry."

Abigail's parents broke down into deep sobs as they exited the room, leaving their comatose child lying naked from the waist up on the double bed.

Chapter Six

"**M**other, I finished stacking the wood in the wood box," Edmund spoke up as he entered the back door.

"Edmund Proft, you know I just washed the floor. You go right back out and take off your boots." "Oh, Mother."

"You heard me, young man. You are eight years old and should be able to figure out you can't wear your boots in the house when I've been on my hands and knees with a scrub brush and a bucket of water. Now, scat and do as you're told. And think next time."

"Yes, Mother." Edmund stood on the plank stoop and unlaced his shoestrings, then used a boot jack to pull off each boot. He went back into the house and sat on a kitchen chair at the polished, round, worn, oak table with a red-and-white checkered cloth.

"Sorry, Mother." Edmund shuffled his stocking feet back and forth on the clean floor.

"That's fine, son. Have a thick slice of the bread I baked yesterday. Put some jelly on it and get a glass of milk." She placed the china plate and glass on the table and turned back to the cook stove. "I'm making Lancashire pie for supper from the leftovers of last night's beef."

"I love your crabapple jelly, Mother. Guess what? In school, my teacher was telling the class about the Alamo. I raised my hand and said you and father were there."

Cecilia, using a thick cloth, picked up a pan of hot water as her son said the word Alamo. Her back stiffened, and her hand slipped until it touched the hot handle. She dropped the pan on the stove and gasped in pain.

"Mother, what happened?"

"I just burned my hand a bit, son. Fetch the jar of goose grease for me, will you?"

"Sure." Edmund went to the shelf and returned to the table with the jar. His mother sat down. Edmund removed the lid and massaged some grease on her fingers.

"That is much better. I'll tie a cloth strip around it, and it will be fine."

"You're sure? It looks red."

"Yes, son. I mixed the goose grease with butter churned in May, so it will be just fine."

"Why does it have to be May butter?"

Maybe this will distract him, and he will forget about the Alamo.

"I don't really know. I guess the grass in May is fresh and good for the cow, which then gives its best cream that we churn into butter. Here, put the jar back on the shelf, and finish your bread. I'll peel the potatoes at the table."

"Will you tell me about the Alamo, Mother, while you're peeling?"

Cecilia sighed. "Your father and I weren't at the Alamo, son. We were about thirty miles from it when it fell to Santa Anna. Your father wanted to start a freight line from New Orleans, Louisiana, to various areas in Texas. Here, you grind these raw potatoes while I rest my hand for a bit."

Edmund stood and turned the wheel as he fed the grinder. "Mother, you talk better than my reading a history book. Tell me about you and Father in Texas."

She allowed her back to rest against the straight-back chair. Her lower lip trembled.

"Mother, are you crying" Is it your burned hand? Should I go and get Father?

She wiped her eyes on the hem of her apron. "No, Edmund. I don't need your father. My hand smarts a bit. That's all. Your father will be home soon, and I need to finish supper. Tonight, he can tell you the story. Run along to your room and memorize your Bible verse for church."

✻ ✻ ✻

After supper, Michael sent Edmund to get his pipe and tobacco. When Edmund was out of earshot, Michael whispered to Cecilia, "What did you tell Him?"

"Nothing, really. You should tell him, only leave out the worst part. He doesn't need to know everything, does he?" Cecilia blinked away tears that were forming in her eyes, threatening to spill out.

"Don't tell him about," she took a sobbing breath, "what we lost." She put her hand on Michael's. "And what we found."

"Leave it to me. A boy wants adventure. I'll tell him enough so he will think it was exciting, like in a dime novel, and that everything turns out happy at the end."

Michael gave his wife a squeeze as Edmund entered with the pipe and tobacco.

Cecilia sat in her rocker and picked up her knitting needles and yarn. Michael sat by the small table in the sitting room. Edmund sat at his father's feet, eager to hear a story about the wild west.

"Hurry, Father. Tell me about you and Ma in Texas."

Michael smiled and tapped his tobacco in his pipe. He got up and took a piece of kindling from the stove, put it in the flames, and lit his pipe. Tossing the wood into the fire, he sat down at the table.

"It was March in 1836, and a whole world away from here. I wanted to start a freight business in Texas to bring out goods to the early settlers. Your mother and I were walking by our ox cart in east Texas when "

Cecilia listened to her husband tell their story as if it were an exciting adventure. She rocked and automatically knitted as her mind traveled back to her reality. Everything played out as if it happened to other people, young people named Michael and Cecilia

※ ※ ※

The iron-rimmed ox-cart wheels creaked as they ground over the sand and dirt. Scrub grass dotted the dry land as the sun beat down. A young woman brushed away a fly buzzing about her. She smeared the wet charcoal painted around her eyes and on her nose to cut down the glare of the sun, even though her face was shaded by a wide-brimmed hat. She stopped walking by the oxen's heads and pointed to a dune in the distance.

"Michael, what is jerking over there?"

Michael shaded his charcoal-blacked eyes with his hand and squinted. "Looks like someone in trouble. You stay here unless I call you over. Keep your rifle handy." Squaring his shoulders and holding his Baker musket at the ready, his lean six-foot frame approached the distant object. As he neared it, he heard the huff of pain escape the animal's nostrils. He raised his rifle.

The crack shattered the hot air, causing Cecilia to jump. He motioned for his wife to come closer. She led the oxen to Michael and saw a horse, its head lying in a small pool of blood, with an obviously shattered leg. A man pinned under the animal's heavy body gasped for air. Michael got the canteen from the wagon and gave him a drink.

"*Gracias, Señor, gracias.*"

Michael fastened a rope around the dead horse's front legs and tied the other end around the oxen yoke. He led them forward, and they pulled the still beast off the man as he screamed in pain.

Cecilia walked on the wagon's far side.

The Mexican lay quiet, his eyes closed to the sun, his face sunburned and blistering.

Michael checked the man's legs and said, "I don't think they're broken. Can you stand?"

"I don't know. I have been under the horse for over a day. I cannot feel my legs. My sombrero blew away. Do you see it?"

"I do. "Cecilia ran to the dune, and picked it up, and brought it to him.

Michael helped the Mexican man up and held him as they stumbled to the back end of the cart.

"*Gracias, Señor and Señora.*" The Mexican sat on the flat bed of the wagon and put his hat on.

"My name is Michael Proft, and this is my wife, Cecilia."

"I'm Humberto Herrera. I was on my way to the Alamo mission when my horse caught his leg in a hole, and it broke yesterday afternoon. My caballo suffered, but I could not reach my gun. I thank you for putting him out of his misery."

"It had to be. I'll get your saddle and things off it, and you can ride in the back of the cart. We're heading to a place near Gonzales to build a home and start a business. You're welcome to come with us that far."

"That sounds good. Gonzales is not far from the Alamo. I will be fine once I can feel my legs and walk. To repay you, I will help you build your house. By that time, I should be able to move easily, and I will go on to the Alamo."

Chapter Seven

Days later, Michael and Humberto were building their home. The land was hard and gritty. Coarse bull muhly grass covered the soil, and quaking aspens, arroyo willows, and Freemont cottonwoods were scattered about.

"Michael, we are doing a splendid job. Our house will be so wonderful when it's finished." Cecilia stood by what would be the front doorway and looked in.

Michael stood from where he had knelt by the second row of an adobe brick wall. "I couldn't have done it without Humberto working and showing me every step. It will be weeks before we're finished, as it takes time for the bricks to dry in the sun, but we will get there. Right, Humberto?"

"*Si.* It will take more time than most adobe houses, as your husband is a smart man, *Señora.* He wants the house to last a long time, so we hauled plenty of stone for the foundation. Later, we will put a coat of adobe on the foundation and first row of bricks, so when the rains come, the water in the ground will not cause the lower layers of adobe to fall apart. Not everyone does that, and then in a few years the foundation starts to crumble. *Si,* your husband thinks ahead and works hard. Much hard work to haul stones and make adobe clay bricks. Much hard." Humberto turned back to placing another layer of brick as he started the third row.

"I'm making corn cakes, even though I don't have an oven. I hope they will turn out tasty anyway." She went to the campfire, where she put two cups of cornmeal in the hot water and stirred it until the grains were swollen. As it was cooling, she took out the last two eggs from the cask of preserving brine.

She combined the egg yolks with water, then stirred them into the corn mush. She added melted fat from the last animal kill. With a wooden spoon, she whipped the egg whites until stiff and folded them into the batter. Placing an iron spider on the low campfire, she poured a spoonful on the hot griddle. *Sure wish I had an oven, as this should be baked. Maybe by the time the little one comes we will have one.* She smiled as she scooped out each little fried cake when it turned brown. When the batter bowl was empty, she scooped the cakes onto tin plates and brought them to the men.

"Time to eat." She set two plates down on a wood bench and sat with her plate on a small pile of dried bricks.

The men stopped and washed their hands in a bucket of water, then dried them on their shirt tails. They ate with their fingers.

"*Señora*, very good."

"You think that because you are hungry. They really aren't so good." She blushed with the flattery.

Michael smacked his lips as he said, "The best corn cakes ever. You won't need an adobe oven. You can cook over a fire all the time." He grinned at his wife with a mischievous twinkle in his eye.

"Michael Proft, if I don't get an oven after the house is built, all you will get is beans, beans, and more beans." She pretended to pout but couldn't help ending her scold with a grin back at him.

Humberto pointed, warning, "*Señor*, rider is coming, coming fast." Michael and Cecelia looked in the direction Humberto indicated. Michael stood and picked up his rifle as he took a few steps forward. The rider reined in two yards from the campsite. "Good day. My name is William Livergood. Folks around here call me Red." William removed his Stetson, and his carrot-colored hair blew in the breeze. "All right if I come in closer?"

"Come ahead. We're the Profts, and this here friend is Humberto Herrera."

"Yeah, I heard about you folks moving here. I live near Gonzales, too, only a bit north. I came to tell you two things. First, two men, a Mr. Archibald Smothers and a Mr. Nunnelley, were out cutting trees and making boards when they were ambushed and killed by Comanches. Watch out for those raiders."

Cecilia moved closer to Michael.

"I thank you for coming with the news. We sure appreciate it," Michael said.

"The bad news ain't done yet, folks. You all hear about the Alamo?"

"We heard men were gathering there to fight a general called Santa Anna. Haven't heard anything since."

"Santa Anna has an army of a thousand or more and has our men trapped in the Alamo. Colonel Travis sent word out that he needs help. He's only got about two hundred men."

"Two hundred against a thousand?" Cecilia asked.

"Yes, ma'am, or so I heered. Sorry I speak so graphic-like, ma'am, but all the settlers near Gonzales are asked to come into town right away. Colonel Fannin is at Goliad with the militia and wants more men to join so they can march to the Alamo and help. Folks are to head into Gonzales to receive more information. The menfolk are needed. You comin'?"

"I'll be there," Humberto said.

"I'll be there, and I'll bring my wife. I'm not leaving her out here, with the Comanches on the prowl. We'll come in soon as we can."

Red replaced his wide-brimmed hat, grinned, reined his horse, and trotted off calling back, "I'm going out to tell more folks. See ya."

"Come. We will make as many bricks as we can before we leave for Gonzales. Hopefully, we will come back late tomorrow and turn the blocks. It's time-consuming to wait each day for them to dry evenly, but I don't want to waste a minute. We need to get the house built if the Comanches are raiding." Michael put his arm around his wife's shoulders as they walked over to the brick setup. The three had a sense of urgency. They removed their shoes. Michael, using a hoe, mixed the straw. Humberto poured in the wet, red clay from his bucket. After the straw was stirred, the three tramped upon the mixture with bare feet. The men poured the mixture into wooden molds with four sides and an open top and bottom. They laid the forms out in the sun to dry.

Their legs ached, but they didn't stop to rest. They washed their feet in a bucket of water by the campfire. They ate the corn cakes as they worked. The two men hitched the oxen to the wagon while Cecilia straightened up the campsite and put their belongings into the two- wheeled cart. They put on their shoes and headed for town.

Chapter Eight

Michael tied up the oxen by the livery. The three headed down the dirt street toward the main buildings in the town.

"Dear, look at the people." Cecilia edged closer to her husband and held his arm. Everyone stood in small groups, talking in low voices.

"Something has happened, all right. I see Red standing with that group of men near the general mercantile. Let's find out from him." He led the way to the gathering.

"What's happening?"

"The Alamo fell."

"No!".

Michael kicked a stone with his boot. Humberto swallowed hard and averted his eyes.

"Deaf Smith was sent out to get as close as he could to see if it was true. A few hours before he got there, he met Mrs. Dickerson and several other women and children running this way. They confirmed that the report was true. Come, we are all going over to the middle of the town. Everyone is gathering there. Mrs. Dickerson is going to tell us about the battle."

"Bad news, very bad," said Humberto.

"Yep. It sure is," said Red.

They joined other groups of men and crying women as they made their way to the town's center. Everyone stood in the blazing heat facing the boarding house. Mrs. Dickerson came out the door, carrying her child. Two

Negro men stood on her left side. The crowd hushed. A man followed them, moved forward, and stood in front.

"I'm General Houston. I arrived a short time ago with about two hundred men. We were heading for the defenders of the Alamo when we stopped here at Gonzales, and I met with Mrs. Susannah Dickerson, this lady right here." He turned and indicated the woman holding a little girl. General Houston gave a weak smile and added,

"This is her daughter, Anelina." Mrs. Dickerson nodded and hugged her child closer. Their faces were dirty, and tear stained. Their clothing was covered with dried bloodstains.

"The men on my left are Sam, the servant of Colonel Travis, and Ben, a free Negro and servant to Lieutenant Almonte Dickerson. He was Travis's aide." The Negroes nodded. "They helped Mrs. Dickerson and the other women as they ran from Fort Alamo." The crowd bobbed their heads in recognition, and a few said, "Good for you."

"Good men."

"Mrs. Dickerson and I talked. She does not feel up to telling you the news, so I will speak for her. We had over two hundred men, American and Mexicans, fighting against Santa Anna's thousands. Within just two hours, Santa Anna's forces overwhelmed our brave men." The crowd sucked in its breath as if through one throat. "Most were killed. Many died in hand-to-hand fighting when the men ran out of ammunition or did not have time to reload. That includes Mr. Dickerson, Travis, Bowie, and Crockett. Two of Crockett's friends, one who identified himself only as a bee hunter and the other by the name of Thimblerig, and two hundred more Americans and Mexicans who believed in Texan Independence from Mexico were killed without mercy."

A few men in the crowd yelled, "Independence! Freedom from the tyrants!"

A woman shouted, "Weren't there any prisoners? Surely, there were prisoners."

Colonel Houston looked down at the plank board porch and then back at the crowd before he continued. "About thirty men were taken prisoner. They were brought before Santa Anna. He ordered them killed. Susannah Dickerson heard with her own ears one of his officers refusing to obey. But,

Santa Anna ordered it again and the Mexicans standing around the prisoners fell upon them, and with their knives and swords, hacked them all to death." The crowd again gasped.

"Their bodies were dragged out and flung into the fire consuming the bodies of the other defenders. One body was given to a Santa Anna soldier who wanted to bury his brother in their hometown in Mexico. The Mexican wives and children clung to the bodies of their loved ones. As they shrieked in grief for mercy to bury their dead, the remains were torn from their arms. The bodies were cast into the fire. Mrs. Dickerson said the stench from the burning flesh was unbearable and sickening."

The sobs of the women in the crowd added to the sound of the men shuffling their feet in the dust as they fought to control their emotions.

Mrs. Dickerson spoke up. "I must tell you that our small force acquitted themselves so bravely." She choked back a sob. "So many of Santa Anna's army fell that we could not walk without stepping over their bodies. I think it will take several days for Santa Anna to bury his troops." She stepped back and hid her face in the child clutched in her arms.

General Houston said, "Thank you, Mrs. Dickerson. That knowledge will help the families of the fallen. Would you like to add anything else to what I've said?"

She shook her head, then changed her mind and began, "Yes, yes, I would. All of us women were back in a little room off the main church. We held our children and tried to comfort them. The cannon fire, the rifle shots, our men's screams were terrifying to us all." She stopped speaking, and with tears running down her ashen face, her eyes searched the faces in the crowd. Her gaze stopped on a gray-haired lady in the middle of the throng. "Mrs. Gaston, your boy Johnny found me in the back room. He tried to tell me something, but I think both his jaws were broken. I could not understand him. I believe he wanted me to tell you he loved you. He turned and went back into a wall of bullets. He died a true hero."

Mrs. Gaston covered her mouth with her hands and sank to her knees. Three women went to her side to comfort her.

"Santa Anna parceled out two dollars and a blanket to each woman. He ordered us to flee Texas and not return. Several of us ran this way. Some fell on the way, exhausted from the weeks of ordeal, the heat and lack of food. I would have succumbed, too, if Deaf Smith and the men with him had not found us and helped us get here. I have told you all I can, except that Santa Anna shows no mercy." Mrs. Dickerson was shaking as she turned and went back into the house.

General Houston then spoke: "My officers and I will discuss our next course of action. You will be notified of our decision." He followed Mrs. Dickerson into the boarding house. Sam and Ben trailed behind the General.

The women broke up into little groups, sobbing, wailing, hugging, and supporting each other.

The men also broke up into groups, ill at ease, not knowing what to say or how to comfort the women.

Michael's hands shook as he turned to Cecilia. He took her arm when he saw the pallor on her face. "Come; let's go back to our wagon. We can have some coffee and sleep there tonight."

Humberto led the oxen off to the back of the blacksmith's and helped Michael start a fire. They made chicory coffee. Cecilia tried to help but found her knees too weak to stand for long. They sat quietly as the sun lit the sky in pinks and lavenders that deepened into gray and then black.

After drinking his coffee, Humberto put down his tin cup and said, "I'm going into town to see if I can learn anything more. I'll come back later. It might be very late, so don't worry about me." He walked away from the wagon and was soon swallowed up in the black night.

Michael and Cecilia whispered till the moon was high in the sky, casting shadows. They curled up in blankets and lay down next to each other.

"Michael, what will those women do without their men? There must have been twenty or thirty women in the crowd who'd lost their menfolk."

"I don't know, Cecilia. I don't know." He put his arm around his wife and she laid her head against his shoulder.

They lay in silence, staring into the night sky, with thoughts tumbling over and over. In the stillness, they heard footsteps running toward the wagon. Michael jumped up and grabbed his rifle. Cecilia rose and stood behind him.

"Michael, it's me, Humberto. Quick, put the fire out. Get the oxen hitched. We must leave town now!"

"What has happened?" Cecilia asked as Michael ran to hitch the oxen.

"General Houston ordered all his men to get the horses ready and leave. Everyone is in confusion and scrambling, not sure of what is happening. The rumor is that Houston's going to lead the army out of town and retreat to Peach Creek, about twenty miles east of here. Someone said he ordered the whole town burned, right down to the ground, every last building. Everyone is to leave. They say that Santa Anna's got a huge army marching right for us and will be here at any time."

"Who says?"

"Everyone."

"Michael, should we go home?"

"No, we'd best go to Peach Creek with everyone else. The army will need all the guns they can get, and we wouldn't stand a chance by ourselves against the Mexican army. I don't reckon they would spare us if they found us at our unfinished adobe, that's for sure."

Within minutes, the three were heading east. People were streaming out of the town, some on horses going pell-mell, others in wagons pulled by horses or mules. Some folks were running--women, children, men. Everyone was passing their wagon as the oxen plodded on through the dark night.

They looked back and saw the spires of fire leaping into the sky from the burning buildings. The cries of shouting men, weeping women and children--the few who had not left the town--rang in the air and settled into heavy hearts.

An hour later, the ox cart caught up with children and women who had been running beside the road and had fallen in weariness. Cecilia helped them up onto the wagon so they could get some rest. The dark night concealed everyone's face, but fear wrapped around their shoulders like a shawl.

Chapter Nine

Three days later, several people staggered next to the oxen. The wagon now carried the burden of three widows worn out with grief and seven children. The march seemed endless. They passed people lying by the side of the path, too weak and exhausted to go on.

Michael and Humberto left the wagon to scrounge for any food they could find, returning at night with nothing.

One night, Michael leaned his rifle against the wagon. "Cecilia, the army needs food. The women and children need food."

She held a little girl in her lap in order to give her mother some rest. *I wonder if our baby will be a girl.* She considered the gathering of dejected children and women around the wagon and campfire. "I know."

"I'm going to take Buck and Bright to the army. They can divide up the meat amongst the military and civilians."

She cast a weary eye at their faithful beasts. *Their friends that worked without complaint, privy to long conversations, and never uttered a word in return or divulged any secrets I told them on our long journey. Faithful friends.* She looked away and nodded, then listened to Michael's footsteps crunch off into the darkness. She hummed a soft song to the little girl as she rocked back and forth to cover up the sound of the hoof steps disappearing into the night.

❋ ❋ ❋

The next two days and nights, it rained steadily. The earth turned to slick mud and sucked at their feet with each step. They removed their shoes when they became too heavy with mud. The women lifted the hems of their skirts and petticoats and tied them around their waists. Everyone was covered in grime, and the women's hair hung past their shoulders in dirty clumps.

Without Buck and Bright they left their cart and carried a few things tied in blankets.

Twice they came upon men digging narrow trenches along the road. The dead, covered in mud, were lowered, sometimes thrown, into the trenches and buried. No words of Christian burial, no mourners. Cecilia turned her head. It was too heartbreaking. Rumors flew that people were dying of measles, pneumonia, and smallpox.

The journey to Peach Creek seemed an eternity, but at last General Houston called a halt. A day of rest, taking shelter from the rain, trying to wash off the mud was a blessing. Michael caught a rabbit in a snare, as ammunition was too scarce to waste on hunting. Humberto found a handful of corn at an abandoned homestead.

The oxen meat had been parceled out. Michael was given a small amount of meat, since he had supplied the animals. Cecilia boiled it in their cast-iron pot and doled out a half-cup of the broth and a bit of the meat to their exhausted companions.

Michael said, "Hopefully, we will stay here for a while to rest. Houston might be getting ready to go after the Mexican Army now that more volunteers have joined him."

"Humberto? Is he going to leave us?"

"Yes, if Houston marches with his army towards Santa Anna." Cecilia shook and stammered out the words she feared to say but could not hold back. "Are you going with Houston? Are you signing up?" Michael took her in his arms. "No. We are going to face what comes together. I won't leave you."

She felt her body sink into his arms until his strength was holding her upright.

Humberto ran into the campsite. "Michael, General Houston says we need to move out. He wants us to cross the Colorado River."

"Why?"

Humberto drew circles in the mud with the toe of his worn boot.

"A rider just came into the army's camp. General Urrea of Santa Anna's forces forced Colonel Fannin and the American troops at Goliad to surrender when they ran out of food and ammunition. The fort is near Gonzales. They took 300 prisoners and…."

"And?" asked Michael.

"Marched them out of Goliad and massacred all three hundred. Even the sick and wounded. They burned the bodies."

Cecilia collapsed in Michael's arms. He picked her up and took her to one of the women seated by the trail. He turned to Humberto.

"We will start right away."

"You'll have plenty of company. Everyone is trying to get away. If we thought it was bad before, you ain't seen it all yet. People from every town, home, and encampment from here to the Texas border are fleeing with what they can carry, some with nothing except fear."

※ ※ ※

The march continued. Michael put his arm around Cecilia's waist and supported her as they trekked forward. The rain ended, and the sun dried out the soil. The mud ruts made by those ahead became hard, dusty, toe-tripping furrows for those trailing behind.

Each night, Michael and Humberto searched for food. One evening, Michael returned to the campsite with another man, whom he introduced: "This is Edward Miles. He has fought against Santa Anna's army in skirmishes. He just found out from General Houston about what the General is planning. I asked him to come and talk to us, and those traveling with us, so we know what we are in for."

The women held their children in their laps. One woman sat with empty arms. She stared into the firelight as it flickered among the coals. She moved when someone held her arm and directed her. She never spoke.

Cecilia brushed the woman's hair back from her face. Tears pooled in her eyes as she thought, *I don't think anything can be worse than losing a child.* She stood as she brushed the tears that had spilled down her cheeks. She greeted the men and motioned for them to sit by the fire.

"Please, Mr. Miles, tell us all you know. The not knowing is worse than knowing what we have to face," she said. The women nodded.

"Ladies, I'll do just that. Now that we have crossed the Colorado River, our army is about 800 in volunteers."

"That's good. We only had 200 ten days ago," said one of the mothers rocking her three-year-old in her arms.

"Yes'm, it is. But Santa Anna has more than doubled the number." Moans rose from weary lips.

"The General knows if he keeps retreating, he will lose most of the volunteers, so he is spreading the word. He is going to take a stand at a place called San Jacinto."

"Ain't never heard of it," said a mother as she cut a strip of leather from her worn shoe and gave it to her child to suck.

"It's got some high ground, prairie-like, and is bounded by Galveston Bay and its marsh land, Buffalo Bayou, San Jacinto River, and Vinces Bayou. Now, we got to get there first for two reasons. One, we need the higher ground, as that is much easier to defend, and the other is two pieces of hollow ware, ah cannons, six-pounders. Houston calls them the Twin Sisters. Some businessmen in Cincinnati, Ohio, wanted to help with this war, so they raised the money for the two pieces to be manufactured, mounted, and supplied with shot and sent to New Orleans and then to Brasoria. Then it was decided the Twin Sisters would be too close to Santa Anna if he came that way, so the cannons were loaded onto a schooner called *Pennsylvania*. They were sent to Galveston Island and then to Harrisburg. They are there now. Horses will haul them the rest of the way to Houston's army. But, we need to get there before Santa Anna gets to them first.

"Captain Zumwalt has been placed in charge of getting the civilians to the Sabine River. He is calling our journey "The Runaway Scrape", or some folks call it the "Chute to the Sabine." If Santa Anna wins and defeats our forces, Zumwalt is to do all he can to get the civilians across the Sabine to safety. Louisiana is on the other side of the river, and it is not far from San Jacinto."

Cecilia looked around at the gathering of women and children. She choked back a sob that wanted to erupt from her throat. She knew if she let it out, it would open a floodgate of hysteria. *Will any of us make it to the Sabine*

River? How can we? We're exhausted, weak from lack of food, and hopeless in despair. We had to give up our homes, our dreams. Many lost loved ones, and here we sat in misery, and we were asked to give more. Do we have it in us? Do I have it in me?*

❈ ❈ ❈

Before dawn, thousands of worn-out people stumbled forward. As they neared towns, more people joined them. Some people shared the food they had, and others didn't. Soon, people were attacked and robbed for food or anything of value. One morning, Michael led the group past dead bodies of folks murdered for their possessions. No one stopped to bury them. No one had the strength to do it.

That night, while Cecilia and Michael lay in each other arms, Cecilia gasped and grasped Michael's arm. Her fingers dug into his flesh.

"Cecilia, what is it?" Michael sat up.

"Something is wrong with the baby. Michael, something is awfully wrong." She gasped in pain.

Michael called out to the woman with the three-year-old girl.

"Mrs. Britton, come here and help me."

The woman moved away from her sleeping child and crawled over to Michael. "What's wrong?"

"Stay with Cecilia while I find a doctor. I'll be back as soon as I can." He stood and was running into the dark before he finished the sentence.

❈ ❈ ❈

A circle of women holding tattered blankets and dresses formed a privacy barrier. They knelt around Cecilia.

The doctor stood and left the makeshift pallet where Cecilia lay. He put his hand on Michael's arm. "I'm sorry I could not save your baby. It was a boy."

Michael swallowed hard. "Will Cecilia be all right?"

"Her heart is affected. She will need care and rest. And she won't be able to have any children. I am sorry."

Michael looked at his wife. The women were straightening the area. One held a wrapped bundle in her arms. Cecilia's thin body, and the dirty, tangled hair that framed her ashen face, lay still with her eyes closed. Michael could see the tears clinging to her eyelashes. "I'll dig a grave and find a preacher who can say the proper words. There must be some in this mob of misery."

※ ※ ※

Michael searched the refugees for over two hours, looking for Humberto. Then he scoured Houston's camp. Not finding his friend, he decided to return to Cecilia. As he neared their camp, Humberto walked up to him.

"I've been looking for you. I wanted to let you know I'm going to try to get Cecilia away from here and take her home. I didn't want to leave without letting you know."

"And I came to get you. A slave boy from Santa Anna's camp informed Houston that Santa Anna is just a mile from us, and a mulatto slave woman named Emily is at the camp and wants to get information to us. I told Houston I would get you, and we would scout out the camp and try to contact Emily. If they are only a mile away, they could wipe us out in no time. Maybe Emily knows something that could save us, at least buy us more time. Are you for this?"

"Cecilia can't take any more of this. I have to know what is going to happen. I'll go with you. This has to end, one way or another."

※ ※ ※

Humberto and Michael each carried a musket with a bag of lead balls and a horn of powder. They jogged toward the forest and entered it. The farther they treaded into the woods the more cautious they became. The air was still and stifling. Flies and mosquitoes, attracted by their sweat, buzzed and bit. The underbrush caught at their feet and snapped with thunderous cracks in the still air. At the edge of the forest they crawled on their bellies, inching their way in the moss and rank rotting undergrowth.

The men saw a huge red-and-white striped tent in the center of the Mexican encampment. Rifles were stacked in groups around the main area.

Soldiers in dirty uniforms sat, lounged, and ambled about with no idea of being watched.

"Humberto, do you think that mulatto woman with the buckets is Emily?" Michael pointed with his chin to a young woman in bare feet and a long red skirt with a pink off-the-shoulder blouse. She was going toward a small pond.

"Could be. Let's edge our way around the trees to get closer to the water."

The two men crawled back into a thicker area of trees and then did a running crouch as they headed towards the lake. Just as they arrived at the edge of the trees close to the lake, she stood from kneeling on the sand. Humberto tossed a pebble into the water, and it made a small splash. She looked up, startled. She saw their faces and held her finger to her lips. She glanced around to see if anyone in the camp was watching. Kneeling back down and emptying a bucket in the water, she refilled it as she whispered, "Who are you? I am Emily, slave to Colonel Morgan."

"Thank the Lord. The slave boy got your message to Houston. What else can you tell us?" Humberto whispered.

"Santa Anna captured me while I was trying to get Colonel Thomas Morgan's property to safety. I knew from the way the president looked at me, he liked me. I told him I would wait on him and serve him at his pleasure. He sent his mistress back to Mexico. He trusts me, as he thinks I do not like Colonel Morgan, which is a lie. He treats me like family. The slave boy has the run of the camp, and no one realized it whenever he left camp. He told me Houston's army was only a mile ahead on the

other side of the woods. I asked Santa Anna if he would camp here for a few days to give me, the other slaves, and his soldiers time to rest. He agreed. He travels with the best of accommodations, and he wants to enjoy them. He has fine silver and crystal and a luxury carpet on the floor of his tent with many rooms. He travels with champagne, fine chocolates, and other delicacies at his disposal. Even now, at noon, he is still wearing his silk gown and has not indicated he will dress today. I convinced him not to set pickets around the camp and give everyone time to rest. He does not know Houston's army is so close."

Emily rose and picked up the handles of the two buckets. "I must return before he becomes suspicious. Tell Houston he must decide what he is going to do soon, or his forces will be discovered. Santa Anna has more than a thousand men at his command. If he learns where the Americans are, he will wipe them out. He has told his officers to 'kill every enemy with a gun.'" She turned, and her bare feet left small prints in the hot sand.

The men belly-slid deep into the undergrowth before standing and running. Tearing through the woods, ducking under low branches, jumping over fallen trees, they emerged from the forest breathless. Stopping long enough to take two deep breaths, they ran across the trampled field where Houston's army camped. As they approached his tent, they called out, "Houston! General Houston!"

The general stepped out of his tent. "What is it? Report!"

"The slave boy was right. We talked with Emily Morgan. We can take Santa Anna by surprise. He doesn't know we are so close. He isn't ready." Humberto and Michael gasped out the news intermittently, taking turns.

Houston yelled for his officers to come to his tent. Men scurried off in different directions to relay the message.

Within the hour, the officers left the command tent and rounded up their men to carry out the battle plan. The 800 men marched to the woods. On entering the tree line, they broke formation and stepped forward with determination. Under orders not to talk and to make as little noise as possible, each man watched for hand signals from the officers leading the way.

Michael and Humberto and the lead officers stopped twenty yards from the edge of the woods. Houston gave the hand signal to stop, and it was passed back to the men behind. A slight breeze stirred the treetops, but the air hung heavily at the base of the trees. The birds were silent, and the small animals had scurried into the underbrush. Houston gave the signal to fan out. The men, some barefoot, some in worn boots, and some in foot rags, moved to the edge of the tree line, which reached halfway around Anna's encampment.

Houston yelled, "Charge!!"

The men yelled as they ran into the open. Some knelt and steadied their rifles, fired, reloaded, and ran forward. Other men stood and fired at the stunned Mexican soldiers.

Some of Santa Anna's men ran to get their weapons. Others just ran. Michael ran forward from the trees, stopped, fired, and saw an unarmed soldier fall. He reloaded and fired again. Another man fell. He ran into the camp, jumping over the bodies of men. The yelling of commands, the firing, and the screaming of pain and of fear forced him to stop. He glanced down and saw he had just stepped over a man whose dead eyes stared up at him. He looked about him. He watched his comrades chase the confused and unarmed soldiers. They shot at their fleeing backs. Other Americans were clubbing and knifing the fallen. *Vengeance for the Alamo and Goliad rule this battlefield."* Michael swallowed hard as he looked at the carnage. *After weeks of misery and running, it only took twenty minutes to destroy the Mexican army.*

❋ ❋ ❋

As soon as the fighting ended, the looting began. Michael took off his shirt, loaded as much food as he could into it, and slung it over his back. Carrying his rifle, he jogged back to his campsite. Twice he stopped to talk with men he knew and trusted. The news of the victory had already spread, and many were running forward to join the looters. Cecilia sat on the ground with her back against a boulder. She smiled when she saw her husband drop his bundle on the ground by the dying campfire. "I heard the war is over, but you weren't here with me. I thought you were dead." Tears coursed their way down the grime on her face.

"I have food. And, we are going home."

"Home? It's so far to Gonzales. I can't make it."

"Not to Gonzales. To Connecticut. I will go into the dray business with my brother, and we will get a little house for us. A quiet, clean place with a little yard. This place is not for us. It will be a long time before there is a government in control. People will be looting and killing. We will go back to Connecticut." Michael smiled at his wife as he smoothed her tangled hair off her face.

Cecilia broke into sobs. "I can't. Michael. I can't make such a long trip. I want to--oh, how I want to--but I can't make it."

"Yes, you can. We're going to rest here for a while. I've been talking to others. There is a group of us that want to go east, out of Texas, even back across the Mississippi. We're going to pool everything we have and go together. We will have one wagon to carry the supplies, and you will ride in it. The rest of us will walk, pulling the wagon until we can get an ox, mule, or horse. We'll work our way east, bit by bit. It will take time, but we can do it. And with food and rest, you will get better. You will get better." Tears flowed freely down his face. He sat down next to Cecilia and wrapped his arms around her. "I need you!"

❋ ❋ ❋

Cecilia was absent-mindedly rocking in her rocker, her knitting laying in her lap. She pulled herself out of her memories, took up her knitting, and listened to her husband.

"It was April 21st 1836. I'll not forget that date. When you hear the song 'The Yellow Rose of Texas,' it is Emily Morgan who is the Yellow Rose. She was the slave who gave the Americans the information needed to attack Anna's army.

"Didn't Santa Anna get captured?" Edmund asked.

"Yes, the next day. He was found hiding in tall grass, wearing some discarded clothing from a soldier or slave. He later signed the Treaty of Velasco, which recognized Texas's Independence. He was sent as an exile to New York, and in 1837, President Andrew Jackson allowed him to return to Mexico."

"The battle at the Alamo must have been exciting, and you and Mother were heroes, but once the war was over, why did you and Mother not go back and finish making your adobe house?"

Cecilia dropped a stitch. She picked it up as she listened to Michael's answer.

"Your mother and I had lost so much of our property. We didn't even have our oxen. We were worn out, and the new Texas government was just forming. Everything seemed to be in chaos. We decided we would come back to where we were born, here in Stamford, Connecticut. I knew I could get work with my brother in the dray business. It took us two years to work our way back, but here we are."

What happened to Humberto?" Edmund asked.

"I gave him my land and the beginning of the house. He earned it and more. I am sure your mother and I would not have survived those hard days without him."

"And I was born on your way home. I wish you had stayed in Texas. It would have been exciting, fighting the Indians and living off the land," Edmund said.

Michael and Cecilia exchanged looks.

"Yes, we got you on our way home, while we were in the New Mexico Territories." The exhaustion he'd felt in the Chute for the Sabine again entered Michael's body and drained his energy. He wanted to close the telling and turn Edmund's mind to other thoughts.

"Now, your mother and I have told you our story. How about you telling us the Bible verse you are to say in church?"

Edmund took a deep breath, smiled, and said, "And we know that all things work together for good to them that love God, to them who are the called according to his purpose. Romans 8:28."

Cecilia gazed at her husband as tears slid down her cheeks. "Yes, indeed."

Chapter Ten

"Good day, Mr. Farris." Edmund grabbed the doorframe of the tonsorial parlor to stop his feet. He reached down and unstrapped the rollers from his shoes.

"Hello, Edmund. School's over for the day, I see. How are those dry land skates?"

"Great! Real bumpy on the cobblestone streets, but that makes it more fun. I can only go straight. The wheels can't turn corners."

"A bright boy like you could invent a pair that can turn."

"Maybe. But I was wondering, now that your hired man, Tim, has gone off to join the Union Army, could I take his place? Maybe learn to be a barber, like you?" Edmund put his books and skates on the clean plank floor and fingered the shaving cups with the customers' names. He saw his father's cup with "Michael Proft" written on it. "I want to quit school. I'm tired of sitting all day learning out of books. I want to learn important stuff. I'm fourteen now."

"Like shaving and cutting hair at low pay? I don't think your folks would like that. You'd better discuss it with them. I don't want your father to be angry with me."

"I'll tell them I'll quit school and either work for you or join the Union forces. They would rather I worked for you. Thanks."

"Not so fast. If Tim does come back from Grant's army, I am going to give him his old job back, if he wants it."

"That's okay." Edmund opened the door, scooped his books up from the floor, and turned back to look at Mr. Farris. Pointing to the top book, he said, "This book is called *Kit Carson: The Prince of the Gold Hunters*. It's a blood-and-thunder book by Charles Averill. It's real good. If Tim wants his job back after the Civil War, I can join the Union Army. Maybe I'll get sent to fight the Navahos with Colonel Carson in the New Mexican Territories. He's a real hero." Edmund left the shop, carrying his skates on top of his books.

Mr. Farris shook his head and muttered, "The youth of today. No sense."

❈ ❈ ❈

Edmund ran down the Connecticut streets, dodging the freight wagons, the carriages, and pedestrians. He waved at the shopkeepers and people he knew as he headed to the white frame house on the edge of town. He leaped over a picket fence and ran to the backyard. Moving past the privy, he snapped an apple from a tree and bit into it as he went through the back door of his house. Dropping his skates by the door and slinging his books, bundled together with a leather strap, onto the kitchen table, he announced, "Mother, I'm home. Whose rig just left from the front?"

A man with gray mutton-chop whiskers walked into the kitchen.

"Quiet, Edmund."

"Father, why are you home so early? What's wrong?"

"I had a delivery to make in this area, so I stopped in to have lunch with your mother. I found her feeling ill. I called the doctor. He just left."

"Is she all right?"

"Son, it's her heart. It's wearing out."

"Is she going to die?" Edmund's voice quivered.

"No. The doctor left some medicine to help her, but she needs rest. She'll spend a few days in bed, and when she does get up, she can't work so hard. No more chopping wood for the stove and hauling water. No more standing in the kitchen for hours putting up preserves and cooking. No more standing over washtubs doing laundry. We need to step up and help more here at home."

"I'll quit school and do all the chores."

"No, you won't. Get that idea out of your head this minute. Your mother and I have dreamed for years that you'll attend the university to become a lawyer or a minister, or maybe a judge. A couple more years of schooling, and you'll be ready for university. Your mother and I are going to live to see you graduate with a degree. Don't you disappoint us." Edmund's father put his arm around his son's shoulders.

Edmund looked down at his feet. "I'll try not to." His body shivered. All thoughts of joining the Union Army or working in the tonsorial parlor left his mind. He knew he couldn't consider it again.

"Come, your mother and I have been waiting a long time to talk something over with you. We think today is the day."

His father led the way into a bedroom. A slight, round-shouldered, gray-haired woman lay on the bed, propped up with pillows. A smile flashed on her face when she saw her husband and son. "Edmund, give me a hug."

Edmund walked to the bedside and put his arms around his mother. "Are you all right?"

"I'm fine. A bit tired, that's all. I'll be around for many more years. Now, you sit in the rocking chair while your father sits on the bed and holds my hand."

Edmund moved the wooden chair with its leather seat, so it was on the rag rug near the bed and dropped down into it. His parents held hands and smiled. Michael cleared his throat and looked away. Tears filled his mother's eyes. "That rocker went in the covered wagon with your father and me all the way out to Texas. It came back with us two years later, when we decided your father should go into business with his brother. I rocked you for miles as well as for years in that chair. Do you remember much about our living in the wagon before we moved into our house?"

"No, I remember you held me in your lap and rocked me here in the house, not in a wagon."

"I think he was two or three when we moved into this place, Cecilia," said Michael.

"That's right. Time flies by so fast." The woman reached out her hand, and the boy took it. "We love you, you know that."

"I know." Edmund panted. His chest felt heavy. He swallowed hard as a wave of tension filled the room. He sensed their reluctance to tell him something important.

"The decisions we made, we made for you."

"Yes, I know." Edmund took a deep breath.

The woman disengaged her other hand from her husband's. She reached over to the nightstand and picked up a battered brown leather book. "This is yours. It has been all along. We think you are old enough now to read it. We hope you understand."

Edmund opened the cover. "It says it was written by Elizabeth. Who is she?"

"Son, go to your room, and read the entire book, all the way to the last paper in the back cover. Then you'll know why it's your book. When you're finished, we'll talk more." Michael Proft held his wife's hand again.

Edmund got up. He looked at his parents and then the book.

Afraid to speak as his throat felt tight, he left the room.

Tears flowed from the eyes of the two sitting on the bed.

"Did we do right? Is he old enough to understand?"

"I hope so."

❋ ❋ ❋

Edmund walked to his room, closed the door behind him, and stepped to his bed. Using a boot jack, he removed his ankle-high boots, swung his feet up on the quilt, propped a pillow behind his back, and held the journal on his lap. With trepidation, he opened the cover. Paper had been hand stitched together through the center and then stitched through a brown cowhide cover. Many pages were curled on the corners; some were torn at the edges, and some pages were almost hanging onto the stitching.

He read, "As I begin married life in the year of our Lord 1847, with my husband Garrett and the new adventures it will surely contain, I decided to write these happenings as they occur in a journal for my future children's children to read."

Edmund shivered. *Why do Mother and Father want me to read this? Why does the book belong to me?* He continued to read. "Garrett and I have been married for several hours already. The day is nearly done. Immediately after the ceremony, we said a joyful—at the same time a sad and tearful--good-bye to our families and friends. We know we may never see each other again. It is hard to part, but at the same time Garrett and I look forward to our future.

"We packed our goods into a mover's wagon, and we are ready to go. The wagon has wood slabs and is easy to turn, with its front wheels smaller than the rear ones. It has a canvas cover but not as billowing as the Conestogas or, as some call them, Pittsburgh wagons. I was so surprised at all Garrett got into the wagon. It was twelve feet long and only 42 inches deep. We will carry the makings of a tent for staying in at night if the weather requires it, but mostly, he says, we will sleep under the wagon. There is a canvas hammock bag under the wagon, and it will be my job to gather buffalo chips and other kindling for our fire as I walk beside the prairie schooner.

"We will join a wagon train with eighty-some members at the Mississippi River. Garrett says we will travel in some areas on our own, but we will spend a good share of the time with others. I am joyful at hearing this. I have much to learn about our journey, and I hope the other women will be more knowledgeable than I. Garrett hitched up the horses, and we're off to the Mississippi River and Independence, Missouri.

"We hope to go all the way to Texas and see the Alamo, of which we've heard so much. We know one day Texas will be part of this beloved country. There is a great rush of fine folks heading to California to find gold, so we may go on to California.

"Garrett isn't interested in gold mining or panning. He wants to find a place with a good supply of trees for a sawmill. He is a fine craftsman and thinks the new settlers in the West will have need of furniture they'll not be able to bring with them on the long trek. We're both so happy and excited; we've burst into spontaneous laughter several times today. And each of us is trying to help the other get over the sadness of leaving our kith and kin forever."

Edmund turned a page and read a new entry. "We have reached Independence. I went with Garrett to pick out and buy the four oxen we would need to pull the wagon. Garrett said oxen can keep going on a poorer diet than horses or mules, and they are not so skittish but also not so fast. We bought the oxen at the blacksmith's, where they were delivered by the seller.

"Garrett helped the smithy shoe the beasts. Each shoe consisted of two pieces, and because of the weight of the animal the ox can't stand on three legs like the horse can during shoeing. The blacksmith had special shaped stocks to hold the ox still, and with a sling and windlass the animal was raised until the smithy could complete the shoeing, which did not hurt the animals but was fretful to them. It was the first time I had seen the process, and I was sorry for our four gentle giants. "Garrett said oxen cannot sweat, so if they become overheated, they must rest until they cool off, and if the day is hot, we will need to rest more often. Our travel will be slow, maybe five or six miles a day. How does my dear one know so much? He amazes me, and it is easy to trust in his judgment."

❋ ❋ ❋

Three hours later, Edmund opened his bedroom door. He found his father in the bedroom giving his mother a cup of tea. Tears streaming down his cheeks, Edmund slumped against the door frame. He tried to speak, but words would not come. He shook his head and swallowed hard.

Cecilia saw the look on Edmund's face. Tears brimmed in her eyes as she bit her lower lip. Michael straightened up from bending forward. His hand shook as he extended it to Edmund. His other hand he placed on his wife's shoulder.

Edmund began with, "You aren't my parents? Elizabeth and Garrett are my real mother and father?"

The man and woman looking at Edmund spoke together, "That's right."

Cecilia dropped the teaspoon onto the floor. It lay there. Edmund looked at the couple, studied their faces for a moment.

"Everything is changed. My world is all different now. You never said anything about not being my real mother and father before. I am out of place. Strange. Yet, I'm the same, and you are the same."

"Oh, my dear, we didn't want to hurt you. We love you. Please forgive us if we were wrong not to tell you before." A sob broke Cecilia's voice. She grasped her husband's hand.

"Son, your mother and I were newlyweds, and we went by ox cart and later by Conestoga wagon across the Mississippi, across what seemed to be a never-ending plain until we reached what we now call Texas. During the fighting with Santa Anna and his Mexican Army, there was killing by bandits on both sides of the Rio Grande. People were displaced from their homes and towns by the Mexican Army or the bandits. Some people ran with nothing but the clothes on their backs to the next town or settlement, and then that town would be attacked, and they would run again. Mothers couldn't feed their children. The people who had a few possessions were targets of those who had nothing. Texas won its independence, and in 1848 the Gold Rush began, and everything became chaotic again. Your mother and I decided we would come back here, where we grew up. We knew the people. We knew the life. We made our way home, and on the way, we found you and the body of the woman who gave you life and kept you alive."

Edmund sobbed as he stumbled to the bed and sank down on it.

"Why would God let my real parents die? Why did he let all that bad stuff happen?"

Cecilia reached out to him, and he fell into her arms. "I don't know, son. I just know he blesses everything, even the sad things, for good to those who love him. I think that is why he made sure we decided to come back to Connecticut and not stay in the West. He knew you needed us."

"I don't understand it. I just don't. I love you. Elizabeth and Garrett are just names. I don't love them. Isn't that awful? I should love them. They are my parents."

"They are just names to you. You can't love people you don't know." Michael's voice cracked.

"Can you still love us?" Cecilia's lips trembled.

Edmund looked at their tear-stained faces. "You are my mother and father, and no one else. I'm your son, Edmund Proft." The words tumbled out of his mouth.

The three burst into tears as they hugged each other.

"Mother, I'm going to do more chores before school, and I'll come straight home after school to do all the other chores for you. I promise on the Good Book. I lost one mother, even if I don't remember her. I don't want to lose you. Please, please, get better."

Chapter Eleven

Sitting down with his back against a rock, the cavalry officer sipped cold coffee from his tin cup. Cold camps in enemy territory had blessings. Without firelight to dim the heavens, the gleaming stars appeared as diamonds within plucking reach. The brilliant starlight drew his eyes up to the sky as his thoughts turned to his young wife. He smiled. *Josefa will see these same stars tonight in Taos, maybe even at this very moment.*

An officer stole up to him, saluted, and whispered, "Colonel Carson, I have the report from one of our Ute scouts."

Colonel Kit Carson returned the salute with two fingers, tapping his hat as he said, "Sit down, Captain. Have some coffee."

The captain squatted on his heels and declined the cold drink before he said, "The lead Ute scout, Foxtail Grass, says the Navaho camp is five miles west of us. It's a large village with many horses. Foxtail Grass wants his Ute scouts to get the horses after the raid."

Carson sighed and stared into his cup of darkness. "We'll assemble two hours before dawn and raid the village just before sunup. First, we will run off the livestock—all of it, horses, mules, cattle, whatever they have—and kill the sheep. Burn the corn fields and gardens. No foodstuff or crops are to be spared. Destroy the hogans and any baskets that could carry food or water. Shoot only if attacked. When the people see all their food gone, they may surrender. Some will run away, probably to Canyon de Chelly, where the others have run to hide. Let them. That is their last holdout. We will dig them out when their food is gone. From the signs we have encountered, we can figure some of the braves may be off hunting. If so, the battle won't last long.

Tell the Ute scouts they can't have the horses, as everything will be confiscated. They are getting paid for their service. That is all they get. They signed up because they hate the Navajos for past battles. This military campaign will rid them of an effective and feared enemy."

The captain stood and saluted. "Yes, sir." The Colonel returned the salute.

The officer turned and shifted back to the Colonel. "Sir, the War Between the States can't last much longer. Eastern people will move west again. They will call you a hero, give you credit for making the territory safer for settlers."

"Credit, Captain? You and I wouldn't be here, ready to pounce on a sleeping Navaho village, except for Colonel Washington, our illustrious military governor of the New Mexico Territory, who allowed a stupid disagreement over a horse to trigger a fight at the peace talks he ordered Chief Narbona and other Navajos to attend. The governor commanded the troops to fire at the assembled Navajos. Chief Narbona, an old, arthritic warrior, was shot. Then a Union soldier scalped the chief before he was dead. That man should have been court-martialed, not praised. No wonder Narbona's son-in-law Manuelito became a war advocate. He gained influence over the tribes and talked them into this conflagration. John Washington has failed in my opinion. No one is a hero in this mess."

The captain saluted. "Yes, sir." The crunching sound his boots made on the sand and rocks faded into the blackness.

Young officers see glory. I see heartache. For a moment, his first wife's face flashed into his mind. *My lovely Arapaho, Singing Grass. You live on in our daughter, Adeline, but still I miss you.* Then he remembered the loss of his second wife. *Making-Our-Road, I understand why you returned to your Cheyenne people when they migrated to their winter grounds.* He poured the coffee onto the ground. *I'm ready to go home to Josefa and our Jive children, but it won't be until after the Civil War ends and the Navahos are settled on a reservation. Lord, I'm tired of this life.*

❋ ❋ ❋

The column of Mexican volunteer troops moved silently through the early morning, dark hours. Rags and blankets muffled the equipment. Soldiers rode in silence. Orders were passed in whispers. Steam from the nostrils of the tense animals rose in the cool air, forming droplets of moisture on their ear tips.

Colonel Carson held up his right hand to signal a halt when he saw a figure stand from a crouched position near the trail. Kit dismounted and walked his horse to the Ute Scout. They talked more with their breath than with a voice. The Colonel, fluent in the Ute language, did not need any clarifications of the terse message that the Navajo camp was a few hundred yards to the right, and all were asleep except for a few sentries. Foxtail Grass volunteered his fellow scouts to kill the sentries in silence and then join the cavalry in storming the camp.

Colonel Carson stood by his horse's head to keep him still and nodded in agreement. "Kill to keep the alarm from sounding." He breathed words into the air. Kit turned his horse and walked it back to the troops. He signaled for all to dismount and spoke orders in a soft voice to the captain to spread the word for half the men to get a piece of scrub brush or branch. The order passed by whispers from trooper to trooper down the line. Carson then took a coal oil can from the supply wagon and had each man soak a rag in the oil and attach it to the sticks. The pungent, oily smell made the horses jittery; they pawed and backed into each other. Their heads bobbed up and down as they tried to jerk the reins from the men's hands. The slight jingle of the bridles stabbed the silence. The troopers stilled the horses as they stood by them and waited in the darkness. The Mexican volunteers' hearts beat fast, not from fear of the coming battle but from the revenge they were to exact on the Indians for their past raids on Mexican settlements.

Carson gave the signal, and the men walked near the heads of their mounts, ready to stop any nickering. In minutes, they were at the base of a hill of scrub grass and sand. He led them halfway up the hill before he dropped his reins and left his horse standing. He crawled on his stomach to the crest. Using his field glasses, he propped himself up on his elbows and looked down at the camp. A stream cut the wide valley. The Indians' main herd of horses was picketed on this side of the narrow stream, and a few were tethered by the owners' hogans on the other side. Cornfields lay on both sides of the water along with vegetable gardens. The enemy prized horses, so he trained the field glasses on the herd until he spotted the sentries guarding it.

Carson lowered the glasses and saw movement from the corner of his eye. Near a rock outcropping, a Navaho sentry dozed. He blended in with the night and terrain. His arm fell to his side from the rock where it rested. The movement jerked him awake. He crouched, alert now, and looked at the village, stream, and horses. Carson lay flat, not twitching. He held his breath. The Navaho crawled back down to the rock cover and disappeared.

The Ute scout eased himself behind the rock while the Navaho faced the stream. Carson had not seen or heard the Ute, Foxtail Grass, and was as surprised as the sentry when the Ute reached over the rock behind the Navaho and slipped a rawhide thong around the man's neck. The guard grabbed at the string as Foxtail Grass tightened and twisted it. The Navaho's hands went down, and his body slumped against the rock. It all happened in silence, a silence Carson could feel.

He nodded at the Ute and slid back down the hill to the waiting men. At his command, the men mounted, and in less time than was needed to take a deep breath they galloped up the hill and charged down while drawing their rifles from their scabbards.

Yelling at the top of their voices, the troopers fired their rifles into the air and split into two groups. One group, led by the captain, charged into the herd. They smashed down the rope and brush corral. The panicking mustangs ran down the Navaho sentries and galloped off toward the shallow stream and the camp. The careening horses raced through the village, trampling campfire stands, vegetable containers, and leather drying racks.

Colonel Carson led the other half of the cavalry. He rode to a smoldering fire and plunged the end of his branch into its heart. The torch lit, and he held it aloft. The other men raced up to him and lit their torches. Brandishing his fire stick, he led the men, shouting, through the cornfields and gardens, setting everything ablaze.

The sounds of crying babies and screaming women competed with the shouting troops and rifles discharging in continuous bedlam and confusion. The warriors, the young boys, and the old men stumbled out from their hogans with rifles, clubs, and bows and arrows.

Four warriors each knelt on one knee in front of their hogans with their squaws and babies crying inside as they fired arrows into the melee of charging soldiers. Two old men with war clubs ran out the doorways of their homes toward the mounted troopers but fell under the horses' hoofs when pushed off balance by the twisting, churning animals. Warriors with rifles fired at the troops. The crack of the cavalry rifles added to the din as the braves fell.

The riders who had scattered the Indian herd joined their comrades in the village. Within seven minutes, the battle was over. Fires from the Indian lodges lit the sky and competed with the rosy sunrise glow. Women and children stood wailing by their burning homes. The braves put down their rifles and stood helpless as the troops rounded up the people into a small circle.

Colonel Carson sat on his horse, surveying the devastation.

The captain rode up, saluted, and reported, "You were right, Colonel. Most of the braves are out on a raiding party south of here. The Ute scouts say the warriors are in Mexico. This is their base camp. They are not expected back for a week or more."

"Status, Captain."

"Three troopers wounded. Five warriors killed and six wounded, sir." "Very well, Captain. We will escort these captives to Fort Canby to join the others. Then we will root out the holdouts at Canyon de Chelly.

It is sacred ground for them. I'll send the Ute scouts ahead to ascertain the strength and position of tribes taking refuge."

"That is a good defensive place for the Indians, sir. Only a few patrols have ventured in to those canyons, and then not very far. The cliffs are sheer in many places, and there are caves and small structures the natives have built for lookouts. I heard the soldiers will find it hard, if not impossible, to pick the enemy out as they blend in with the rocks. It could be a bloody battle on both sides."

"You may be right, Captain. The scouts' information will be key. For now, we will herd these captives into the fort as soon as the fires are out. Be sure the fire destroys all crops, all foodstuffs, and all baskets for carrying food or water. Leave nothing the returning braves will be able to use."

"Yes, sir." The captain saluted and turned his horse, riding with a straight back and squared shoulders. Carson sat back on his horse as he looked into the eyes of a wailing child. *Josefa, I miss you and the children. The children suffer the most from the mistakes of the adults.*

Chapter Twelve

Jason Wilcox, standing in the wagon bed, hefted two jugs over the side to the man standing in the dirt in front of the saloon. "That's twelve jugs, Mr. Buttwill. Will that do you for the month?"

"It should. Your folks make the best whiskey we ever had."

"I made this batch. I didn't cut any corners. Price is the same. A dollar a jug, if that's okay with you."

"That's fine. How are your folks doing?" Mr. Buttwill handed Jason the money.

Jason stuffed it in his pocket under his gun belt and jumped down from the wagon. He picked up two jugs, stepped up two wooden steps, and entered the saloon. The youth crossed the hard dirt floor to the makeshift bar. "They're both dead. Pa dropped dead in the barn about six weeks back. Ma said I was fourteen and could look after myself, so she started drinking till she died of whiskey poisoning. I buried her last week, next to Pa."

"I'm sorry to hear that. They were good people. How old were they?" Mr. Buttwill carried in two jugs and placed them on a shelf behind his plank bar.

"Ma figured she was more than eighty-seven and Pa likely eighty- nine. She wasn't sure. They walked here all the way from the hill country back east. Went through Boonesbourgh but missed seeing Daniel Boone, as he had already moved on to Indiana. Took them years to get this far, but she wasn't sure how many. They started out when she was thirteen or so."

"With your folks gone, are you going to join the war?"

"Naw. I don't care which side wins. I can hardly feed myself, let alone slaves, so I don't want any. I don't care what the government says about it."

"Are you going to run the ranch and still the whiskey, same as your folks?"

"That's my plan. Plus, a year back or so, Pa showed me how to brew beer, and we brought hops from a place eight days' ride from here. I reckon I'll make enough to sell. It'll be twelve dollars a barrel. Let me know when you want some." Jason kicked at a chicken to shoo it away from the door.

"While you're in town, ain't you worried someone will raid your place for the whiskey?" Buttwill moved a barrel behind the bar.

"I rigged shotguns to kill any Navahos or thieving Mexicans from trying to get at the still when I'm not there, and I carry Pa's rifle and Colt with me at all times. Ma was right. I can take care of myself."

"I noticed you have that smart-looking Winchester."

"Yeah, Pa got it when his brother Charlie died at the Sara Flats Massacre. Pa claimed the body and had it buried at the ranch and then claimed his rifle and Colt."

"Your uncle was at Sara Flats? Right sorry to hear that."

"Yup, it hit Pa hard, that's for sure. He hated the Mexs worse than ever after that."

"Speaking of Mexs and Indians, have you seen the army troops? They came through town last week, led by Colonel Kit Carson himself."

"Yeah, they watered their horses at my ranch. They went on to Lemuel Baxter's to buy mules for the army. Lem sure raises first-rate animals. One of the troopers told me Carson prefers riding a mule over a horse, as the mules have more staying power. And Carson, being such a short cuss, he can git away with it. He don't need the height of a horse." Jase stacked the casks behind the plank bar.

"Anyway, the Colonel said he was going to round up the Navahos and corral them east of here at Bosque Redondo. I'd say it's about time. We've lived with their threat long enough. With Kit Carson and the army after them, they will be catawamptiously chawed up for good. Then we will just have the thieving Mexs to deal with."

Jason walked out of the saloon. "I see Sabilla and John have moved their general store out of the tent and into a frame building. Looks nice. They usually buy a few jugs to sell. I'll head over there."

"Will Marsh's wagon is out front of the store." Mr. Buttwill stood at the door of the saloon and folded his arms over his chest. "You'd better wait until he's gone. He has a mean temper, drunk or sober. That's his missus sitting on the wagon seat."

"They new here?" Jason asked.

"Started a place four hours south of here six or seven months back. Last time they were in town, the missus had her arm in a splint. Talk was her husband likely broke it. Everyone can tell she's afraid of him." Mr. Buttwill spat tobacco juice in the street.

Jason added spit juice on top of Buttwill's and smiled. "I ain't gonna bother him none."

They jerked their heads up and looked when a tall, muscular man banged open the general store door and strutted onto the street with a flour barrel. He dropped it into the back of his wagon with a loud thump, causing the wagon to jolt. Cursing, he went back into the store and carried out a wooden crate with several items in it. He set it next to the barrel. "You folks are thieves. Downright thievery, charging prices like this." He sauntered up to the wagon seat and yelled at the woman, "You're no better. You waste so much of this stuff, we got to come to town for more. You think I got money to spend like it was nothing?"

"I don't waste anything, Will. I'm real careful." The woman sat at the end of the seat and pulled her shawl tight around her shoulders. She tucked her torn brown skirt under her legs and away from where her husband would sit.

Will went to the hitching rail and yanked on the leather strap connecting the horse's bridle to the post. The horse tossed its head high, rolled its eyes, and laid back its ears at the sudden movement.

"I'll teach you to shy away from me." The man took off the wide leather belt with a large brass buckle that held his Colt against his waist. He stuck the gun into his pants waistband.

"Please, Will, don't do it. The horse didn't mean nothin'."

"Hush up your naggin'. This animal needs to know who's boss, and I'm going to teach it once and for all." The man raised his arm and brought the belt down with the buckle, hitting the horse's neck. It tried to back away and rise on his haunches, but Will held onto its bridle. He hit the animal again and again. Its screams of terror and pain filled the street.

"He shouldn't do that," Jason said. "It ain't right."

"Stay out of it, Jason. It's his wife and his horse. It's none of our business." Mr. Buttwill stepped inside the saloon doorway. "That fella is a lot bigger than you. I'm his size, and I don't want to tangle with him."

"I don't aim to fight him. I aim to stop him." Jason stepped into the street and headed for the general store.

A fifth blow followed the fourth. The feeble horse struggled to back away. Blood ran down its withers, neck, and head.

"Mister, don't try to hit that animal again. If you do, I'll take the strap and use it on you."

Will turned and stared at Jason. "You? It's none of your business. Besides, you're just a skinny kid."

"I can't help my age or the meat on my bones. But you ain't hittin' that horse again. You try, and I'll fix your flint."

"You think cuz you're wearin' a gun you can stand up to me?"

"Will, please, leave the boy alone. He doesn't mean anything. He's just a b'hoy. Please, let's go home," the woman pleaded as she mopped tears from her face with the hem of her ripped skirt.

"I told you to shut up. If this kid thinks he's a man, let him prove it." Will dropped the belt. He stood straight for a moment and then raised his right shoulder as his hand went to his waistband and reached for his revolver. The gun was halfway out when a small explosion widened his eyes in surprise. "A no-account kid." He fell to his knees; then his face hit the street. His lips parted, and his tongue hung out onto the dirt. His eyes stared ahead, seeing nothing.

Mrs. Marsh sobbed a gasp and yelled, "Will!" Her hands covered her eyes.

Jason's right hand holstered his Colt on his left hip with the butt facing forward. He stepped over Will's body as he spoke in soft tones to the trembling horse. He took the reins and tied them back on the rail. "I'm real sorry, but I had to do it, ma'am." Jason approached the sobbing woman.

The woman's body shook as she brought her hands down to her lap. She stared at her husband's body lying in the dirt. "It was bound to happen. It isn't really your fault none. It's his." She choked out the words with her sobs. "Are you going to get in trouble for killing Will?"

"No, ma'am. We don't have any law in Wild River. We look after ourselves. Do you have someone to look after you?"

The woman sat, staring at her hands, as her sobs quieted down.

"I guess my brother and his family will take me in. They're good people. They know what Will was like. We just didn't know it when he courted me."

"Where does your brother live?"

"Three or four days east from here."

"I don't know nary a soul who would want to buy this nag, but it don't look like it could make the trip. I'll git you back to your brother's place. Least I can do, I reckon. I'll have my horse pull your wagon."

"You can have the poor beast. Will starved and beat it so much, it's plumb wore out."

"I'll take your horse and my wagon to the livery stable. Sam will take care of your horse until I get back, and his kid will likely go out to look after my place."

"I ain't got money to pay you."

"No need. I'll help you pack up your belongings."

"I thank you for your kind offer, and I'll take you up on it. I'm sorry I called you a b'hoy. I know you ain't a rowdy kid. I wanted my husband not to take notice of your standing up to him."

"That's okay, ma'am. Reckon I am a bit b'hoy."

Jason went across the street and led his horse and wagon back to the woman. He unhitched her horse from the rail and walked both horses and wagons down the street.

At the livery stable, he unhitched the nag and brought it into the corral.

Sam put down his barn shovel and moved to the fence. "You got trouble, Jason?"

"None to speak of, Sam, if 'en you don't mind looking after this critter until I get back to town. I aim to get this here lady to her folks, and it might take a few days. Can your boy go out to my place and look after the barn stock?" He unhitched his horse from the whiskey wagon and hitched it up to the widow's wagon.

"He sure can."

"What should I do about Will's body?" asked the woman.

Jason climbed up on the wagon seat. "The town will bury him."

❋ ❋ ❋

Otis held the mule's bridle as he walked on its left side through the corral gate. He closed the gate behind them and led the animal across the yard toward the barn.

"Hey, Otis. Look here." Silas turned from the huge kettle in the backyard. He picked up a wood bucket and ran up to Otis. Silas put down the pail and stuck his hand into his pocket, and then pulled out his hand, holding silver dollars in his palm.

"Whoo-ee! Did you take them from Pa?"

"You think I want to get killt? Last week, when I was in town helping Pa load the provision on to the wagon and he was dickering with Sabilla and her husband on the prices, I had time to sneak off."

"Where did you go?" Otis's eyes were wide with surprise and admiration.

"I tore off around back of the buildings, and behind the saloon I stumbled over a Mex, passed out. He was corned for sure. I saw the leather money bag tied to his belt and took it."

"Who was he?"

"Don't know, some stranger. Who cares? He'll never know who it was that took the money, and besides, it's his fault. He shouldn't get so drunk he can't take care of his own property."

"How much is it?"

"Six dollars."

"Whoo-ee."

"Let's sneak out tonight after Pa goes to bed."

"Where should we go?"

"To town, of course. Let's go to the saloon. Pa never gives us money. We could get a drink and learn to play poker. I'm sixteen, and you're fifteen. We're men. Pa should be paying us for all the work we do anyway."

"Yeah, but you know he tells us all the time that he had us young'uns to do work. Our pay is our victuals, and our place to sleep, which is better than he had, and he says one day we will own the ranch. He don't think we deserve to be paid."

"Don't you think we deserve some fun for all the work we do?" Silas held out the coins glittering in his palm.

Otis stared at the money. "That's the most money I've seen all at once. But, we daren't. If Pa found out, he'd skin us alive."

"He'll never hear us. He snores so loud he can't hear anything. If Ma hears us, she won't say anything."

Otis fiddled with the bridle as he stared at the gleaming coins.

"Okay. When?"

"Tonight, so don't get undressed. Just pretend to go to bed when Pa does. You better get the mule to the corral gate before Pa sees us talking. I got to get the bucket of ash lye into the outhouse."

"Ain't that Ma's job to freshen up the bucket?"

"Yeah, but she's looking tuckered out. I figured I'd scrape it out of the caldron for her. It's hard on her arms after it boils down so much from the wood ash. It gets hard and stuck to the pot. Might as well bring it here once I got it in the bucket. Don't want the privy smelling. Pa would go after Ma for sure."

"Ain't that the truth." Otis led the mule forward.

Chapter Thirteen

The captain saluted as he handed a dispatch to Colonel Carson.

"Sir, this just came in from General James Carleton."

"Good. I've been waiting for this. You are dismissed, Captain." The man saluted. The captain left the small office at Fort Canby.

The colonel handed the packet to the sergeant standing next to him. "Read this to me." The trooper tore open the dispatch and read it out loud as Carson stood from his desk and turned to face the map on the wall behind his chair. The sergeant did not smile or look surprised when Carson handed the letter to him, as everyone in the cavalry unit knew the Colonel could not read or write. The sergeant did all the correspondence for the Colonel. After reading the lengthy and wordy dispatch from General Carleton, the sergeant asked, "Is there a reply, sir?"

"No. Tell the captain to come back in." The captain entered and saluted.

"The general has denied my request to allow the Navahos holed up in Canyon de Chelly to stay there. They are not a threat. He wants to send a message to the Navahos that they are subdued once and for all. He orders us to proceed against the Navajo in Canyon de Chelly. Another detachment of soldiers from Fort Defiance will join our men. Then we will march to the canyon."

✷ ✷ ✷

Colonel Carson sat on his haunches next to the Ute scout. They both looked up at the red-brown sandstone butte that stood in the middle of the canyon floor between the sheer bluffs.

"They give up soon. Winter is bad time for them. They have no food. They die soon if they no surrender," said the Ute.

"I agree. That is why we have camped at the base of their fortress for weeks. They can't hold out much longer." He surveyed the burned-out peach orchard that the Indians had tended for generations. Carson shook his head in sadness, remembering his order to the troops to cut down and burn all crops. He looked back at the Ute scout. "How did they get up so near the top?"

"Cut notches in tree trunks and use as ladders. They pull up the trees after they climb up."

As the men spoke, a Navaho woman and a small child stood up in the open near the top of the butte. They stood for several minutes with the troopers watching from below. Then more women, children, and a few old people stood up.

Carson ordered, "No one fire." He yelled in Navaho, "If you surrender and come down, you will get food. You will not be killed." His Navaho words echoed through the canyon. More Navahos stood. The younger men lowered the tree trunk ladders, and the people came down to the canyon floor.

Carson called out to a sergeant, "Sergeant Major, divide the Navahos into groups of twenty, and see they all get food and water. We will rest here a day before we march them on to Fort Canby. After a few days of rest, we will combine the Indians at the fort with these and march them all to the Bosque Redondo Reservation."

The sergeant saluted. "Yes, sir."

Carson considered the haggard, dejected throng that huddled on the hot canyon floor. *Will any of these miserable souls be alive a year from now?* An old warrior on spindly legs, leaning on a staff, dropped down onto the rocky soil. *Even a month from now? Lord, have mercy!* He turned and stomped off, barking orders to any trooper he saw not working.

Chapter Fourteen

Connecticut, 1871

The team of six Clydesdales strained forward on the cobblestone street as it wound up from the busy port and warehouses. Ten wooden casks were tied on the bed of the wagon: five on the bottom, four on top of the five, and one at the apex. Each cask was labeled with its contents and destination. Three barrels were for the hardware store, three for the mercantile, and the remaining ones for four different private homes, containing merchandise ordered and shipped from England.

Three ships were in port, and two were lying at anchor, ready to come in to unload as soon as there was room. Michael Proft and his brother, Samuel, scurried to load the wagons and deliver the goods from their warehouse so more ships could come in and store their cargo for later delivery. Samuel drove his dray north to the main business district. Michael turned his south to the upper-class homes and a small business area. He urged his horses forward, calling their names and clucking his tongue. Their sweaty hides glistened in the early-morning mist as they clopped over the cobblestones. Soon they left the smell of the harbor, the brackish water, dead fish, and rotting wood behind as they made their way into the heart of the town, where the smell of freshly baked goods, other sweating horses and occasional piles of horse and dog droppings in the street assailed the nostrils.

"Hallo, there, Proft. How's it going? Did that boy of yours become a doctor?" Mr. Farris, sweeping out his tonsorial parlor, stopped and waved at Michael.

"He sure did. Got his diploma printed right on his sheepskin. Looks right fine. It was lots of work, lots of burning the lamp at night, but he did great. Cecilia and I went to his graduation last weekend and are proud of him," Michael shouted back to Mr. Farris as the dray continued up the street. He didn't want to stop the momentum, as it would be hard for the horses to start again, moving uphill with the heavy load.

He listened to the creaking of the wheels and the clopping of the horses' hooves. The sounds represented money-making to his ears.

A wagon wheel hit a hole in the cobblestone pavement. The wagon jolted hard as the wheel hit the depression with a thunk and then came out with a grinding crunch.

Michael felt the jar. He turned and looked over his shoulder at the casks. One of the middle-layer barrels had slipped a bit out of its rope bindings. He twisted in the wagon seat and reached back to adjust the bindings. He pulled hard on the loose section but couldn't get it to slip over the edge of the cask. Putting the reins under his feet to free his hands, he twisted until he was half-standing and pulled the rope with one hand as he steadied the barrel with the other. At the moment he threw his weight at the task, the wagon wheel hit another hole. The dray jolted. Michael felt his body fly sideways. He yelled and tried to catch the cart, but all he got was a moment of air. He fell from the wagon seat to the street. Just as he hit the pavement, the rear wheel rolled over his chest.

Men walking by the shops shouted, and women screamed in horror. Mr. Farris ran down the street to the wagon as men dashed forward and grabbed the horses' bridles to stop them. One woman fainted, and others rushed to her aid. Three men raced to Michael and lifted his limp body, leaving blood on the cobblestones. They laid him down on the narrow cement sidewalk. A pool of blood seeped out around his head and chest. Mr. Farris saw Michael Proft lying in the crimson pool and ran off to find Doctor Edmund Proft.

※ ※ ※

Dr. Proft shook hands with the pastor at the gravesite. "Thank you, Pastor Lingrin, for your words of comfort. And thank you, too, for all your visits these last few months, when Mother could not leave her bed."

The two men looked at the freshly turned earth next to another grave, with "Michael Proft, Beloved Husband and Father" carved on the tombstone.

"It was my honor to preside over her burial. She was a good servant of the Lord. She and your father were in their pew every Sunday with you until you dear father was taken so suddenly in that horrible accident."

"Yes. He died quickly, I'm sure. Telling Mother was the hardest thing I ever had to do. Her heart couldn't take the sadness. I think that is why she left us a few months later." The doctor pulled his wool cape around his shoulders as the blustery wind whipped through the little churchyard.

"You just remember, they loved you and were as proud as could be of your becoming a doctor. They told everyone how you went to New York Medical College and earned your diploma." The pastor went over to the horse-drawn hearse. "They were so happy you didn't take the easy way and pay a doctor to follow him around for a few months and then get a letter saying you were qualified to practice medicine. They were a blessing to you, and you to them. Remember that, son." The pastor put his hand on Edmund's shoulder.

"As soon as Mother's stone is ready, I will have it placed here." Edmund Proft cleared his throat as he felt it tighten. He looked at the other gravestones in the small cemetery. Some names he recognized, as he'd known the men before they'd gone to war. Many had not been buried in the graveyard, as they'd died on the battlefield too far away, so only a stone marked their passing.

"Pastor, how could a loving God allow all this misery?" Edmund swept his arm out in an arc to indicate the new section of the cemetery.

"All these fine men died in the war. Most aren't even buried here. Many of the men who did return are so injured in mind and body, there is little I can do for them. The only thing I am thankful for is that the doctors who were in the war have also returned and know what the men have experienced and can help them more than I can."

"It is a blessing, too, that you became a doctor after the war ended, or you would have had to serve.

"Father's death was the hardest. There was no warning. Mother was so devastated I feel so inept. I don't understand why God would allow this."

The pastor looked at Edmund and then followed his line of sight across the graveyard. "No one can, my boy, no one can. His ways are beyond our understanding. Always have been. Always will be." The pastor patted Edmund's shoulder in comfort. "I do know the Lord doesn't cause misery. Wasn't it one of your mother's favorite verses,

'All things work for good for those who fear and trust in the Lord'? We have to give those things, even the hard things, to the Lord for him to bless. Somehow, some good will come from it, but we must look for it and maybe never see it. It's a matter of faith, my son."

Edmund turned to face his minister. Freezing, stinging snowflakes fell on the old man's weathered face and gray hair. His thin wool cloak was wrapped around his round shoulders and bent back. Edmund didn't want to add to the bitter cold by expressing his doubts about a loving God or even of a god. He smiled, and with three silver dollars in his hand he shook the pastor's hand. "Thank you for your words, again, Pastor. I won't keep you out here in the frigid air any longer." Edmund turned and walked away before any more words could be said. The dark cold he felt in his spirit made the pelting snow unnoticeable.

❊ ❊ ❊

Edmund stepped out of the brougham. It was his first time in such a luxurious vehicle. It was enclosed, protecting him from the blustery wind, but he felt sorry for the driver, who sat outside, and for the horse that pulled the carriage through the narrow streets. He turned back to the vehicle and picked up his doctor's bag. The driver said as the horses moved forward, "That's the servants' door, Doctor. Just knock, and someone will show you the way to the scullery maid's room."

He listened to the hooves clop away on the cobblestoned back street. Sighing with relief, he saw a gas light had been lit over the servants' entrance at the base of three stone steps. He drew his wool cloak closer together at his chest as the wind blew snow down the stairwell, and then he knocked on the entrance. The manservant must have been waiting by the door, for it opened immediately.

"Come in, sir. The Madam said I was to show you the way to Colleen's room the moment you arrived. Mrs. Sterling wishes to see you in the library as soon as you finish your visit with the scullery maid."

Doctor Proft followed the butler up narrow steps to the fourth floor, the attic. The servant left, and the doctor knocked on a low wooden door. A moment later, he heard shuffling footsteps and then a voice.

"Who…who is it?"

"Doctor Proft. Mrs. Sterling requested I see you, as she feels you are ill. She will be responsible for payment."

He heard a chair scrape away from the door and saw the knob turn. It opened a crack. Red, swollen eyes stared at him. The door opened. He bent his head to clear the doorframe. The room was small, with one dirty window looking over the back street. The roof slanted from six feet in height to three. A small washstand with a chipped porcelain pitcher and washbasin stood by the door on one side, and on the other were hooks in the wall. One hook held a gray uniform dress and white bibbed apron; another hook held a tattered shawl, and another had a brown skirt, torn at the waist, with a matching bodice. In a corner, on the floor, was a commode.

"I understand you are not feeling well and refuse to leave your room."

"I need your help. I got a baby growing in me, and I want to get rid of it."

"You're sure you're pregnant?"

"Of course. I haven't had my time for two months, not since Master Sterling forced himself on me."

"What?" Doctor Proft dropped his bag onto the only chair in the room and faced the girl. "You can't be more than twelve years."

"I'm thirteen, almost. The Sterlings paid for my steerage passage from Ireland when I was eleven for my work in the kitchen for five years. Master Sterling came home from school for December holidays, and one night, when his parents were out, he came after me."

"Didn't the other servants come to your aid?"

"Of course not. They would lose their positions. I will lose mine when they see I am with child. Jobs are impossible to find."

"The Sterlings would not turn you away when they learned the infant is their grandchild."

Colleen moved away from the door to sit on the bed. Its squeak as the wood joints scraped against each other accented her sarcastic laugh. "They don't want their blue blood contaminated with the likes of mine. They will pay you for your services, and I will keep my job." Doctor Proft fiddled with the clasp of his bag. He pulled out his stethoscope and said, "I'll listen for a heartbeat. If there isn't any, we won't have a problem."

Colleen sat still on the bed. Proft listened and then straightened his back.

"There is a heartbeat."

"Make it stop."

"I can't do that. I took an oath to preserve life and not destroy it. My professors at the medical college would not sanction this. You must carry the child to term. You can give it up for adoption. I will see to it that you keep your job, if you really want it."

"If I want it? I have no other place to go. I have no money. I'd freeze within a week or die from starvation. I have to keep this job. I'll be fired once I start showing."

"I will talk to Mrs. Sterling tonight. I will tell her she has no choice but to keep you on. Trust me, I'll handle this." Doctor Proft put away his stethoscope, closed his bag, and moved to the door. "I'll be back next week to see you. Don't worry." He put his hand on the latch.

"Doctor, you don't know what my life will be like. You don't know." Colleen sobbed and curled up on the bed.

"I'll be back next week." Doctor Proft opened the door and closed it with a soft click. He went down the steps and found the butler, who showed him into the library. Mrs. Sterling stood from the Victorian chair near the fireplace.

"Is everything taken care of, Doctor Proft?"

"Yes, it is. I have assured Colleen that I will be back next week to check on her. I told her she will not be fired, and she will deliver the child and put it up for adoption."

"How dare you! I will not have that…that bastard linked to this house."

"Yes, you will. If you fire that girl or get another doctor to do this thing, I will let rumors fly about your aristocratic son and his proclivity for young, defenseless servant girls. Those stories will reach your high- tone social circle. You will be the talk of all society."

"You wouldn't dare. You can't discuss your patients."

"Your son is not my patient. Colleen is." The doctor pulled his cloak about him. "Now, you may have your butler notify the coachman to take me home. Goodnight." Doctor Proft strode swiftly from the room.

Mrs. Sterling stared at his back. *If he thinks he is going to force me with blackmail to keep that wench in this house, he is wrong, dead wrong.*

❋ ❋ ❋

Placing a crate in the back of a small, one horse-drawn wagon next to five other boxes, Doctor Edmund Proft stepped back. "Thank you, Mrs. Tootleman, for coming every day to help me care for Mother. I'm glad you are taking her things to give to the poor. I know she would want them used. I kept a few articles of clothing. I will take them to one of my patients. She has almost nothing." He gave a slight bow to the elderly lady standing next to him and took her gloved hand in his two bare hands.

"I'm glad I could help her. She was a dear lady. Her poor heart wept every day since your father's passing."

"Yes, his accident was so sudden, as all are, but still it is hard for us to bear. The past four months have been horrible, and now she is gone. The two people I loved, I couldn't help." The doctor blew on his hands to warm them and to hide his emotions.

"They were both very proud of you and loved you dearly. You must remember that."

The woman pulled her cape tight against her shoulders and wrapped her scarf around her throat another time. Gray clouds sent down a burst of flakes. "Are you going to continue to live in your parents' home?"

"Yes, I guess. I have patients to see. My practice is growing."

"I must say, it is. Isn't that a swank carriage coming up behind my wagon? I'll leave so you can find out who needs you. My, you are coming up in the world. Also, I want to get home before it's candlelight time."

"Yes, it will soon be dusk."

Edmund helped Mrs. Tootleman onto the wagon seat. She picked up the reins and drove it from the curb as the carriage behind her stopped.

"Doctor Proft."

"Yes."

"Mrs. Sterling says you will not be needed any further to tend to Colleen the scullery maid."

Doctor Proft chuckled. "Really? Well, that won't work. I will be by to see Colleen tomorrow."

"You can't, doctor. She climbed out her room window onto the roof and jumped. She's dead."

"Are you sure?" The doctor stiffened and sucked in his breath, forgetting the cold.

"Yes, sir. I helped the undertaker take the body to potter's field. Mr. Sterling paid the cleric from his church to say the proper words, and he represented the family at the burial. They sent this letter for you." The coachman handed Doctor Proft the envelope and drove off. Edmund staggered as he entered his house. It was quiet, somber, and dark. He looked at the small stack of clothing he'd been planning to take to Colleen.

He tore open the seal on the envelope, and a sheet of paper fell out with two silver coins. He picked up the letter and left the dollars lying on the floor.

Doctor Proft, this money should more than pay for your services. It is a pity you did not help the poor girl as requested, but that was your decision, and you shall have to live with it. If any unfortunate rumors should circulate about this matter, I am sure those rumors will be about your competence and abilities. We do hope that will not happen, as you would lose your practice if patients do not have confidence in their doctor. The letter was unsigned. Edmund read and reread the letter in disbelief. His hands shook until he lost control of his fingers, and the paper floated to the floor.

Didn't Colleen believe me when I said I would take care of everything? Did the family pressure her? Should I have done what she wanted? Is it my fault? Did I do the right thing? What point is it to be a doctor and not save people? What good am I?

Chapter Fifteen

"**A**bigail, come here."

Abigail left the bread she was kneading and went to the little parlor to sit next to her mother on a polished oak parson's bench. She noticed the paper in her mother's trembling hand. Her other hand held a handkerchief to her eyes. Tears stained her mother's cheeks.

"Ma, what is it?"

"Your father dropped off this letter from your Uncle Lemuel before he went out to the barn to help Jack. It just arrived in town. I couldn't wait until tonight to read it. You remember my sister Martha, the one who married Lemuel the same time I married your pa? They went out to the New Mexico Territories."

"Of course. I remember him from Aunt Martha's letters. Is someone ill?"

"No, dear." Alvina shuddered. "Your Aunt Martha has died."

"Oh, Ma, I'm so sorry." Abigail got up and knelt in front of her mother. She kissed her face and brushed back a strand of gray hair. "What happened? Did Uncle Lemuel say?"

"You read the letter, dear. Out loud. I can't believe my eyes. Perhaps I'll believe my ears." Alvina's hand shook as she handed the paper to Abigail. Abigail got up and sat on a straight-back chair by the fireplace.

She read:

"In this year of the Lord, 1871, "To Alvina Lester and her kin,

"I take pen in hand to bring to you sad news. Martha, my wife of twenty-four years, hung herself from the rafters in our sitting room while I was working in the barn. I fault her not, as she was melancholy for more than a year. Our sons, Silas and Otis, took it in their foolish heads to go to California to look for gold. They left in the night, taking two of my best riding horses. Martha said she knew they were going, as she'd prepared some provisions for them and given them all the egg money she had been saving. If I had known what those two fools were planning, I would have stopped them for sure.

"Just when those two were raised to be of help on the ranch, they ran off and left Martha and me to do everything. Martha got more and more melancholy each day the boys were gone. She missed them, and I think she was afeared they would not come back, even though they said they would when they struck it rich. Not likely, I told her time and again.

"I need help here with the housework, cooking, and the like. From your letters to Martha, I know you have a daughter, Abigail by name, that is grow'd but not able to find a husband because of her disfigurement. I also understand your son Jack has posted banns in the church to get married. After the wedding, you stated the couple will live at your farm, as the boy inherits the property, which is the proper thing. As a new woman will be in the house to help you and Abigail an extra mouth to feed, likely not wanted once the new woman moves in, I propose that she come here to live on my ranch. She could come for a month to see if she is up to the work. If I find she is hearty, I will provide a respectable place for her in my house. She would be the only woman and in charge of all female things. I do not require a handsome woman to be my partner in this life; I require only willing hands and a sturdy body.

"Discuss this, and if she decides to come, send me word when she is to arrive in Wild River, and I will meet her there and bring her out to the ranch.

"I am a God-fearing man. I do not drink, nor do I gamble. They are the works of the devil. Everyone in town knows I am a good rancher and a hard worker. Send me word on your decision at the earliest.

"Your brother-in-law and widow,

"Lemuel Baxter"

Abigail's hand shook, and her lower lip trembled. "He's right, Ma. After Jack's wife moves in, I will be the odd one out, a fifth wheel on the cart, not wanted."

"Nonsense, dear. We love you and want you. Jack, too. We will work things out. We'll find a way."

Abigail stared at the floor. *I knew when Jack started courting Libby, I would need to leave someday. But, to go where? I am a recluse. I seldom go to town, and when I do, it is such a stressful time I hate it. I know I could never work in town with the eyes of some staring at my face and others averting their eyes when they see me. And all feeling pity for me. Maybe working for Uncle Lemuel at a ranch a good distance from town and neighbors could be the answer. Couldn't it?*

Chapter Sixteen

*T*his can't be Wild River. This must be a mistake! I thought it would be much bigger and more settled by now. The stage stopped in front of a building boasting "Wild River Grand Hotel" on the sign that swung in the hot wind. Edmund stepped off the stagecoach and stretched his aching muscles. A gust of wind blew sand and dust into his eyes, causing them to burn. After closing his eyelids for a moment and wiping them with a linen handkerchief, he surveyed the weathered buildings lining the dusty street. A gunsmith store, a tonsorial parlor, and a harness shop were at one end of the street; the general store, the hotel, saloon, and freight office filled in the middle; and the road ended with the jail, livery, and blacksmith. The buildings were unevenly dispersed. Houses appeared between the stores and at the street ends. A weathered frame house, which seemed to be the oldest building in the town, stood at the elevated end of the road. The village layout appeared haphazard, the buildings, like wind-blown weeds, sprouting up by chance.

He felt boxed in. Men unloaded a freight wagon in front of the Overland Freight Office and jostled the stage driver as he unloaded the luggage and mailbag. One man unhitched the six horses from the coach and then led them to the livery as a new team arrived to take their place for the next twenty miles of the route. The men moved through the haze of the heat at a slow pace and cursed the animals in their charge. Three women, their dresses and bonnets faded from the grueling sun, stood in front of the general store and conversed. They ceased their conversation when a man barreled by them, carrying a crate of squawking chickens into the shop. All the inhabitants trudged as if weighed down. *Elizabeth's journal said everything was green and fresh and the people young and cheerful. The people I see look worn and used-up.*

He shook his head and forced a smile as he turned his attention back to the coach. He extended his gray-kid gloved hand to a young lady's gloved hand and helped her down. The lace scarf wrapped around her head allowed her eyes, nose, and mouth to be visible. He remembered the material had been white when he'd encountered her as she'd gotten off the train at Saint Louis, but now, like her gloves, it showed the gray discoloration of the long journey.

"Thank you, Dr. Proft. You've been very kind. Without you, this trip would have been unbearable." The woman, her hands trembling, pulled her scarf tighter against the right side of her face.

"It's I who should thank you, Miss Lester, for your companionship, which made the trip more pleasant. I'm sorry we were the only two hapless souls to cushion each other during the jerks and jolts for the last fifty miles. The driver must have aimed the coach for every rock and hole in the road. I don't think there is much life left in the springs in this conveyance."

"We did get tossed around a bit, didn't we?"

"Yes, and you were forgiving when I landed on your feet." He smiled. *She has such lovely deep brown eyes... it's a shame her face is so disfigured.*

"Excuse me. You are Miss Abigail Lester, aren't you? I heard you were arriving today," a middle-aged woman said as she approached the couple. The woman stopped talking and stared at Abigail's face, blinking several times at the sight of the blotched and scarred face showing through the thin scarf. She averted her eyes and looked past Abigail. She began stammering. "Your...your uncle said you...you were coming to live at the ranch with him. My name is Sabilla Platt. My husband and I own the general store. I wanted to greet you and extend an invitation to church services."

Abigail turned the unscarred side of her face to Sabilla and bit her lower lip before answering, "Yes, I'm Miss Lester."

Edmund Proft sensed Abigail's embarrassment and decided to draw Sabilla's attention away from her. "My name is "

"Don't be rude. I was speaking to Miss Lester." Sabilla had regained her composure and faced Abigail's profile. "We don't have a preacher, so Sheriff Clement and his wife Hortensia hold informal church services at their house on Sundays at ten o'clock." She pointed to the frame house at the higher end of the street. "Afterward, we have a potluck lunch or picnic. Everyone brings an item of food and their own eating utensils. Your uncle and cousins have been invited, but your uncle says too much time is lost from chores. Perhaps with you at the ranch he will change his mind. Please, try to persuade him." Sabilla extended her callused hand and laid it on Abigail's arm.

"We would love to have you come, my dear."

"I'll do what I can." Abigail stared down at the dirt.

Sabilla faced Edmund. She squared her shoulders. "As for you, you are indeed invited, but we don't expect you to come, of course. You should get married. Maybe your wife could drag you to our service." Sabilla looked up the street. "I see my husband is waiting for me. I must say goodbye." She hustled off, her high-button shoes kicking up dust. "Do you know her?" Abigail watched Mrs. Platt as she headed to the general store.

"No, I don't know anyone outside of my hometown in Connecticut. She is an odd duck if there ever was one. I wonder why she thinks I need a wife to drag me to church service." Edmund looked at Abigail, and they burst into laughter.

"Abigail, is this your trunk?" a harsh voice demanded.

Startled, they turned. An older man in a short-sleeved, cotton underwear union suit and bib overalls marched up to them. The armpits of the underwear were black from sweat.

"Yes, it is. Are you Uncle Lemuel?"

Edmund stepped toward the man when he saw Abigail's posture stiffen.

"Yup. Hurry up. We got a long way to go. I want to git to the ranch afore nightfall. Your two cousins came back from the gold fields without a nugget in their pockets. They're not worth a nickel in getting chores done if 'n I ain't there to hound them. Come. I'll put your claptrap in the wagon." He lifted the trunk and heaved it into the cart.

"Uncle Lemuel, I want you to meet Doctor...."

Lemuel looked at Edmund as he got up on the wagon seat. "Told you, we ain't got time for socializing. Git in." He picked up the reins and made it plain the next movement would be to urge the mules forward.

"I am truly sorry, Dr. Proft." Abigail averted her eyes.

"Don't be. I understand. I'll help you get seated."

Edmund carried her portmanteau as they walked to the side of the wagon seat and set it next to her trunk as he helped her settle in.

"She'll be no good to me at the ranch if she can't get into a wagon on her own." Lemuel snapped the reins on the mules' rumps, and the cart jolted forward.

Edmund heard the two exchange a few words.

"Uncle, you weren't polite to the doctor."

"Humph. The likes of him ain't no doctor."

"What do you mean?" The iron-rimmed wheels spat dust as the wagon rumbled and creaked down the street.

She has a tough life ahead, but at least she has relatives to take her in and provide for her. A renewed sense of loss for his parents shot through him for a moment. Suppressing his emotions, he brushed his suit coat and derby hat with his hand. The dust billowed off his attire before it settled down, some back onto his clothes. He took his suitcase and a leather bag from the frowning driver, who smelled of horses and sweat. *I heard the West was hard, but I hadn't thought the people were.*

A slam in his back jolted him a step forward.

"Move, mister."

He spun to face the voice. The man backed up a step and stammered, "Oh! Right sorry. I didn't know it was you. I was just getting the mailbag. No offense meant."

"No offense taken." The doctor raised his voice as the stranger grabbed the mailbag and stalked off before looking back with a grimace.

Dr. Proft clenched his bags. Marching toward the hotel, he muttered, "The manners of these people are no better than their slovenly appearance." *My parents could never have lived here. They were genteel people. Now I realize why they returned to Connecticut to raise me. And this place would not be to Elizabeth's liking, I'm sure. I must be in the wrong place."*

He stepped onto wooden planks laid together in the dirt to form what he suspected was the town's attempt at a boardwalk. The loose wood led to the hotel and ended as if its job were done. *Either the town ran out of wood or money to continue the walk, or the rest of the buildings on this side of the street are not considered worthy of a boardwalk.* The hotel looked newer than the other buildings, as its wooden sides were more yellow than gray. He took note of the sign again: "Wild River Grand Hotel."

Going across the plank floor to the counter, he heard the sand grind under the soles of his shoes. A man's back was toward him. He swatted flies buzzing around a sticky stain on the wall. Dr. Proft picked up the pen. Wiping the tip clean on the register's side, he dipped the pen into the ink bottle and signed his name. The hotel owner turned around.

"I ain't never seen anyone so dandy fide before. Ah, no offense, but you sure are lookin' fancy. How come you're here? Not that you need to explain anything to me. No siree. Just curious is all, and "

Edmund put down the pen with a sigh. *Just my luck. This guy is a prattler, and I'm too tired, hot, and hungry to be polite.* He broke into the man's speech.

"My name is Doctor Edmund Proft, and I assure you, I want a room. Now!"

"Sure. Take number six. Overlooks the front street. It's no never mind to me if you want to spend two bits a night to stay here and call yourself a doctor. Ain't no never mind to me. No, never mind." The man's voice trembled.

Edmund interrupted again, "Do you have bathing facilities here?" He needed a bath, even if the other residents of the town didn't see the need to smell and look clean.

"Of course. The bathing room is at the end of the hall. Just twenty cents extra for me to haul two buckets of hot water up to the tub. I'll bring the water up directly. Towels and soap an extra five cents."

"That's fine. Bring the water as soon as possible." Edmund took the key and carried his luggage to his room. He unpacked and brought clean clothing into the bathing room. The focus of the room was a metal tub with four squat metal legs that looked like animal paws. After bathing he tipped the tub, and the water spilled through a hole in the floor near the wall. It flowed down an open, long box to the ground outside the building, where it splashed onto the hard dirt, making a mud puddle until it dried in the heat.

❋ ❋ ❋

After his bath, Edmund settled into his room. He opened his carpet bag and took out a leather-bound book. Opening the front cover, he slid out a gray daguerreotype of a young couple. The man was dressed in a white shirt, a frock coat, and a string black tie, his face tilted to the side. He was clean-shaven except for a mustache and stood behind a seated woman with his hand resting on her shoulder. With her hands folded in her lap, she sat at an angle, half facing the man. Her waist-length hair was tied back with a ribbon. She wore a white muslin, high-necked dress with mutton sleeves.

As Edmund looked at the picture, he touched his upper lip and mustache. *I thought I understood them, but now I don't. Elizabeth's journal is filled with the hardships of her journey, but the people she described were young and friendly. She wrote that they crossed the Wild River. Maybe it is a different river than the one near this town.* He rifled through the pages of the book. *This was to be an adventure to retrace their journey. I thought I could connect with them and know them better. But, this place and people are not like them. This was a journey of a thousand miles for nothing but misery.* He replaced the book and closed the bag.

He shaved his day-old whiskers, trimmed his mustache, scrubbed his shirt in a washbasin, and hung it on the back of a chair to dry. He washed his handkerchief to remove the stains from the tobacco spit he'd wiped off the train seat. Brushing his brown suit, he shook it several times and frowned when he saw it had a few cinder burns acquired from his train ride to St. Louis. He'd had to sit near the window to get some fresh air in the dusty, black gritty, foul-smelling train car. The pungent cigar smoke choking the air with its blue stench had given him and other passengers a dry, hacking cough. He'd preferred contending with the coal cinders blowing in through the window and landing on his tailored suit. *From the way people dress out here in this forsaken land, I doubt the holes will be noticed.*

A wind gust blew the leather curtain taking the place of glass on the one window in the room. He looked out and searched for something green; instead he saw only brown and gray. He rolled up the cloth and tied it with a strap hanging down from the top edge, deciding the dust was preferable to the infernal flapping and snapping of the leather.

He finished dressing and hurried down the staircase without touching the dusty handrail. The same man brandished the fly swatter behind the desk.

"Where can I get something to eat?"

The clerk blinked as if he didn't understand the question.

"Eat," Edmund prompted. He snapped his fingers. "Food!"

"Same place. My brother Buster's saloon. Steak, eggs, and coffee. Cost fifteen cents. It ain't changed none." The condescending tone of the clerk irritated Edmund.

"I've never been here before. You act as if I should know where to eat. What's the matter with this town?" He shook his head and walked next door to the saloon. The smell of whiskey and warm beer assailed his nostrils as he pushed aside the half-open door. The floor was covered with a thin layer of wood shavings and sawdust. Three men slumped in chairs at a table were drinking beer. The doctor saw their dirty necks, their grimy clothes, and their filthy, torn fingernails. *They haven't washed in weeks*. Edmund looked at his clean nails and smiled.

He stepped up to rough boards supported by wooden barrels. A husky bartender wiped sweat from his face and used the same cloth to wipe a glass. On the other side of the planks, an unshaven man was drinking whiskey between hacking coughs. *Dust pneumonia. He doesn't have too much time left*. The bartender did a double-take and stared at him when Edmund asked what he could get for supper.

"What do you think?" quizzed the bartender. "I serve the same thing to everyone."

"Fine. I'll have it," snapped Edmund. *How would I know what he serves? Everyone must be slow-witted to survive out here. The next coach east will take me back home. I belong where I was raised and not where I was born.* He went to a back table and wiped sawdust and a chicken feather off the chair seat with his handkerchief, then sat down on a creaky straight-back chair.

He studied the room. Sand and dirt blew into the saloon and swirled around before settling to coat everything. This included two chickens wandering in and pecking at whatever they fancied on the dirt and sawdust floor as they left behind their droppings.

He listened to the men at the table. They wagered whether a man named Clement could hold his own against a Miranda. Edmund tried to figure out if they were talking about a contest like horseshoes or a fisticuffs bout.

The bartender came with his meal. He brushed the flies off the table and set down a burnt steak. The edges flopped over the rim of the tin plate. Three eggs with runny yolks and whites sat on top of the meat. The black coffee sloshed in the cup as the man put it down with a fork and a hunting knife.

Edmund picked up the huge knife, asking, "What's this for?"

"To cut the meat, what else?" the bartender said as he walked away. His tone implied, "What's wrong with you?"

Edmund sawed the steak and, with effort, cut off a gristly portion. The inside was red. The blood flowed onto the half-cooked eggs. He slammed the knife down. *Disgusting! How can people live this way*? He pushed the tin cup and plate away as the saloon door opened wider.

"Hey. It's happening right now. Hurry!" The excited voice ceased, and the door swung on its hinges. The customers and the barkeep left their places and scrambled down the side of the street.

"What's going on?" Edmund joined the men. Two men in the harness shop stepped out onto the boardwalk. Three women stood by the general store. The stable man and freight men stopped unloading a wagon. Glancing around, Edmund saw nothing out of the ordinary.

The bartender said, "It's Miranda, all right. You can tell he is looking for a fight." The bartender stared at one end of the street.

Edmund turned his gaze in that direction. A man moved step by step down the side of the street. Edmund looked at the other end. A taller man approached with a deliberate pace. The two men stopped fifty feet apart.

Edmund sucked in air as his eyes widened when an explosion startled him. The shorter man lay in the dirt with a gun in his hand. The other man stood clutching pistols. A light wisp of smoke drifted up from the guns until the wind blew it into a million particles as if it had never existed.

Edmund's mouth dropped. He watched the crowd and the shooter in disbelief. "You're all crazy. This can't happen. It happens only in… in dime novels. Not in civilized life. People don't live this way. There are laws!"

His words were lost in the commotion of "Well done," "Good riddance," and "Served him right, the thief." Everyone talked at the same time.

Edmund ran to the figure in the dirt. He stooped and felt for a pulse in the man's neck. None. He didn't expect any when he saw a bleeding wound in the chest where the heart should be pumping. He fell on one knee as a sense of defeat welled up in him. With a gentle hand, he closed the man's eyes. "I can't help him," he muttered to no one.

Boot steps ground into the dirt behind him. A man's shadow with guns in his hands fell across the body.

"You killed him. You're a murderer!" Edmund stood and turned to face the gunman as he repeated, "You're a murderer!" Gasping, he stared into his mirror image. The man had the same build and wavy black hair as he. Underneath the three-day whiskers and dirt was the same line of the mouth, the pointed jaw, but most of all, his deep-set gray eyes. Edmund's head jerked back as his mouth fell open, sucking air. He felt his heart skip a beat before it started racing.

People edged around the two men. "Hey, what's this?"

"What do you make of this?"

"Who's the fella in the fancy suit?"

"He looks like Jason, sort of." Their voices sounded sharp and critical.

The hotel owner raised his voice above the din. "This here fella," he declared as he pointed to Edmund, "registered at the hotel as Doctor Edmund Proft. I saw right away something was odd. He sure does look like Jason."

"My brother Hiram is right. When the stranger ordered his supper at the saloon, I thought he was Jason, only daft," said Buster Buttwill.

"Yup, I mistook him for Jason, all right. I thought no never mind to me if Jason wants to stay at the hotel. Yup, I did."

Edmund heard the droning of the clerk, but he concentrated on the man standing before him. He thought the stranger seemed to be as bewildered as he was. But in a blink, he saw the man's face become hard and his eyes turn cold. The man holstered his guns and turned away with contempt.

A voice in the crowd rang out, "Stop, Jason. You're under arrest." The shooter stiffened, crossed his hands in front of him, and grasped his gun butts.

Chapter Seventeen

"It was a fair fight, sheriff," yelled a voice from the crowd. Other voices joined in with, "It was fair. I'll swear to it."

Edmund shook his head in disbelief. *Killing is fair?*

The crowd parted to allow a balding man with a handlebar mustache and a sheriff's badge pinned on his cotton shirt to come close to the dead man.

"You got to go to jail, Jason. We'll have a hearing soon as the judge gets to town on Monday. You'll be treated fair. You know that." Jason drew his guns. The crowd stepped back. The sheriff and Jason stared into each other's eyes for a moment. Suddenly, the gunman flipped the Colts, so the butts were toward the sheriff.

"Sure, Clement. I could use a night or two in jail. But I need someone to tend to my stock, and can your wife cook the suppers?"

"She sure will. And Sam's boy, Kenny, will be happy to go out to your place and look after things, like he's done afore." The sheriff grasped the pistols in his gnarled hands. The two men walked together to a small shack. The title "Jail" was hand-lettered on a board and nailed over the door.

Three men picked up the dead man and carried him toward the livery.

"Why are they taking the man there?" The doctor stood with the remaining crowd.

"They'll throw him in a wagon, and the livery man will haul him out to boot hill. He gets paid for each grave he digs," the bartender explained.

"That's all there is to it? A man just died! Civilized people don't kill people in the middle of the street in broad daylight." Edmund choked as he spoke. He forced down a swallow of saliva to ease his dry throat.

"It happens here, mister. Ain't nothin' more can be done. That's what I say." The hotel clerk left with the crowd following him. Everyone talked about how peculiar it was for the stranger and Jason to look so much alike.

Edmund stood frozen. The blood on the ground was almost covered by the sand as the wind whipped up the street. He let out a deep sigh as he held onto his derby and marched to the Butterfield Overland Stage Office and Freight building.

✻ ✻ ✻

"Hortensia, did you hear Miguel Miranda is dead?"

A woman straightened her back and leaned on a hoe. She arranged her poke bonnet to shield her eyes from the sun as she answered,

"Yes, I did, Sabilla. And how are you on this hot day?"

"Breathing better now that Miranda is dead. He vowed he was going to kill Jason, the judge, and your husband. I just saw the men carrying his body to the livery. What would this town do if he had killed Clem? We need him here as sheriff."

"Thank you, Sabilla. I appreciate him, too." Hortensia pulled over a crate leaning against the side of her small frame house and sat down.

"Of course, dear. What would you do without him? I feel sorry for you, as it must be such a worry with him being in such a dangerous job. And he must feel awful having to put Jason in jail, you being such good friends with him and all. But folks will speak up for Jason come Monday. I know I will."

"Fine." Hortensia had begun to weed her garden earlier in an effort to calm her fears when she'd heard Miranda was in town looking for her husband. Then, guilty feelings over her happiness at his death demanded an outlet, and whacking weeds in the garden answered that need. Sabilla's speaking ill of the dead brought chills to her spine, though. Hortensia felt tension creep back into her body. She again straightened her back as she prepared to stand. "If you'll excuse me, I need to start fixing the biscuits and stew for Clem and Jason. I've some elderberry jam for the biscuits, and I'm going to put a few pine nuts in Jason's stew, as he likes them so. My Clem is allergic to them. Breaks out something awful."

"Before you go in, did you know there is a stranger in town who says he's a doctor? All the way from back East. And of all things, he's the spitting image of Jason, 'cept they don't dress the same, of course."

"No. I didn't hear that. I think the nearest real doctor is over two hundred miles from here. Won't it be fine to have a doctor in town?"

Hortensia, pulling her body upright with the hoe, stood and took a few swipes at her vegetable garden.

"I'm afraid not. He just bought a ticket from the Overland Stage Office. He's going back. Just got here and is going home, ain't that strange? And him, lookin' like Jason. They could be twins. I heard about twins afore, but I ain't ever seen any. I thought they had to have the same ma and pa and get born the same time. And it is certain sure Old Eli would have found two infants when he found one, unless maybe one drowned, but then he couldn't come here as a doctor. It makes little sense. What do you think?"

"I have no idea, Sabilla, but I do need to check on my stew."

"All right, then. Give my regards to Clem. I'm glad he weren't killt."

"I will, Sabilla." Hortensia stopped hoeing and arched her back

to ease the ache as she rubbed her callused hands. She leaned the hoe against the back wall of the house and stepped into the kitchen, where she removed her bonnet and pinned back gray strands straggling out of the bun at the base of her neck.

After wiping the perspiration from her face with the hem of her apron, she lifted the lid from a pot and savored the aroma of the simmering contents. She stirred the stew with her cast-iron spoon and tasted it. Smacking her lips to get all the rich gravy, she replaced the lid to let it cook a bit more. She spread jam on biscuits before she wrapped them in a cloth. Licking drops of dark, sticky jam from her fingers, she studied a sheaf of dried elderberries hanging near the stove. *I'm glad I cooked some of the berries. But I should move these uncooked ones away from the stove. They're poisonous when raw, and I don't want any to fall into the food. Imagine, a doctor in town. Someone who looks like Jason. A twin. Could be possible, given what happened years ago. And we do need a doctor. So many bad things happen with all the new settlers-- more accidents, more illnesses, and more violence. If he had to stay around a few days and take care of someone sick, he might change his mind...especially if that someone was Jase.* She stared at the berries. *Of course, it's not a nice thing for me to do.*

Hortensia ladled stew into two metal pails with lids. Picking a few elderberries from the vine, she mixed them in one pail. *Just a few. I hope the stranger is a good doctor.* She sprinkled pine nuts on top. She wrote "Jason" on a piece of scrap brown paper. She pinned the paper with Jason's name to the pail of pine nuts, elderberries, and stew.

❋ ❋ ❋

"Can't I do it, Pa? Can't I? I know how real good."

The livery owner stopped harnessing the two horses to the wagon. He turned and looked into his son's eyes, as he breathed heavily and leaned against the horse's withers.

"I could earn the money all by myself. I'll put it with the shiny Indian cent Jason gave me a long time ago. Do you want to see it, Pa? Do you?"

"Sure, Kenny. I want to see it." Sam figured this was about the hundredth time his son had shown him the coin.

The young, lanky man took a red bandana from his pants pocket and untied a knot he had made in the corner. On the cloth lay a shiny copper piece. "Ain't it pretty, Pa?"

"You have done real good in taking care of it. You can dig the grave and get the two cents."

"Can I drive the wagon by myself too, Pa?" Kenny tied up his coin.

"Sure. I'll ride in the back with the body. I can help you find the right spot to dig the hole, but you can do the digging, I promise. First, you need to get something. What is it?"

Kenny looked around. "We got the wagon, we got the horses, we got the body. We got everything, Pa."

"To dig a hole, we bring…."

"The pick and shovel, Pa! I'll get them." Kenny sprinted with his long, skinny legs into the barn.

"Bring a canteen of water, too. We'll need it with this heat." Sam spread a ragged blanket in the back of the wagon and sat on it with his feet dangling over the edge. He felt more than heard the wheeze in his chest. *I'm all he's got. What will happen to him when I'm gone? Lord, I don't know.*

Kenny returned with the grave-digging tools and canteens. "I brought two canteens, so we have plenty for the horses and us. Don't look so worried, Pa. I can drive the team real good." Sitting on the front seat, he gave a light slap of the reins on the horses' rumps. They lowered their heads and pulled forward. Kenny sat up straight, his smile stretching from ear to ear as he took up the slack in the reins.

❋ ❋ ❋

Sam tethered the horses under a stand of cottonwoods. He sat in the shade and watched his son work for his pennies as the horses swatted flies with their tails. No trees or fence sectioned off the graveyard. It blended in with the dry, flat, red and brown earth.

Kenny shoveled the last scoop of dirt on top of the grave, then gulped warm water from a canteen. With the shovel over his shoulder, he left the small section of unmarked graves and went over to another section containing old wooden crosses, some made of sturdy planed wood and some of skinny tree branches denuded of leaves and tied in a cross shape with bull muhly grass twisted into a rope. The planed crosses bore a name and some even a date. Two crosses had tipped over, one all the way to the ground. Kenny righted each one and tamped more dirt around the base, then braced them with rocks he gathered from the stony cemetery.

He went back to the cottonwoods. "Pa, I'm done. You want to take a look-see? I did good."

"I know you did. I don't need to look. Let's give the horses a drink and go home." Sam put a hand against the tree trunk to steady himself as he stood. Looking at the road as it curled its way back to town, he saw a wagon approaching slowly. He reached into his cart and grabbed his rifle.

"I think I've seen these folks before." Carrying his rifle at his side, he walked to the road and arrived just as the wagon stopped, pulled by an old black nag. He focused a wary eye on the older man and woman on the seat. "You folks need something?"

"*Si, Señor*. My wife and I want to put flowers on our son's grave."

"Your son is Miguel Miranda?"

"*Si*." The man and woman kept their eyes on the ground. The wildflowers in the woman's hand trembled.

"It's fine, I reckon. Kenny, help the Señora down, and bring the canteen to water the flowers."

"*Gracias.*"

Kenny held his hand out to the woman as she stepped down from the wagon. The couple made their way to the fresh grave. They knelt and prayed for a moment, and the woman dug a small hole in the fresh-turned earth with her fingers to place wild buckwheats and desert trumpets in it. She patted the dirt around them and drizzled water over the soil. Sam and Kenny waited behind them until the couple got to their feet. The four together went back to the wagon.

"I've seen you two in town on occasion. You took over Miguel's place after he went to jail, right? Didn't know you were related," Sam said.

"*Si*. We came from Mexico when he was in prison. We thought we could keep it going so he would have a home when he got out. But when he came back, he was not our boy anymore. He was hard and mean." The father shook his head and put his arm around his wife.

She cried into a handkerchief and leaned against her husband.

"He said he was going to kill the men who sent him to hell--his name for the prison. We tried to talk him out of it, but he would not listen to us. He was a good boy once."

"He stole one time to feed his animals. He tried to buy the feed, but the storekeeper asked for double the price because he was a Mexican. Our son could not pay it, but his horse was getting sick just grazing on grass," *Señor* Miranda explained.

"You folks get charged double, too?" Sam asked.

"*Si*, we do in Wild River, so we go to Mexico when we need to buy something. We raise vegetables to sell or trade, also chickens and eggs."

"Everyone should pay the same price. If you folks need items from town, let me know. I'll buy them, and you can pay me the regular price. I run the livery stable."

"*Gracias.*" The man took off his sombrero. "Would you be able to buy a plow mule for us? We talked to Mr. Baxter. He said the price was two hundred and fifty dollars. We do not have so much. I offered to pay a hundred now and the rest later, but he laughed at me."

"Yeah, Lemuel sold me a couple mules once for two hundred a head, but he wanted the money up front. If you get another hundred dollars together, I'll buy it for you."

"*Gracias*! It will take a long time before we will have the money. A long time."

Kenny helped the woman climb back onto the wagon seat. A tear fell on her empty hands. She looked up at the graveyard to pick out her son's place with her eyes. A breeze made the bluebonnets sway. Kenny watched her face; seeing her eyes were red and puffy, he said, "I didn't know he had a ma and pa. I thought he was just a thief and a dirty Mex."

"Kenny! That's not nice."

Kenny seemed surprised. "I'm sorry, Pa. I didn't know I said something bad. Everyone says it."

"Not everyone, Kenny. I don't, and I don't want you talking that way, either. Apologize to the *señora*."

"I'm sorry, *Señora*. I didn't mean to say a bad thing. I'll put more water on the flowers before we go, if you like."

"That would be nice of you. *Gracias.*" Tears spilled out onto her lashes. "You're a good boy."

Sam turned his face to the horse to hide his embarrassment. He didn't like what Kenny said, and he remembered the old blanket he'd wrapped around the body. He knew he could have found something better. To distract everyone but mostly to get his mind off his feelings, he felt the legs of the horse and studied its teeth. "Do you know how to skin a horse properly?"

"*Si.*"

"When the time comes, I'll buy the skin for six bits. The meat is likely tough, but I might get a little for it if you want me to sell it for you."

"You are most kind. He is old, but I think with good care he will last a year or two more. When the day comes, I will remember your words." Mr. Miranda sat on the wagon seat and picked up the reins. He slapped them with a gentle hand and clucked his tongue. The horse pulled forward down the road away from town.

"Pa, I'm glad I did a good job on the grave for their son." "Me, too."

❋ ❋ ❋

Abigail climbed down from the wagon. Feeling awkward and jittery, she fidgeted with her veil as she stepped over to the mules' heads. She put her face against the neck of the animal her uncle called Obadiah. Breathing in the sweat smell brought a quick smile.

"Your remind me of Rosie, my father's mule in Ohio." She studied the nearest corral. Three burros stood near the fence. The next corral, behind the barn, had six mares and six young mule foals. In the distance, she saw several full-grown mules grazing. She again smiled. *The animals look well cared-for. Uncle Lemuel must be a caring person, for all of his stern talk.*

Lemuel Baxter took her trunk and carpetbag from the wagon and shoved them through the door of the tool shed. "I got a cot in here for you to sleep on. It wouldn't be fittin' for you to sleep in the house unless we were married." He reached into his pocket and pulled out a nail. Handing it to her, he said, "You can pound this nail in the wall to hang up your things. Hit it straight, so when I remove it, it will still be good, and I won't have to bend it back. Bending weakens them. They cost money. Do you need two, or will one do?"

"Oh, the one will do, I'm sure." Abigail took the hard metal. She felt small, like the nail, only bent and weak, as she entered the dark tool shed. *I could use many more than two, but I'd better not say so.* The light from the doorway showed a room filled with harnesses, tools, and wood stacked around the walls. Her nose wrinkled at the smell of old leather, rotting wood, and dust filling the hot air. She touched the rough wood of the cot. The creak of its joints made her doubt its strength. Her foot kicked against an unlit candle and holder on the floor. She noticed the scrape marks in the dirt where some things had been moved to fit the cot into the shed, but just enough.

"There isn't room for my bag and trunk. Where should they go?"

"Your one bag is small enough to go under the bed. You can keep the trunk outside along the wall. I can't move anything out of the shed, as I don't want it getting wet if there's rain."

She saw him studying her. "As I said in my letter, I'll give it a month's trial. If you can handle the work, I'll keep my promise and provide you with a home, and we can put your belongings in a permanent place in the house." Lemuel stood outside at the doorway.

"You'd best go on to the house and get familiar with the kitchen. We need supper tonight, me and the boys. Martha ate after we finished so we could get back to work. Expect you to do the same."

"Of course, Uncle." Abigail went out the door, squinting in the bright sunlight. *My family always ate breakfast and supper together. I think Uncle is saying I am a servant in his house.* She bowed her head, followed her uncle to the house, and went in behind him.

"Hey, what are you two doing in here? Get out and finish your chores." Lemuel held the kitchen door wide open. "So long as you're here, meet your cousin, Abigail." He stepped aside as Abigail came forward.

"Reason we're here, Pa. Is she as ugly as you said she might be?" The taller of two men got up from the bench and lunged at Abigail. He tore the lace shawl from her head and threw it on the table.

"Whoo-ee! She's uglier than we thought, ain't she, Otis?"

"Yeah, Silas, she's one awful-lookin' woman."

Abigail lurched back when Silas snatched the shawl from her. She tried to cover her face with her hands. Tears filled her eyes.

"How did you get like that?" Silas's jeering smile seemed natural on his face.

"When I was nine, I fell against a hot stove and a pan of boiling water fell on me. One side of my face, an arm, and a hand were burned."

"Whoo-ee! Bet it smarted, huh?" Otis got up. He ran his fingers through his shoulder-length, unwashed hair.

Abigail thought he wanted to touch her skin and hair, so she stepped back farther. "I nearly died. I was sick for months."

"You boys, leave her be. She came here to cook and take your ma's place. Don't matter what she looks like. You get out and finish your chores. She's got supper to make."

Silas, Otis, and Lemuel tromped out the door, leaving it open. Abigail listened to her cousins laughing and hooting as Lemuel nagged at them to get back to their chores. Her legs felt weak and unable to hold her. Avoiding the only chair at the head of the plank table, she sat on one of the two benches on either side. She yanked a handkerchief out of her pocket. Sobs burst out of her as the tears gushed into the cloth. *God, I just want to curl up and die. Please, let me.* When the handkerchief was soaked, she pulled up the hem of her dress to her face. Voices coming from the barn broke into her awareness. She glanced out the door. *I can't let them see I care what they say, or they will continue to taunt me. I know it.* Forcing herself to stand, she staggered to the washtub used for the dishes. She dipped water from a bucket on the floor and gulped it. Splashing the tepid water on her face, she rubbed hard to get rid of the tearstains. Letting out a deep breath, she looked at the dirty, unkempt room serving as a kitchen and sitting room. The rancid grease in the cast-iron skillets assailed her nose like skunk spray. She put the pans in the washtub, poured water on them, and then investigated the bins and shelves to see what food was available.

A smile curled up her mouth when she saw the pie safe. *Ma said Grandpa made his two girls matching pie safes, as they married on the same day. Just like Ma's, only Aunt Martha's is more scratched.* She ran her hands over it. The two side ends of the wood cupboard had blue-gray metal plates inserted. Each had a flower design punched into it. The front doors had the same design, only larger and in more detail. Each punch produced a small hole going through the metal, small enough to let in air but not flies. She traced each hole with her fingers.

Abigail opened the doors. *Ants!* She looked at the four legs of the cupboard. Each stood on a small wooden block inserted in a shallow tin. *I see. The water evaporated, and some time ago, it looks like.* She put three dippers of water in each of the tin plates. *Now the ants won't be able to get in, and I can scrub out the cupboard.* Abigail stood straight and tall. *I am needed here.*

Chapter Eighteen

A smile fluttered across Edmund's face. Memory glimpses flickered in his brain like a candle flame: Mr. Farris polishing the shaving cups embossed with the names of each customer of his tonsorial parlor; Mrs. Tootleman planting geraniums, the deepest red, like brilliant rubies, dancing in the summer breeze; Mr. Claxton white-washing his picket fence a dazzling white at this time every year; and the green of the leaves and grass, so glossy and brilliant, basking in the sunshine to the point of hurting the eyes. All these memories transported him home.

"Mister, you heered me?"

"What?" Edmund jerked his head up and shifted his gaze from the cold, ink-black liquid the bartender called coffee to a lanky man standing by the table. The kerosene lamps cast flickering shadows like gray smoke around the saloon. The din of the customers talking, laughing, and arguing swarmed into his ears like stinging wasps.

"I axed if I could sit and talk with you a minute."

"I suppose," said Edmund. An involuntary sigh shuddered through him.

"Hey, dummy, your pa doesn't want you in here. I don't want him riled with me for letting you in." The bartender put a glass of beer in front of a customer as he yelled.

"Yes, Mr. Buttwill. I got to speak to the doctor for a minute. Then I'll go."

"See that you do."

"Yes, sir."

The young man sat down at Edmund's table. "My name is Kenny, and I was walkin' by the jail when the sheriff hollered out the window and axed me to fetch you."

"Why?"

"Jason Wilcox is sick. He's vomiting and has chills and fever. The sheriff's worried it might be dipothea or something that's catching."

"You mean diphtheria?"

"I guess. I like Jason. Look, he gave me this shiny Indian cent." Kenny took out his bandana and opened the knot at the corner. He smoothed the handkerchief on the table. "Ain't it purty?"

Edmund softened in his resolve and said, "Yes, it is. I'm sure Mr. Wilcox is fine. I saw him a few hours ago when he killed the man in the street. He looked well."

"Yeah, I buried that man. The town will pay me two cents. I'm going to save it with my Indian piece." Kenny tied up his coin and stuck it back into his overalls pocket. "I don't want the sheriff to get sick, too. He and Jason don't call me dummy like most folks. Will you come?"

Edmund sighed. "Even killers get sick, I suppose. You'd better go home and stay away from the jail."

Kenny rose. "Do you get paid cash money?" Edmund smiled. "Yes." Kenny looked down at his hands. He bit his lower lip. Taking a deep breath he blurted, "If Jason ain't got cash money, I'll…I'll pay you my penny and the two cents owed me when I get it. Is that enough?"

Edmund's smile broadened. "I'm sure that what I charge, Mr. Wilcox will be able to pay. You keep your money."

"Thanks, Doc!" The words leaped from Kenny as he fled the saloon.

❊ ❊ ❊

Edmund got up, paid for his coffee, and strode to his room, taking two steps of the stairs at a time. The doctor checked his bag to be sure the bottles and paper packets were intact. He checked each of the medicines: bismuth, Dover's Powder, morphine, podophyllin, mercury with chalk, compound cathartic pills, bromide of potassium, tincture aconite, mercurous chloride, fluid extract of ergot, tincture belladonna, and tincture hydrastis. Everything had survived well the long, bouncy trip from Connecticut.

Edmund opened his suitcase and took out the leather journal. He stroked the worn, tattered leather for a moment. He opened it and turned the yellowing papers with care. The stitching fastening pages to the leather was fraying. *I hate the thought of sharing it. I don't want to acknowledge to him we're connected. What if he won't return it? Or worse, what if he throws it away? He's hard enough not to care.* He took a deep breath through his nose, held it a moment, and let it out in a whoosh like a bellows. His hand shaking, he placed the book into his doctor's bag and marched to the jail.

❋ ❋ ❋

"Clem, I told you I don't need a doctor. I'll be fine." Jason leaned forward on the cell bunk with his arms across his stomach.

"You don't want to be responsible for maybe making other folks sick, do you?" Clement paced.

"I ain't gonna make no one sick. I don't want a doctor, especially that one. He called me a murderer."

"I know, but he's new to our town. He doesn't know any better." The two men stopped talking when the door opened, and Edmund entered. He stood silently in the office lit by a kerosene lamp on the sheriff's desk.

Jase also stood. He pulled the blanket wrapped around his shoulders tighter.

"It sure is uncanny. You two are the same height, have the same hair color, you carry your shoulders the same, and you walk the same. Even your voices sound the same. It's like seeing and hearing double." Clement shook his head.

"Except one of us believes in shaving and washing." Edmund stared at Jason.

"I don't want him here, Clement."

"Don't you listen to him none." Clem picked up a small table from the front office, placed it in the only jail cell, and set a kerosene lamp on it then lit the wick. "He's shivering and vomiting and running out back to the privy."

"I ain't ever seen a doctor in my life, and I don't like him looking like me. It ain't natural." Jason glared at Edmund.

"You've killed one man today. Do you want to kill off the whole town with a disease to add to your accomplishments?" Edmund opened his bag. "Sheriff, will you please heat some water?"

"Sure thing." Clement filled up a coffee pot with water from a bucket and put the pot on the stove. He added a few sticks to the fire box to make the low embers burst into flame.

"The man vowed he was gonna kill me. I had to get him first," Jase said. "Bet you wish I was the one that got planted?"

Edmund opened his bag. "I'm not here to discuss the right or wrong of it."

"Do what you want. I ain't gonna stop you." Jason's legs felt wobbly, like a newborn foal's. He sat down on the cot. *I ain't gonna pull apart like frayed rope in front of this snoot-nosed stranger.* He sat with his back straight and removed the blanket from his shoulders.

Jase watched the doctor take a small whiskey bottle from his bag and pour a little on a cloth. Then he took out a spoon and wiped it.

"Open your mouth wide." Edmund stuck the spoon in Jason's mouth and pressed it down on his tongue as he peered at his throat. Jase gagged and retched. He grabbed a bucket and vomited a small amount of liquid then had dry heaves. He coughed and gasped for air. "You trying to make me worse?"

"Your throat looks good. Take off your shirt. When did you start feeling sick?"

"About two hours ago," Jase answered as he removed his shirt.

"Have you been near anyone in the past two weeks who was sick?"

"I don't reckon so."

Edmund examined Jason's back. "No rash." He touched a mole behind his patient's left ear. He sighed. "What did you eat or drink last?"

"Supper. Here."

Clem stopped pacing and stood by the cell door. "That's right. We both had my wife's stew and biscuits. She brought it over in dinner pails. I feel fine."

Edmund held the kerosene lamp close to Jason as he examined his chest. "No rash. That's good. Your skin feels warm and clammy. It's good you're getting rid of whatever is in your system. I don't think it's contagious."

"That's a relief," Clement said.

A severe shivering fit hit Jason. He clutched the blanket and lay down. The shame of appearing weak increased his misery.

"I'll make some tea for you to drink. It will help. The worst should be over by morning," Edmund instructed.

Jase watched the doctor pour hot water into a cup and add powders from paper packets he took from his bag. He stared in apprehension as the doctor brought the cup of steaming liquid toward him.

"What's in it?" Jason took the cup and smelled the vapors. Making a face, he held it away from his nose.

"Sulfur, soda, and Senna. It will help settle your stomach." Jason squeezed his eyes shut. Taking a deep breath, he tested the tea. He opened his eyes. "It's swallowable." He sipped at it.

"I'll make more for you in a few hours. I think you have food poisoning," Dr. Proft said.

"Food poisoning? You saying my wife tried to poison him? If 'n you are, you're way wrong. I've been eating her cooking for years. She ain't never poisoned me." Clement made a fist and punched it into his other hand. "And she likes Jase. Don't you go around telling folks my wife poisoned him!" Clement's voice took on a hard edge.

"Clement, cool your horses. The doc's ignorant of our ways, remember? Everyone knows Hortensia wouldn't poison me. Likely, it came from the river water I drank this morning, or something was on my hands when I ate. Right, Doc?"

"Very likely." Edmund glanced at Jase's grimy, callused hands and the torn, dirty nails before he turned and faced the sheriff. "I'm sure your wife is an excellent cook."

"That she is, and don't you forget it." Clement stomped into the office.

"I won't." Edmund smiled in indulgence.

"Ah, thanks, Doctor, for giving me that tea. I think it's helping. I apologize if I seemed ornery. It knocked me sidewise to see someone that looked like me."

"It surprised me, too. I...I've this book you can read-- if you know how to read, that is. It tells why we look alike." Edmund hesitated before his voice emphasized, "I want it back." Edmund handed Jase the journal.

Jason heard the resolve in Edmund's voice. "Yeah, I can read." He glared at the doctor as he detected an insult in his question. "We don't get too much out here to read. I'll take care of it, but I can't see how this can explain why two men born a thousand miles apart be mirror images." Jase took the book and lay down. He pulled the wool blanket to his chin. "Now, go away. You ain't needed," he scolded as he faced the wall. "You go home, too, Clement. I want to sleep."

❈ ❈ ❈

Hortensia pulled the blankets off the bed. Her long nightdress clung to her sweating back. She dipped two cloths into a bowl of water and wrung them out. Handing one to Clement, she lay down again, tense as Clem took off his shirt and pants. He left his summer-weight long johns on and eased his tired body onto the bed.

They rubbed the wet cloths over their sweaty faces and across the back of their necks. Last, they laid the rags on their foreheads.

Hortensia cleared her throat. "How's Jase? Did the doctor help him?"

"Yeah. Just got something in his stomach that weren't good for him, but the doctor knows it wasn't your cooking. I told him I ate the same, and I'm fine. Jase will be well in a day or two."

"Oh, that's a relief. I was worried." Hortensia's body relaxed.

"Me, too. But not just about Jason. I'm worried about us." Hortensia took the cloth off her face, rose up on one elbow, and looked at Clement. "About us?"

"What's to become of us?"

Hortensia asked, "What do you mean?"

"We're getting older. My hands are so crippled with this arthritis, I can't draw a gun to save my soul, and no way could I make a fist if I had to knock someone out. If that Miranda fellow had come after me before Jason, you'd be a widow. The whole town knows I can't do the job anymore. The council will likely fire me if I don't get killed first. Then what will happen to us? We ain't got any money to speak of."

"Now, who could replace you? The only person who can handle a gun worth anything or hold his own in a fight is Jason, and everyone knows he's too hot-tempered for the job. No one wants to see him with a badge." Hortensia lay back down and replaced the wet rag on her face. "Even if you lose your job, what with the town growing, there could be work for you at the livery or the general store." She patted his hand. "Now, don't you worry. With the vegetable garden and my canning for the winter, we'll make out just fine. We always do. Trust in the Lord, dear. He's never failed us yet. He brought a doctor here, didn't he?" Hortensia turned onto her side, away from Clement, and wiped a tear from one eye. "Everything will look better in the morning. It always does."

"I hope you're right. Good night, Sia." Clem turned onto his side, his back to her.

"Night, Clem." Hortensia listened to his breathing as she stared into the dark. *I can't let him see I'm scared, too. What will we do? Lord, help us.* Another tear formed in her eye and rolled down her cheek.

❈ ❈ ❈

Jason set the empty bowl and spoon on the table in his cell. "That was right tasty clabber. Thank Hortensia for it, Clem." He sat on the cot and pulled the blanket around him.

"I'll do that."

The sheriff picked up the bowl. "I'm going to run our dishes home. You need anything?"

"No, Clem. You go." Jason leaned back against the wall and opened the book as the sheriff left the office.

Inside the front cover, written in a fine hand, was "The Journal of Elizabeth, a new bride." *Don't know why he thinks I should read this, but I ain't got nothin' else to do.*

On the facing page he read, "As I begin married life in the year of our Lord 1847, with my husband Garrett and the new adventures it will surely contain, I have decided to write these happenings as they occur in a journal for my future children's children to read."

Jason shivered. *Must still be the miseries. A book sure can't give me chills.* He turned the page. "Garrett and I have been married for several hours already." Jase read pages describing the journey across fast-flowing rivers by ferry to the Mississippi River and the jumping- off place for the wagon trains. He read of the horses that brought the couple to Missouri being sold and the buying of oxen. Jason relaxed as he read Elizabeth's entries. He turned another page. "At the jumping- off place for crossing the Mississippi at Independence, Missouri, we signed up with a train of sixty wagons. We have a captain of the train and a set of rules the men signed for the governance of us all. Garrett talked to many settlers who had returned from going west and learned about some of the supplies we would need. We prepared for over a year to get what we could ready. We knew we could not bring a cow with us; therefore, I churned butter, and we preserved it by boiling and skimming off the scum as it rises until it is clear. We placed it in tin canisters and soldered the lids on. I prepared desiccated vegetables, and to be safe, I also procured citric acid that we can mix with water to ward off scurvy. Garrett knew he needed to bring extra shoes for both of us, two woolen blankets apiece, and for himself woolen pants reinforced on the inside with soft buckskin, woolen socks, stout boots, one gutta-percha poncho, a broad-brimmed hat of soft felt, flannel over-shirts, woolen undershirts, cotton drawers, a rifle with a large bore, flintlocks with four pounds of powder, twelve pounds of lead, a mold to cast the bullets, a hunting knife, a pound of castile soap and three pounds of soap for washing clothes, a belt-knife, and a whetstone. I am to carry a good cloth bag containing linen thread, large needles, beeswax, some buttons, a paper of pins, and a thimble.

"After we signed the wagon train contract, the Wagon Master ordered that Garrett and me pack the following additional supplies: 300 pounds of flour packed in hundred- pound double canvas sacks that have been well stitched; fifty pounds of bacon or pork that should be put in strong sacks, placed in a box surrounded by bran, which helps keep the fat from melting away in the heat, and put in the bottom of the wagon so it will be kept cooler. Also, we are to bring thirty pounds of coffee, fifty pounds of sugar placed in gutta-percha sacks in the wagon where it will not get wet, a good supply of saleratus or yeast powders for making bread, and of course, salt and pepper.

"The Wagon Master also told Garrett to bring spare ox shoes, a ten-gallon water keg, and each ox wagon needs a tar-bucket filled with a mixture of tar or resin and grease.

"We got four oxen. The two yoked on the left side are both called Buck, and the two yoked on the right side are called Bright. I thought this was strange, but Garrett said it kept the oxen from getting confused, and anyone could drive them once they were yoked." Jason continued reading.

"After everyone on the train had packed the supplies, we started on our journey. What a glorious, exciting day it was, even though there was a slight mist in the air for the first three hours.

"For three weeks, we have traveled five to six miles each day. Garrett is so enthusiastic and excited about our journey west that I've not the heart to dampen his spirit with the fears that have crept into me and taken lodging in my mind. My fears of Indians, wild animals, and accidents seem to increase more each day as we progress into the tall prairie grass. I've heard the stories related to each of these occurrences from people we have met on our path. So far, our way has been peaceful and safe, but I fear it will not stay that way. When I walk beside the wagon, the grass is over my head. I feel so insignificant and closed-in. When I sit on the wagon seat, I can see for miles the endless wave of prairie. I feel even smaller."

Jase looked around the cell. He closed his eyes. He remembered the times Eli had taken him to get hops for the beer-brewing. They'd ridden for days without seeing another soul, and the arid land had seemed to be endless. He hadn't let Eli know he'd also felt puny and vulnerable.

He opened his eyes and read, "I think I am with child. This will be our first baby. There may be no doctor or midwife to help when the time draws near. I must calm my fears before I speak of this to Garrett. I don't want to appear less of a helpmeet in his eyes. He feels the whole world is ours. He has no trepidations about the future."

Jason lay the book aside and he stared at it. Moistening his lips, he took a deep breath. *First time I ever read a woman's thoughts and feelings. I never thought a woman had such fears. My ma never talked about being worried. My notion always was that women and men thought the same, just did things different. This journal is sort of private-like. Maybe I shouldn't read it, but I feel drawn to it.*

He went out to the office and poured a cup of coffee from the large pot on the stove. Standing at the entry, he watched people going about their business in the town. Jase lifted his face to the sun and let the warmth settle on him like a hot blanket. A woman with round shoulders came out of the general store. *Hortensia is looking old. I never noticed that afore. Clement has always looked old, but not her.* He drained the coffee cup and walked back to his cell. Picking up the book, he sat down, turned a page, and began reading. "A new day, a beautiful day, and time for a new journal entry. I have not written for several weeks, as Garrett and I have traveled on the west side of the Mississippi with our wagon pulled by Buck and Bright, our four dear oxen. We left the wagon train in the New Mexico Territory and have traveled for days on our own.

"We arrived at a small settlement. There are twenty-six people in this little spot situated on the banks of a quick-flowing creek. Most of the people live in tents or their wagons, but two families do have dugouts.

"We stopped here, as I was soon to deliver our child, and Garrett thought we should have the help of the women in the hamlet. We were going to pitch our little tent, but Armas Talo and his wife Aileana invited us to move into their dugout. It is cut into the side of a hill like part of a cave. The roof and back are the hill, but the front is made of sod slabs stacked on top of each other. There is a door frame and a wooden door, as well as a window frame with oiled skin over the opening to allow some light in, but one cannot see through it. Even with the window it is quite dark, and candles or lamps are needed in the day unless the door is open to allow more light into the home. As kerosene and candles are costly, the door is open as much as is feasible. If need be, the door can be barricaded, and the window can be shuttered.

"Armas is Finnish, and Aileana is Scottish. She said her name means 'green meadow'. It is a lovely name, and it fits this place, as it is quite green with the creek feeding the grass with its life source.

"I agreed to stay in their home until after my child was born. I will share the bed in the corner with Aileana. Armas and Garrett will sleep out in our tent.

"They also have three adorable children. They had five, but two did not live beyond a day or two. The surviving children are two boys and a girl: Kari, which means 'blessed' in Finnish; Timo, which is Finnish for 'God-fearing'; and the girl named Malise, which means 'God's servant' in the Scottish language. Kari is ten and Timo is nine, and both are a huge help with the chores. Each day, Aileana sits them down and makes them do lessons. She puts sand into a frying pan and makes letters and words and sums for the boys to read and copy into other pans of sand to solve. Malise is three and such a delight. She is bubbly and energetic, so much so that her ma and pa and even the two boys have trouble keeping up with her. She sings and coos all day long and is never still a moment. She is a joy.

"The dugout is quite small, with a dirt floor, walls, and thatched roof. The cooking is done outside on a small fire so the smoke does not enter the house. The bed is a three-legged standup attached to the wall at the back of the dugout with a corn husk mattress, which feels great after sleeping on the ground for weeks. Snakes, spiders, and other insects could enter through the roof, so a large canvas is hung over the sleeping area for the grownups and children, to catch the crawlies and slitherers during the night while people sleep. It did happen our first night. Aileana and I were in bed when a rattler came through the roof, but the noise of it thudding onto the canvas cover roused us from our slumber. Aileana got up and killed it with the blade of a shovel, severing its head from its body. I did not go back to sleep again that night, but the children and Aileana did. I stared into the darkness, jerking with every sound I heard in the rafters.

"We are sharing our food with the family, and Garrett is helping Armas. They go every day to a wooded area and cut trees to make a frame house sometime in the future.

I help in the vegetable garden and with cooking and washing as much as I am able, but I am afraid with my time so near, I am not as much help as I should be to repay this kind family.

"The family follows Finnish and Scottish traditions and includes us in them. Armas took Garrett aside and said he wanted him to help them celebrate a Scottish tradition. In Scotland at New Year's they celebrate Hogmanay. Since the family didn't have a house for New Year's Day, Armas decided to celebrate it now in their newly constructed dugout. He said it would please Aileana tremendously, as she misses her family in Scotland. Garrett said he would be glad to help. When Armas told Aileana they were going to celebrate Hogmanay, her face lit up.

"Just before the New Year, the house is given a thorough cleaning, which does not amount to much with a house made of mud and sod, but Aileana and

I washed and swept what we could. Then we baked small oat cakes, made with white flour Aileana had been saving for a special occasion and butter. She also made shortbread and blackbun, which is a cake with raisins and spices she brought from back East and covered in a pastry.

"When all was ready, Aileana went to the other families in the settlement and gave them some oat cakes, which they were to give to her children when they came to their domicile on the special night. The neighbors could keep some of the cakes for themselves as well.

"She taught her children to go to the homes and say, 'Hogmanay, troll-ol, troll-aye, give your white bread and none of your gray. My feet are cold, my shoes are thin, give me cakes and let me in.' At dusk that night the children went to each tent, wagon, and the one other dugout and said the little ditty. The people gave them each some oat cakes.

"The boys returned with their hats full to the brims, and the little girl, Malise, danced in delight as she emptied her apron full of sweet cakes onto the plank table.

"Aileana wanted to sweep the old year out the back door, but the dugout has only one door, so she swept it out the front door and carried the dirt around to the back to symbolize the old year of living on the trail as behind them.

"For this special time, if the first person in the door after midnight, called the first-footer, has black hair, it is a good sign. As Garrett's is brown, Armas cut some hair from his horse's tail, and Garret tied it into his own. At midnight, he knocked on the door carrying a pan with glowing embers in it to stand for warmth in the new house, and he had a loaf of fresh bread to symbolize food for the coming year. As Garrett entered the house, he said, 'Good health to this house and all in it.'

"I write this happy experience in my journal to show my children what fine people we have met in our travels and to inspire our children to help other newcomers during their day.

"Now, for the very special entry! The very next day, I went into labor, and to our great joy I delivered twin boys."

Jason's hands shook. *Twin boys!* He read the entry again. "I delivered twin boys. We named one child Edmund. The other boy is Ethan. He has a small mole behind his left ear. That is the only difference in our sons." Jason's hands continued to shake. He put his hand behind his left ear and felt the mole.

"Ethan?" he said to himself.

❋ ❋ ❋

Abigail set the lighted candle on the empty crate's wooden slat. The small glow bounced off cobwebs, worn baskets, old harness leather, spider webs, a double saw, a sledgehammer, nails, a rusty plow, and a broken rocker. Many items lost in the darkness filled the rest of the tool shed. *I should have come out here earlier, while it was still light.*

The cot with one blanket and no pillow stood just in the doorway. She sat down. *Once I blow out the candle, the only light I'll have until dawn is whatever moonlight seeps in through the cracks between the boards. I'll take off my shoes and dress and sleep in my petticoats tonight. I'm too tired to care what I sleep in.*

She unlaced her shoes and pulled her feet out. Wiggling her toes and rubbing her arches, she sighed with weariness. *I think soaking my feet in a tub of hot water is a luxury I won't have very often here.* She hung her dress on the one nail pounded into the wall for her convenience. *Not much like home.* She missed her own clean room with a wardrobe closet, nightstand, kerosene lamp, and a bed with a feather mattress. *I took it for granted I'd have the same here. But I can put up with it until Uncle decides if I should stay. I just have to be sure not to displease him.*

She stretched out on the bed and blew out the candle. Black swallowed up the room. *I wish the tool shed were closer to the house. But I can't let Uncle know I'm afraid. He might think I'm not suited to live here.* She gasped, and her heart jumped. *What's that?* A scratching sound came from the corner of the shed, and then something made a sound as it scurried across the floor. *It must be mice. Of course, it has to be mice.* She lay stiff, with scarce breath.

A coyote howled. A moment later, it howled and yipped closer. Abigail curled up, facing away from the wall. She heard it sniffing outside the shed. She gasped in air as she stuffed a corner of the blanket in her mouth. The beast howled a piercing wail outside the tool shed. She froze.

She jerked her head toward the wall. *Is that someone snickering? Could it be the boys?* Seconds slipped by in silence. A scratching and soft whining, like an animal trying to dig its way in, broke the hot stillness. Her ears strained to hear in the night. She exhaled as she heard snickering and a harsh whisper, "Shh, she'll know it's us." *It must be Otis and Silas. Why are they doing this? Are they playing pranks, or do they want to scare me away?*

Chapter Nineteen

Stepping from the glaring sunlight to the barn's darker interior, Edmund squinted. Breathing in the fresh hay smell, he called, "Anybody here?"

"Yep, I'm here, Mister. Name's Sam. Can I help you?" A stooped man, holding curry brushes in each hand, looked at him across a horse's back.

"I'd like to rent a buggy and horse."

"You're the doctor who arrived the other day?"

"Yes."

"Where do you want to go?"

"To Lemuel Baxter's mule ranch. Can you give me directions?"

"Sure, ain't hard to find his place. Head west to the fork in the road, take the right, and at the next fork take a left. Stay on the road, and you'll come to it. Takes two hours, but in this heat, go slower and give the horse a break in the shade."

Edmund noticed Sam eyeing his derby.

"I don't suppose you want water in your hat?" Sam asked.

"Of course not."

"I'll put a water bucket in the rig and float a wood piece in it so it won't slosh much. Water the horse at the stand of cottonwoods you'll see on the side of the road, ah, about halfway there. But don't let him drink a lot. Don't let him get bloated. I'll put a canteen of water on the seat." Sam studied the doctor in his suit. "You drive much?"

"No. Back in Connecticut, I hired a horse cab to visit my housebound patients. Sometimes I walked to them if they didn't come to my office, and of course, there was also the horse-drawn streetcar." Sam rolled his eyes a bit, and his face held a slight smirk. "I'll hitch up Jack. He's steady, won't shy on you, and has a tough mouth.

He doesn't mind a heavy hand."

"Thank you. How much do I owe you?"

"Four bits is fine."

❈ ❈ ❈

Edmund slapped the reins. Jack bobbed his head in time to each step.

I hope I don't get lost. I'm used to seeing stores, houses, and people. This is empty, barren land. Gads, I hate it here. He checked his pocket watch and noted he had traveled for an hour when he sighted four trees on the side of the road at the first fork. He stopped and gave Jack a drink from the wooden bucket. The horse remained in the shade as Edmund sat on the ground with his back against a tree, placing the canteen nearby.

These trees are the only ones in sight on this vast, empty land. Miles of nothing but bleak misery and heat waves swimming in the air. He took his hat off and wiped his forehead, face, and neck with a white linen handkerchief, covering it with streaks of grime from his sweat. He then took a drink from the canteen. A quick movement by his right hand caught his eye. His eyes widened as he stared at a small, green-brown, fat lizard. *I wonder what that is.* It scurried off to a boulder. There, it climbed up and positioned itself on top, where it seemed to move up and down with its belly as it kept its feet on the rock. Edmund chuckled as he thought, *It looks like it is doing push-ups.* His laughter caused Jack to raise his head from the patch of grass he was nibbling and look at him.

Jack shook his head to toss his mane and tail and disturb the flies. Then he lowered his head to chew on the lower bark of the tree.

Edmund stopped laughing and rested his head back against the rough tree bark. The fat lizard scuttled off the rock and disappeared. Edmund viewed his surroundings with renewed interest. The land was flat, with an occasional roll of earth that petered out into the flat plain again. The soil was brown, giving over to rusty red, streaking into sandy brown, and ending back in deep brown. Green plants grew in clumps and in solitary positions over the terrain. There were tall, spiky blades, while some plants appeared to him to be spindly half- bushes and half- trees. He knew a few plants were cactus, but this was the first time he'd noticed different types. He looked at the horizon and marveled at the rows of tall mountains with huge, flat tops. *I learned from geography class in high school that the mountains are mesas, but I don't remember if we studied what created them. In the sunlight, they do look beautiful. I wonder why they have almost straight bands of color.*

He got up, brushed off his clothes, and put on his hat before placing the canteen and water bucket into the buggy. He settled in and slapped the reins on the animal's back, sighing in relief when it walked forward. He pulled on the right rein, and to his amazement it took the right fork. A short distance later, the road forked again, and Edmund pulled on the left rein. Jack plodded forward to the left. Another sigh escaped his lips when he saw a ranch house and barn. Putting Jack into a trot, he covered the distance in no time and reined in at the house.

Lemuel came from the corral and strode over to the buggy. "You the fella on the stage with Abigail, ain't ya?"

"Yes." Edmund held out his hand.

"What you mean, driving a limping horse?"

"Limp? I didn't notice a limp." Edmund put his hand down.

Lemuel went to the left front hoof. He leaned his weight against the horse's shoulder and ran his hand down the leg to the ankle. Jack lifted his hoof. Lemuel pulled a metal pick from his overalls and dug out a pebble lodged between the metal shoe and the hoof frog. He examined the foot and let it go as Jack put his hoof down.

"Well, the stone weren't in there long, or the hoof would be bruised. Guess he just picked it up. But you got to watch for these things. Ain't right to lame a horse. Why did you come out here?"

"I'm Doctor Proft"

"I know. Abigail told me. Why are you here?"

"I'd like to visit with Miss Lester and invite her to the Sunday services at the sheriff's house in Wild River. We're both new in town, and I thought it would be a good way for us to get acquainted with folks. I find I need to stay in town for a week or two before I can head back to Connecticut."

"Abigail ain't got time to go to town on Sundays. It's more than a four-hour round trip. She's got chores to do. But, seeing as how you put this horse to work to get you out here, I guess you can sit with her on the porch. Just don't lollygag too long."

Edmund stepped down from the buggy as Lemuel led the horse to shade by the barn. As Abigail came out the door, Edmund could sense she was embarrassed.

"I didn't know anyone was coming to visit. I'm not wearing my shoes. They hurt my feet, and they're hot." Abigail adjusted her thin scarf over her head. She tucked the ends into the dress neckline.

"Your bare feet are just fine. My shoes are hot, too, though I don't think your uncle would approve of my taking them off." Edmund laughed.

"Heavens, no!" Abigail smiled. "Please, sit on the rocking chair, and I'll get one from the kitchen table."

"Let me."

Edmund noticed Abigail appeared flustered.

"I'll go to the well and pull up the buttermilk can. It stays cool there," Abigail responded.

She's surprised someone offered to help her. Edmund sat in the straight-back kitchen chair and insisted Abigail sit in the rocker.

She moved the rocker, so the doctor saw the smooth skin on the left side of her face.

"I know you heard what your uncle said concerning church, but I'll come out and get you and bring you back."

"No. He's right, there's work to do, and I need to do my share, or someone else has to do it. There's the vegetable garden to tend, the cow to milk, the chickens to feed, the cooking, and the house to keep clean. And I'm trying to get caught up on the laundry." Abigail fingered her scarf and glanced away from Edmund. "Besides, I don't enjoy meeting people."

"I'm sure it is harder than I can imagine. But you must get over it. You have much to offer as a friend, and people will enjoy your company once they get to know you."

"I have little to offer anyone."

"Yes, you do." Edmund, surprised by his forceful tone, leaned forward and put his hand under her chin and turned her face toward him. "Traveling in the stage with you, I saw your humor. Remember how we laughed over the jolts and bumps and guessed how long it would be 'til the next one?" He released her chin.

Abigail nodded. "It was funny. Sometimes we didn't have time to say how many seconds or minutes it would be."

"I'd slide off the seat or you would, when we went down a steep embankment."

"And once, your derby landed on my head." Abigail laughed and held her sides.

"Most people would not find humor in the trip. They'd complain and fuss. You were patient when the stagecoach changed horses or when it was late arriving at a station. And the awful food! I must say, what is served at the saloon is worse, but not by much."

"The food was terrible, but the silly wagers we made on the ingredients of the next meal were hilarious. I'll never forget you guessed rattlesnake, and I said chicken and I won. You had to touch your nose with your tongue." Abigail laughed until she gasped for air.

Edmund's smile faded as her face became serious.

"I'm sorry the meals aren't good at the saloon. I wish I could offer you the bread I baked today, but I don't think Uncle would like it."

"Don't you worry. I'll do just fine. See, it is just like you to fret over others when you have enough to take care of here." He leaned back in the chair. "I'm sorry you need to live here."

"It's not bad. I'll just have to get used to it. Soon, it will become routine, and easier. In a month, Uncle Lemuel will decide whether he will provide a place for me to live. I have hopes. It's better than being a financial burden to my family back home." Abigail shifted her gaze to her uncle in the corral. "Did you find any trace of your mother and father?"

Edmund sighed and stared down at the porch floor. He shook his head. "No. When I saw what the town of Wild River was like and knew it got its name from the nearby river, I hoped Elizabeth had confused the name of the water she'd crossed. But, she didn't. The people she wrote about in her journal were caring and helpful. It colored my outlook on what to expect." He studied the porch ceiling of rough wood and cobwebs. "I didn't tell you I had a twin brother, as I believed he'd drowned with my father. But I discovered he didn't. I wish he had."

"Oh! That's an awful thing to wish." Abigail stared at him. "How do you know he didn't?"

"I saw him in town. I'm sure it's him. He's my exact double. He has a cattle ranch, makes whiskey, and brews beer."

"Is that bad?"

"No, but he killed a man in a gunfight the day we arrived. The sheriff put him in jail. He's known for using his gun. Remember Sabilla Platt and the way she spoke to me at the stage? She thought I was Jason, my brother." Edmund watched an ant scurry across the wood floor. "The man who runs the hotel said Jason has been in jail often. Everyone in town acts like being thrown in jail is just a formality. The sheriff said the judge would let Jason go as soon as he arrives in town. Right now, my brother is sick. I decided to stay until he's well. Later, I'm going back to civilization." Edmund stomped his heel on the ant. He turned his face away from Abigail.

She let her breath out. "Life is different out here. It's not what I expected, either. I knew the work would be hard, but not the people-

-not my own family."

Edmund heard the sorrow in her voice. He sipped the buttermilk, then put the cup down on the floor. Changing the subject, he hoped he could get her to smile. "Remember how we were afraid we would be attacked by the Indians? I haven't seen any."

"I've seen a few in the distance. Uncle says we don't need to worry too much. The Navahos live on a reservation now. They were on a reservation farther away for four years, but now they reside on a reservation called Canyon de Chelly. He says we can thank Colonel Kit Carson for making the territory safer."

They watched Lemuel come up to the porch, leading the horse and buggy. "Abigail, you got chores to finish. Dr. Proft, your horse has rested up. No reason you can't head to town."

Abigail and Edmund rose together.

"Uncle is right, Dr. Proft. Thank you for the visit, and I hope you have a pleasant journey back East. I won't be able to go to the Sunday service, but if you have a chance to visit again, it would be nice." Abigail shot a glance at her uncle. "Is it all right, Uncle?"

"Don't see any reason for it. We feel fine. No sense wasting his time or ours." Lemuel walked off.

"I'm sorry, Dr. Proft," said Abigail.

"I'm sorry, too. I enjoyed our visit. I wish the best for you. Good day." He tipped his hat and climbed into the buggy.

Jack trotted forward. Abigail waved from the porch, and Edmund waved back as she dashed into the kitchen. Lemuel stepped up on the porch and watched the departing doctor.

Edmund took a deep breath to dispel the smothering loneliness, as he squinted his eyes against the sun's glare. Abigail's dark, sad eyes were still peering at him in the distance.

❈ ❈ ❈

Jason stared at the journal lying on his jail cot. He rubbed his shaking and sweating hands on his pants as he paced back and forth in the cell. Feeling closed in, he opened the door and paced in the office area. Jase lifted the coffee pot to pour a cup, but it shook, and the lid rattled so hard it nearly fell off, so he placed it back on the small wood stove. He strode outside into the brilliant sunlight and leaned against the post supporting the hanging porch roof. The intensity of the sun struck him, as the roof had a missing plank. He breathed in the hot air, feeling as if he had run a mile over rough ground.

He ambled back into the office and then the cell, where he sat on the cot and picked up the journal. Swallowing hard, he leafed through its pages until he came to the place where he'd left off reading.

"Garrett is beside himself with joy and wonderment. He is even more anxious to find the best place to settle and provide for us. The little settlement has been most kind, and all the good folks have been by to see the boys. Aileana and Armas have been so very considerate and helpful. I do not know what I would have done without Aileana's help during and after the delivery.

I had the bed to myself for several nights, as she slept on the floor with her children. Little Malise is awestruck by the twin babies. She loves to hold them, rock them in her arms, and sing to them. They sleep with me in the bed, and often Malise crawls in with us and lies still with her arms around the two bundles. To see her lie so still for long stretches of time is amazing.

"This is the day we left at daylight. Garrett is eager to set out again. Before dawn, he had the oxen yoked and the wagon packed. The Taloes sent us off with cold food to eat when we stop for lunch. Poor Malise was sobbing in her mother's arms. She did not want us to go, at least not the babies. She asked Garrett and me to leave the little ones with her. She was inconsolable when we said we couldn't. Then she reached out to me as I sat on the wagon seat and asked me to take her with us. I told her she needed to stay with her family, as they loved her and would be sad if she left them. She said she would return at nighttime and be with us during the day. We tried to explain that we were going very far away, and she would not be able to return at night, but she could not understand. Everyone in the settlement was waving, except for poor little Malise, who was sobbing as if her heart would break. I felt very sorry for her as our wagon took us away."

❋ ❋ ❋

Edmund returned the horse and buggy to the livery and took the boardwalk, where it existed, toward the hotel.

Clement barreled into him at the hotel door. "Hey, Doc, I was looking for you. Come on. Hortensia is waiting supper on us." Clement grabbed the doctor by the arm and steered him up the street to the frame house.

"Thank you for the invitation, but I don't want to put you folks to a bother."

"Heck, ain't any." Clement led the doctor to the porch. "We'll eat out here, as it's cooler. Hortensia, we're here. Supper ready? Sit down, Doctor." Clement pulled straight-back chairs around a table of planks on wood barrels.

Dr. Proft scrambled to his feet when Hortensia came out with a tray of metal plates and eating utensils. "Doctor Proft, please call me Hortensia, and do sit down. I am so honored you are going to have dinner with us." She returned to her kitchen and brought out bowls of food.

"It's my honor, and I'm happy to accept the invitation." Edmund saw the glint of pride as she set the table with her prize home-cooked dishes. He held the chair as Hortensia sat down. The thickened tomato dish and the cooked cucumbers were filling and savory. Clement poured cool well water into tin cups.

While they ate, Hortensia and Clement asked Edmund about Connecticut. After the main course had been devoured, Hortensia stood, and Dr. Proft stood as well. "Please, sit down. We have vinegar pie for dessert. It's my specialty. Clem, pour us all a cup of coffee." She went into the kitchen and returned with the pie and a knife, which she set on the table with a beaming face.

"Dear, you haven't made anything that ain't downright tasty. Doc, you ever seen a real lemon?" Clem cut the pie and put a slice on each plate.

"Yes, some, back in Connecticut. Mother made lemon pie for special occasions."

"Well, sir, vinegar pie is our answer to lemon pie. We don't get lemons much, and they are dear. I made Hortensia a small barrel with a bunghole. She puts in a bit of last year's vinegar, rainwater if we get rain, or else well water, and all the peelings and cores from dried apples we can get. She adds sweetening by putting in the skimmings of the preserve kettle and molasses-barrel rinsings. After a month of bubbling and an extra month of souring, it is the best vinegar in these parts. And when she adds some to her pie fixings, I'll wager it is better than lemon pie."

Hortensia's face glowed. "Now, Clement, you do go on."

They each put their forks into their slice and slid it into their mouths. The trio savored the pie in silence.

"Clement is right, Hortensia. That pie rivals any lemon pie I ever had. You folks have treated me to the best meal I've had in months." Edmund was pleased as he put his fork on his empty plate.

Hortensia could not hide the delight his words gave her. She radiated with pride and wriggled in her chair as she crossed her ankles.

"If you folks don't think I'm out of line, I'd like to ask you about Jason. Did you know the people who raised him?"

"Did we know them? Landsakes, yes. Stay seated, Doctor," Hortensia said as she picked up dishes. "You tell him, Clem, while I clean up." Hortensia left the men on the porch, finishing their coffee.

"Doc, you asked the right folks. I reckon we know more about old Eli Wilcox and Wilma than anyone hereabouts." Clem tipped the chair on its back legs to lean against the wall. "When Hortensia and I came, back in 1847, there wasn't a town here. No, sir. The Wilcoxes were the only white folks for a hundred miles or more, I guess. They had this old shanty not far from the river. Even back then, they made whiskey and sold it to troopers, people in the wagon trains, Mexicans, and some Indians, too, I suspect." Clem ran his fingers through his handlebar mustache. "Eli didn't believe in washing or combing his hair or the like. He looked wild, like a deranged hermit, his long gray hair and whiskers down to his waist. Wilma didn't look much better."

"Did they have the cattle ranch?" Edmund asked.

"Yeah, they called it that. Had thirty or forty head. Hortensia and I left the wagon train we were in, along with Sam, who started the livery, and Buster Buttwill. He ran the saloon with the whiskey from Eli. Twenty years later, Buster talked his brother Hiram into building the hotel. We call Buster 'Saloon Buttwill' and his brother 'Hotel Buttwill'." Clement rubbed his arthritic hands. "Hortensia and me ran cattle and had some goats. We lived out of our old wagon and a tent for a year, hoping a town would develop, as the river is close with the cottonwoods, ironwoods, and the good grazing along the riverbeds. Sure enough, it happened, but slow-like."

Edmund finished his coffee and placed the cup on the table planks. He picked up his hat and fanned his face.

Clem took out his bandana and wiped his brow. "We got a general store--Sabilla and John opened it--first out the back of a wagon, then a tent, now a building. More folks came.

"Several smaller rivers feed into Wild River from the mountains. When a storm up yonder dumps rain, it roars down, gathers momentum as it pushes and drags rocks and trees. Nothing much can stand in its way."

Edmund swallowed hard and coughed. His mind flashed to Elizabeth's account of crossing the river.

Hortensia came out of the kitchen and sat next to the men. She fanned herself with her apron. "The dishes are soaking. They can wait. Remember, Clem, when we saw Eli and Wilma come tearing into town? The horses galloped in, their eyes rolling and wild. Wilma clutched a bundle and hung onto the wagon seat as it swayed and bounced. We heard the bawling of what we thought at first was an injured animal."

"Yep, and Eli looked like a banshee standing up and whipping away at those horses."

"Clem, you don't know what a banshee looks like," Hortensia scolded.

"I do so. The word tells me. How would you describe Eli?" Hortensia thought before she answered. "A banshee."

Edmund chuckled. His thoughts wandered back to his childhood and the kitchen table conversations in the little house on the tree-lined avenue. Cecilia and Michael would go back and forth, and he could hear the love underneath it all. *Despite their appearances, Hortensia and Clement are much like my parents.*

Hortensia continued. "Wilma unwrapped the soggy quilt, and there was this dirty, miserable babe." Hortensia used a buttonhook and undid her shoes. She slipped them off and wiggled her toes.

Edmund, afraid Hortensia would stop talking, asked, "The baby was Jason, right?"

"Of course. Eli had been riding near the river when he heard crying. He found a cradle lodged in tree branches snagged in the water, near the shore. He hauled it in and discovered a blessing."

"Yep, you're right there, Hortensia," Clem said. He grinned at the memory. "None of us saw it that way-- not at first. Everyone in town gathered around the old couple and told them how to care for the child. Oh, we were afraid for the baby, and we talked about taking the little one, but Eli cocked his rifle and said God gave them the baby. Finders keepers. No one was about to argue with him, not with his determination. We soon saw they did well. Yep." Clem wiped the sweat from his forehead and face and blew his nose into the bandana.

"It was a blessing, to be sure. They cleaned up their home. The barn didn't need fixing, as they took better care of the animals than themselves. They cleaned themselves up considerable, too." Hortensia's eyes gleamed as she recounted the story. "They cut back on their whiskey drinking. I never saw them drunk after they got the boy. Wilma still chewed tobacco but was careful where she spat. They both came from the Ozark Mountains. I wonder if the women there chew baccey-- Wilma's name for it. Do you know, Doctor?"

"I'm sorry. I don't know anything about the Ozarks." Edmund leaned forward as he entwined and squeezed his fingers. "Did you see Jason much?"

"They brought him along every time they came to town-- once every two, three months or so. When he was eight or nine, Eli and Wilma left Jason here for five months so Hortensia could teach him reading and writing and such. He did chores about the place to earn his keep." Clem brought his chair legs down on the floor. Using a bootjack, he pulled off his left boot. His big toe stuck out through the sock.

"Give the sock to me, and I'll darn it before bed." Hortensia reached over and pulled the sock from Clem's foot. "I think the Wilcoxes were miserable when Jason stayed here. They came to town a lot, just to see him, I reckon. The day I told them Jason could read and do his sums, they burst into halleluiahs. Took him home that very day. Clem and I gave him a Bible. I taught him from it, and we wanted him to keep up his reading. Wilma told me later they had Jase read from it every night, just to listen to him."

"Was Miranda the first person he killed?" Edmund sucked in a deep breath. He was afraid to hear the answer but felt he had to know. He put his elbows on his knees and stared at the floor.

"No. The first time he shot someone was just after his folks died. A fella by the name of Marsh beat on his horse something fierce, right here in town. I was out looking after my stock. I wasn't the sheriff then. We had none. Hortensia, you tell what happened next, as you seen it for yourself."

Hortensia gazed out at the horizon. Her somber face reflected the tone of her voice.

"Marsh's wife added her screams to those of the poor beast her husband was beating. We all came out to see what was happening. We stood and stared.

It was horrible. Jase didn't stand still for a second. He walked right up to the man. Jase was fourteen or so, and Marsh was more than a head taller." Hortensia took a breath. "Jase tried to get him to back off, but he wouldn't. Marsh started to draw, but he died before he finished." Hortensia sighed.

"I'll tell ya, Doc, if I had been there, I'd have shot the man myself." Clem's gnarled hands pulled out his pistol and stroked it.

"The town knew Jase did what was right. He wouldn't have been arrested, even if we'd had a sheriff back then. He drove the woman ninety miles to her relatives. He cared for the abused animal for two years. Then one day, it lay down in the corral and died. The skin wasn't much good, with all the scars on it, but it was worth something if he skinned it. But, Jase said, 'The animal has suffered enough in its life, and it ought to keep its hide.' He dug a hole and buried it." Clem slapped his gun. "There's been a few other times where Jase had to protect his property from thieving Mexicans or Indians. They ain't thieving anymore." Clem shoved his gun back into his holster and filled his pipe with tobacco from a small leather pouch.

Edmund shuffled his feet against the floor and cleared his throat. He wanted to change the topic. His aversion to Jason's being his brother increased with each word he heard about him.

"Did you folks ever hear of the Talo family? They lived in a dugout by a creek about twenty-some years back. They were starting to collect wood for a frame house--probably have one built by now." Clem stared off into the distance as he held his pipe in his hand.

"Nope. Name don't sound familiar to me. How about you, Hortensia? You got a memory a mite better than mine."

Hortensia stared down at the porch floorboards. "That is an odd-sounding name. Think I should remember it if I heard it afore, but I don't. You say there were some dugouts by a creek?"

"Yes, many years ago," Edmund answered.

"Clem, weren't there a couple dugouts that were abandoned on Sims Creek after we had that dry spell for two years and many of the creeks dried up? The dirt got so dry, it turned to dust and blew around somethin' fierce-like."

"Now that you talk about it, I do 'member there were some folks up that way."

Edmund sat up straight. "Where is it, or was it? This Sims Creek?"

"'Bout five days from here by horse. Creek never did amount to much after that drought. Everybody moved away long time back. Wasn't there a tragic thing happen up there, Hortensia?" He lit his pipe.

"You're right, Clem. Seems like a little girl went out to play and wandered off, and her folks couldn't find her. They looked for weeks. Some folks thought Indians took her. The ma thought the little one wanted to follow some settlers that stayed with them for a while. The girl was taken with the babies and wanted to live with the family just so she could be with the little ones. Her folks nigh went crazy looking for her. Months later, if I remember right, her body was found under an old log out in some flat land. Maybe she crawled under it to get out of the sun, or she got bit by a rattler or just died of thirst. We never knew for certain sure, and I don't think her parents did, either. After she was buried, her ma and pa and their boys packed up and went to Minnesota. They had family there in a town settled by Finnish immigrants that was called Embarrass. They might have gone there. I remember that, because Clem and I came from Minnesota.

Edmund asked, "Do you remember if the little girl's name was Malise?"

"By gum! That was it. A right pretty name. Never heard it afore, and it kind of stuck with me. Yep, Malise it was. You be too young to know those folks. How come you askin' 'bout them?"

"Just read about them in an old journal is all. I thought they…. Well, no matter. It was a long time ago." He rose to his feet. "It is getting late. Thank you for the delicious meal and the information. I appreciate it." He picked up his derby.

"Thank you for the visit. Stop by tomorrow in the afternoon. I'll have a loaf of fresh bread for you and some sponge gingerbread. The food at the saloon is terrible," Hortensia offered.

"Thank you, I'll do that."

Edmund left Hortensia and Clement sitting on the porch and strode up the street to the hotel. He ignored Mr. Buttwill and went to his room. He lay on the bed and thought of his life in a clean Connecticut town of law and order, and of his brother's life in the territory. At that, he fell asleep. His dreams of gunfights in the raging water and horses running through saloons, gingerbread in whiskey glasses, and a little girl's sad eyes looking for babies lost in cobblestones aroused him to wakefulness before he sank back into another restless sleep.

Chapter Twenty

I can't be a twin. I never thought of having a brother. I can't be Ethan.
The next page of the journal brought a slight smile to Jason's face as he read Elizabeth's script. "We only expected one child.

Garrett made a handsome cradle out of a wood barrel. I lined it with a quilt my mother made for me when I was born. The two boys will share the cradle, as they are small. Later, they will take turns using it and a large basket until my two lusty sons sleep in trundle beds. I say lusty, for their lung power is beyond comprehension for such small lads. Our wagon must be a sight to see from a distance. I wash the diapers and use thorns to hang them on the canvas of our traveler's wagon, but many folks call it a prairie schooner.

"It is such a good name for our wagon, as it crosses what seems to be an unending sea of grass, like a ship on the waves. Now we are in an area of more scrub grass, bull muhly grass, buffalo grass, and mesquite. We see razor-sharp limestone rocks; mountains of sandstone in bands of reds, browns, yellows, and even black; some cottonwood trees; and wild oregano."

Jason's eyes raced through several pages, drinking in the words like cool water on burning sand. He read of the family's travels across the land, searching for the dream spot to settle. A few pages near the middle of the journal, the handwriting changed from a strong hand to a shaky, faint, and almost illegible script.

"I haven't written for days. I couldn't bear it. Things are so horrible, I fear I shall lose my senses. We arrived at a river's edge. We believe it's Wild River. Garrett thought there had been heavy rain farther north, causing the water and debris to fill the banks. He made a raft for our goods, the babies, and me to float on. Making the raft took all day. The next day, he fastened a double rope to the trees on our side of the bank and swam across the river to the other bank while dodging a few small branches. On reaching the land, he climbed a tree and tied the two ends of the rope around a stout branch. The ropes were high enough not to hang into the water and yet low enough so I could reach them while standing on the raft. He swam back to us and rested, as the current in the river was strong. I tucked this journal and the ink and pen into Edmund's sleeping basket. Garrett left the oxen on the banks to graze until he could go back and swim them across.

"We stood on the raft and pulled on the ropes fastened to the trees on the opposite bank. After we left the shore, Garrett jumped into the water and pushed from the back as I pulled on the rope. The water was soon over Garrett's head, and he had to swim as he pushed. Some water washed up onto the raft, but Garrett had packed well and all the things that needed to be kept dry, like our flour and such, he had positioned on top of what would not be harmed by wetness. We fought the strong, swirling tug of the current. My arms began aching within minutes, as I was straining hard on the ropes. I could tell Garrett was expending all his might in pushing and steadying the raft.

"Despite the river's strength and our exhaustion, I thought we would succeed, until a roaring, crashing tumult filled the air when we were just past the middle. Huge torrents of water came tearing down upon us, filled with trees and branches. Garrett lost hold of the raft. It hit debris churning in the water. I grabbed for the cradle and basket but was only able to get hold of one child before another tree struck and shook the raft so hard it split into pieces. One section, with the cradle and sweet Ethan, was swept downstream.

"I think a log or part of the raft hit Garrett as I saw his ashen face covered by a mask of pain. He saw the cradle and yelled, 'I'll get him!' He swam with the current as it tore down the riverbed. Ethan and Garrett were out of sight within moments around a bend.

"I fell into the river but was able to hang onto the section of the raft with Edmund. It took my strength, more than I knew I had, to reach safety. The raft struck tree roots near the bank. I crawled onto it and collapsed next to the basket. I don't know how long I lay there. It was nightfall and pounding rain when I awakened to Edmund crying. I dragged us up the steep bank and under the shelter of trees.

"I had no way to make a fire. The river and rain were frigid. It is now three days since that horrific occurrence, and my clothing is still damp. The nights are cold and frightful. I hear many sounds in the woods. I keep hoping it's Garrett with Ethan, but it's only the night animals.

"I have a deep, hard cough. I'm too weak to walk far, and I fear if I leave the riverbank Garrett will not find us, if indeed he still lives. If help does not come soon, I shall perish. What will become of my baby?" The writing in the journal ended, so Jason put down the book. He wiped his eyes and got up from the cell bed to circle around the office and head out the door to the street. He leaned against the post holding up the overhanging roof. His eyes filled again. There wasn't a cloud to be seen, and the sun was merciless. *The sun sure makes my eyes water.* He returned to the cell, taking deep breaths, hoping to quell his jumpy stomach. Jase opened the journal. Flipping through the empty pages to the back, he found a creased, thin, yellow sheet of paper. He opened it and read the handwriting of another woman.

"My name is Cecilia Proft. My husband, Michael, and I were traveling by Conestoga wagon through the Territory of New Mexico when we heard a baby crying. We had not seen another living soul for over a week, so we searched out the source of the cry. We came upon a dead woman lying by a riverbank. She appeared to have died a few hours, perhaps a day, earlier. Lying in her arms was a pitiful baby boy wrapped in a blanket. He was dirty, cold, and hungry. This journal was found in a basket. Michael and I buried the woman a bit up from the bank and took the child with us. We made inquiries as to his family whenever we came across passing travelers. We were not successful in our search but are not disappointed. We will raise Edmund as our own. As Elizabeth never indicated her last name in the journal, we will give him ours, but we will honor the given name of Edmund. We are going to Connecticut, where my husband is going into the dray business with his brother. We will give this journal to Edmund when he is old enough to understand."

Jason closed the journal as Edmund entered the office. He looked away for a moment and blinked several times, then swallowed hard to force down a lump. He got up and handed the book to Edmund. Clearing his throat, he asked, "You figure we're Elizabeth and Garrett's two boys?"

"Yes, I do."

"You reckon I'm the one she named Ethan?"

"Yes."

"I don't like Ethan. Jason is better." He turned away from his brother and sat on the desk chair, his legs wobbly.

Edmund stared at the cold stove to hide his disappointment. Everyone knew him as Jason, so the decision to keep that name was logical, but the hard tone of his voice seemed heartless.

"I could use Ethan as a middle name, I suppose."

"I'm sure it would please Elizabeth and Garrett." Edmund felt a renewed sense of hope for his brother.

The office door swung open. Clement entered, followed by a man in a worn, dusty, brown suit. "Hi, Doc. This here is our circuit judge, McHenry. Judge, meet Jason's brother, Dr. Edmund Proft. You two are brothers, ain't ya?"

"Yes, Clement, we are." Jason stood and shook hands with the judge. His legs felt weaker after answering the question.

The judge took a double look at Edmund and scrutinized his face as they shook hands. Turning to Jason, he said, "Jase, I talked with folks here in town and the sheriff. Everyone said it was a fair fight. You may as well go home. I got to get on to the next town. Nice to meet you, Doctor. I'll pass the word around you're here." He turned and was out of the office before Edmund could speak.

"I wish he wouldn't tell people I'm here. I'm going back East."

"Yeah, you should, but I've been thinking you might want to come to my ranch and spend some time there first. I could show you the cradle and the place where Eli found me-- if you're interested, that is."

Edmund regarded Jason for a moment. At last, he said, "Yes, I would like that." *It's taken me months to come this far to find my past. I might as well see it through to the end.*

"We'll rent you a horse at the livery. You ride much?"

"Never."

Jason closed his eyes, opened them, and shook his head. "Okay."

❋ ❋ ❋

Silas tromped into the kitchen. "Pa's impressed with the work you've done. He thinks you might work out. What's my comely cousin making for supper?" He scraped one work boot against another to loosen the dirt. The wet clumps fell on the floor. The odor of the corral muck overwhelmed the scent of the fresh bread from the oven. Abigail kept her back to him as she rubbed the last of the six cold cooked potatoes through the colander. "It was nice of you to give me the compliment of saying I was comely. Even though I know, and you know it isn't true, still it lifts my spirits." Abigail did not feel a pang of guilt in lying to Silas. "We are having potato pudding with butter, and minced pork sausage." Abigail knew it was useless to remind Silas to use the boot scraper before entering the house, as she was sure it was one of his ways to torment her by making her work harder. She listened in disgust as he walked to the water bucket and dipped out a drink. He swished the water around in his mouth and spat it on the floor.

"Silas, a drink from the well will be colder and more refreshing."

"I like this better. Besides, it gives me a chance to visit my cousin, with her delicate, fair skin."

"Thank you for the compliments, though you're jesting, and thank you for the company. It's appreciated." *He wants to rub in his barbs, but I will not let him see my disgust. He'd taunt me with more flint-hearted behavior.*

Silas threw the dipper into the bucket. He tore away the shawl draped over her head and let it fall to the wet patch on the floor.

Abigail put the potato mash into her bowl of beaten eggs, milk, and sugar. She began mixing the ingredients as she stepped to the table. Picking up the scarf, she tossed it to a corner of the room.

"Did you hear the noises last night? I bet you were scared out there in the tool shed."

"Noises? I didn't hear any. I must have slept right through. What were they like?" Abigail smiled at her cousin. *He's not going to know how terrified I was.*

"Animals, I guess." A sneer covered his face. "You know, people can see you through the cracks of the shed walls."

"People? There's only my uncle and cousins here, and I'm sure you are gentlemen and wouldn't think of such a thing," was Abigail's saucy reply. "Besides, during the day, all there is to see are harnesses and tools, and at night it's too dark to see me. It would be a waste of time, which would be better spent in sleeping to be ready for the next day's work, don't you think?"

"I'd prefer to be a man than a gentleman. I'll prove it to you one of these days." Silas touched the edge of her bodice with his finger.

Abigail saw his yellow and brown teeth in his sneer. She forced herself not to draw back from his putrid breath. She picked up the cast-iron skillet with the hot sausage and grease. "Be careful. I don't want to burn you. I need to finish supper."

Silas withdrew his fingers when he saw the hot pan coming close to his hand. "I got chores to finish. If you know what's good for you, supper better be on time. Tomorrow, I'm leaving at sunup for two days to check on the herd on the range. I'll be doing it every week. Make sure I've got food to take with me." He banged the door behind him.

Abigail put down the pan and reopened the door to watch where he went and to bring fresh air into the room. She eyed the rocker on the porch with longing. *If Uncle sees me sitting in the middle of the day, he'll have a fit.* She went into the kitchen and cleaned up the floor. After rinsing out her scarf, she hung it on a chair to dry. Sitting down, she stared out the door at the corral.

Why can't my relatives be as considerate as Doctor Proft, a stranger? He made the stagecoach ride pleasurable. It was thoughtful of him to visit with me. He has a kind heart. Should I have stayed in town before coming out here? People might not have stared at me. I thought this would be a good place to hide. Poor Aunt Martha. I'm sure she loved her family, but I don't think I can live with these dirty, slovenly, mean-spirited people. Silas saying he'd show me he was a man could mean....

She stiffened. She felt a dark and ugly thought creep into her brain like a rodent. Bolting to her feet, she darted past the table to the middle of the room, where she stared at the uppermost beam in the ceiling. *Uncle Lemuel said Aunt Martha began acting strange after the boys left for California to search for gold. She wouldn't do the chores and cook, even when he took a strap to her. One day, he found her up there when he came in from the barn. Hanging from the highest beam.* Abigail stumbled back toward the kitchen. She stared at the two open doors on the back wall. One room had bunk beds. The other room had a double bed with a faded, torn quilt in a heap on the floor. *A permanent place for my things? Where? In there? When he introduced me, he said, "and take your ma's place." That's why he wanted me to come here, to take her place in doing the chores, and to* She stared at the double bed. Shaking with violent tremors, she held onto the table. Her stomach retched and her mouth filled with hot, sour fluid. *I've got less than a month to think what to do. Oh, Lord, less than a month.*

✼ ✼ ✼

Silas left just before dawn to check on the stock grazing on the open range as he headed in the direction of Pine Town. He timed his arrival for sundown. He tied his tired horse to the hitching rail in front of the Pine Town Saloon. The light from inside gleamed on the dirt and lit his way to the single door. He opened it and stood still as he took in a deep breath; the air smelled of cigar, cigarette smoke, whiskey, and stale, sweaty bodies of the men at the bar and tables. He grinned as he closed the door behind him and went over to the bar, where he put his left arm around the waist of a plump, disheveled, dirty-haired woman who looked to be in her forties. Her makeup was thick and streaked. Her flashy, red, low-cut dress exposed major portions of her breasts. Her mesh stockings had holes and ended in old faded red shoes.

"How's my Dora doing?" Silas gave her ample waist a squeeze.

The bartender set two glasses in front of the pair and poured whiskey into each.

"Silas, I've missed you. Where you been?"

"Slavin' for my old man. Where else! But I sure missed you. So much so, I took time away from rounding up some jackasses to come and see you. What my pa don't know won't hurt him. Let me play a bit of poker, and after I win, we'll go upstairs for a while."

"Lookin' forward to it, honey. Hope you win big, so you can help your friend Dora out. I'm sure in need of some dinero."

He chucked her under the chin and took his drink to a table where three men sat with cards.

"Need some new money here, gents?"

"Sure, Silas. We ain't seen you for a spell. Glad to have your money," one of the players said.

"We'll see about that."

❈ ❈ ❈

Silas dismounted and closed the corral gate after the last mule entered. He led his horse to the barn stall.

"Hey, Silas. You're back. Did you bring the herd in from the range?" Otis dragged a bale of hay to the back stalls and faced Silas.

"Sure did. It took two days and nights, but I got twenty-one of the critters in the corral." Silas lifted the saddle from his horse and placed it on the rack. "I even took time to go to Pine Town, and I won a bit at poker."

Otis walked over, grabbed a curry brush, and began brushing one side of Silas's horse as Silas started on the other side.

"Thanks. I am tired to the bone." Silas swept a brush against the backbone of the horse with one hand as he wiped a rag over the sweat marks with his other hand.

Otis smiled. "You help me plenty. Where'd you get money for poker?"

"Oh, I found a way. I'll tell you about it someday. I'll show you how to play poker, too, sometime when Pa can't find out." Silas cocked his head as he looked at his brother. "Otis, you remind me of Ma when you smile. And your hair color is like hers when she was younger and we were kids, sort of a soft yellow reddish-brown. You're a lot like her. I miss her."

Otis quit brushing for a moment and then resumed. "Yeah, me too. I wish we didn't take off for the gold fields and leave her. I think she died cuz she got so lonesome."

"Yeah, I think so, too. But, it's mostly my fault."

Otis stopped brushing again and, across the horse's back, asked Silas, "How so?"

"When I got old enough, I should've stepped between her and Pa more. I did some, but I reckon it wasn't enough. I was too afraid of him. I ain't now, but that don't help Ma none." Silas threw the brush into a wood bin. "And I'm mad he brought Abigail here to take her place, like everything goes on the same as before, that it don't make a difference if it's Ma or Abigail. Well, I think it does. They're both going to learn that Ma's dying ain't a good thing for either of them." Silas kicked an empty bucket as he led his horse to the corral.

※ ※ ※

Jason and Edmund walked to the mercantile, where Jason pointed out the clothes appropriate for ranch life. Edmund bought two blue flannel overshirts, which opened in the front and buttoned down. He bought a pair of riding boots, two pairs of cotton socks, and a broad-brimmed hat of soft felt; Jason called it a Seritilli. Wool pants completed the outfit. He also bought a woolen blanket, a gutta-percha poncho, and a pound of castile soap for washing. Edmund showed him how to pack it all into a bedroll with the poncho as the outside layer.

"Elizabeth wrote in her journal about a gutta-percha poncho... so this is what it is."

"Yeah, don't they have them back East?"

"No, people use wool coats and capes."

"That ain't good for rain. Wool smells when it gets wet, and leather stretches, then shrinks when it dries. The poncho cloth is soaked in white, thick juicy sap. When it dries, it blocks the rain from coming through. Good for keeping the dust off the clothes, too, but I don't mind the clothes getting dusty." Jason spoke to the store owner,

"John, you got a second-hand pistol and rifle my brother can buy?"

"Jason, I don't want any guns. I'm against them."

"How can you take care of yourself out here without at least a handgun? A rifle is good for hunting, though you likely ain't going to do that, but you need a pistol for protection."

"From what?"

"Snakes, for one thing. Maybe a coyote, including the two-legged kind."

"I'm not going to be here long enough to need a gun. I'm planning to go back home in a month or two."

"You need to be prepared. John, do you have a revolver?"

"Sure do."

"No guns, Jason. I mean it." Edmund picked up his purchases and headed out the door.

Jase took the gun John had placed on the counter. "Put it on his bill." He tucked it into his pants belt under his gun belt and followed Edmund out to the boardwalk.

After Edmund took his purchases to the hotel and changed, he followed Jason to the livery. Sam introduced him to Maggie, a quiet bay fourteen hands high. Sam had a second-hand saddle, fourteen inches from cantle to knee, which was a perfect fit for Edmund.

Jason and Sam showed Edmund how to saddle and bridle Maggie, then led the horse to the corral. After a few practice rides around the enclosure, Jason said, "I think you'll be able to handle the ride to the ranch without falling off."

Jason led the way on Jasper, keeping an eye on Edmund. After trotting, walking, and an occasional light canter, they arrived at his ranch by the late afternoon.

Jason dismounted at the hitching rail by the cabin and led his horse into the barn. Edmund followed suit.

"Never clean, saddle, or bridle a horse in a narrow stall. Make sure you have plenty of room to move around." Jason cooled off Jasper with a dry rag, then used a cool, wet rag. He used the dry one again and finished with a brushing. "You never want to let a horse trap you against the walls of a stall."

Edmund listened and watched Jason, then did the same with Maggie. He found his arms ached from rubbing and brushing the horse, which matched the stiffness in his back and legs from the ride. Jason helped Edmund get Maggie to lift her hooves, one at a time, so they could be cleaned with a hoof prick.

"You need to check the hooves after every ride. If a stone gets lodged in the hoof it could cripple the animal, and it might go down with you."

Edmund nodded.

After the animals were cooled, the men fed them grain and filled the water buckets. While the horses ate and drank, Edmund and Jason cleaned the stalls, put in fresh hay, and carted the old hay outside to a pit in back of the barn. Jason removed the water buckets from the stalls before he closed the barn door.

The two men then went to the cabin. After removing his gun belt and holsters, Jason began putting wood into the cook stove.

"Put your bedroll in the bedroom over there." He indicated a small room at the back of the cabin, next to the larger bedroom.

"Come back out here and help with supper."

Edmund placed the bedroll on a single bed. It had one pillow of feather ticking and a cotton ticking mattress filled with corn husks that rustled when he touched it. He noticed it didn't have sheets or a blanket. A cane-back wood chair was next to a two-drawer dresser. On the dresser was a metal pan to be used as a wash basin and a cotton rag for a towel.

He stepped back into the main room where Jase had a small fire going in the cook stove. He handed Edmund a metal coffee pot. "Fill it at the pump out front."

When Edmund brought the coffee pot back inside, Jase asked, "Anything you interested in seeing or doing while we're here?"

"I was wondering, now that you have read the journal, if we could find where Elizabeth gave birth to us and where she is buried."

"We can give it a try. We'll need to be out for a few days if you think you can stand it."

"I'm sore, but I'm sure I can keep going."

"Good. In that case, I'll cook up some biscuits and extra cornmeal mush. They're good for traveling. And I'll bring cold flour."

"What's cold flour?"

"It's parched corn that I've pounded down, so it's like coarse cornmeal. I add a little sugar and cinnamon. I pack it dry, and when we get hungry or thirsty, we add a little to water and drink it. Keeps a man going for a long time on just a small amount. I heard folks say a half bushel can keep a man's strength up for a month, but I ain't ever needed to go that long.

"The biscuits and mush are tastier to me. The biscuits are just milk, lard, a bit of sugar, some salt, and enough flour to make stiff dough. I knead it good and make small mounds by rolling it around in my hand. I'll bake it in the oven, and they will last for weeks if they are kept dry. Right tasty."

"Sounds good. All right if I make the corn mush? My mother taught me how so it could be fried when cold."

"That's just what I was thinkin'. Go to it."

Edmund filled a kettle with fresh water and when it was boiling added salt, stirring while letting the cornmeal sift through his fingers so it would not lump. He added it a bit faster at the end. He sifted in a handful and a half of flour until it was thick and could not be stirred with one hand. He placed the kettle in the oven, where it baked an hour. *Thank you, Mother. I didn't think I'd need your cooking lessons when I was a boy, but I'm grateful now.*

The men lit the kerosene lamp. Jase had put in a clean chimney, so he took the soot-coated one and placed it in a dishpan of cold water, then slowly added hot water so the glass would not break. The smell of the kerosene in the lamp mingled with the pungent odor of coffee as they ate some of the hot cornmeal mush and biscuits.

As they dined, Edmund related to Jase the information Clement and Hortensia remembered about the Talo family and the death of little Malise.

"Yeah, things like that happen." Jason swallowed the last of his coffee.

He doesn't seem bothered by the little girl's tragic death. He's a cold-blooded man. Edmund took a bite of his biscuit to hide his disappointment.

After eating, they cleaned up the kitchen and scrubbed the dishes with hot water and baking soda. Edmund sprinkled a bit of salt on his rag and scrubbed the inside of the glass chimney. The soot was baked on the glass by the heat of the flame. Edmund's hands and fingernails became blackened, and he used salt and baking soda to scrub his hands. They stored the leftover food in the cold oven.

Without saying goodnight, Jason went into the large bedroom. Edmund said, "See you in the morning," and went into his. Sitting on the bed, he removed the boots and his outerwear. As he hadn't brought his nightshirt, he lay on the bed in his short- sleeved cotton long underwear, staring into the dark.

He pushed his thoughts of Jason's callous attitude toward a child's death out of his mind. He thought about the way they'd worked together in making the supper and the food for their journey. He recalled the patience Jase had exhibited in showing him how to ride and take care of Maggie. *The distance that existed between us, at least for now, doesn't seem so great. After today, we are closer.* He drifted off to an exhausted but peaceful sleep.

❋ ❋ ❋

Jase sat on his parents' double bed and pulled off his boots. The heel was out of one sock, so he removed both. *Maybe Hortensia will darn this for me.* He unbuttoned his shirt, yanked it from his pants, and laid it on the floor next to the socks. He unbuckled his belt and pulled the pants off. They joined the clothes on the floor. He placed his gun belt on the edge of the bed. Lying down in his long cotton underwear, he stared up at the dark ceiling. His stern face reflected his somber thoughts. *This idea was a mistake. His ability to ride is awful. He has no idea how to care for himself or his horse, and his life may depend on his horse if he stays out here. Just because he can cook cornmeal mush means nothing. Maggie could throw him easy--more likely he will fall off, get bit by a rattler, or die in the heat. There are many ways to get himself killed. I'm going to have to spend the whole time taking care of him. The distance from where he is and where I am is too great, and it is getting even greater. After today, we are further apart.* Jase fell into a fitful sleep.

❋ ❋ ❋

"Hey, you goin' sleep all day? Coffee's ready. Jasper's saddled. You got to saddle your own horse. Let's go." Jase closed the bedroom door.

Edmund sat up and looked about. The blackness had eased into gray. He ached as he had never ached. Five minutes later, he took a sip of coffee and followed Jase out the door. Jase gave him instructions on how to get Maggie ready and saddled for the trip. Soon, they headed out the yard gate with Jase leading.

Edmund, amazed at the brilliant sunrise, commented on it.

"If you had slept any longer, we would've missed it. We need to do our traveling in the cooler parts of the day."

Edmund did not respond. They rode in silence for five hours. The sun was beating down. Not a cloud in the deep, eye-watering blue. Occasionally, Jase interrupted the quiet with comments. "Sit straight, don't slouch." "Ride with your stomach muscles." "Keep your heels pointed down. Dig a hole in the dirt with the heels." "Watch Maggie's ears. Remember, horses don't think, they act; you need to be ready if she gets spooked." And, "Feel her back muscles with your legs and seat."

At the end of this, Edmund's exasperation surfaced. "How can I possibly feel back muscles through a blanket and saddle? That's ridiculous."

"I know what Jasper is going to do a moment before he does it, I can feel his muscles, as he feels mine. Maggie knows when you drop or raise a shoulder or shift your spine. Fortunately for you, she must be used to poor riders. If I rode as you do, Jasper would be so confused he wouldn't know which way to go."

Edmund held his tongue. He felt Jase was trying to ridicule him and show him what an idiot he was and that he didn't belong. He had no argument.

Suddenly, Jase reined in Jasper. Edmund looked about. He saw bull muhly grass, sagebrush, a few ironwoods, and barren land. Maggie trotted up next to Jasper and stopped. They were on the edge of a river that was coursing through the clay, carving out the depths of a steep ravine. The banks were of the same height, so it was not visible until one was within a few steps of its edge. Water rushed with force down the riverbed.

"This is why you don't run a horse unless you know the land. Some ravines can't be seen until you're right on them." Jason studied the clay and sandy sides.

"Do you think this is the ravine Elizabeth and Garrett tried to cross?"

"No. Her description was of a wide river that was swollen. This ravine is too narrow. Anyway, we need to find a place to cross it." Jase moved his left heel against the horse and reined Jasper to the left. Jasper turned his head and his haunches away from the boot heel pressure as the horse headed up the edge of the ravine.

Maggie followed Jasper.

Twenty minutes later, Jase stopped and pointed to the edge of the ravine. "This is a good place to cross. See, the side going down to the water is not steep and has good footing for the animals. But, more important, right over there " He pointed to the opposite side, two yards up from the entry point. "Where the animals come out of the water is solid footing, not slippery and muddy, and the climb to the top is not steep. Dismount."

Jase and Edmund dismounted. Edmund, not sure if his aching, half-asleep legs would support him, was hesitant as he swung his right leg over to the ground. He hung onto the saddle horn as he used his other hand to pull his left foot out of the stirrup. To his amazement his legs held, although they were a bit shaky. The men walked the horses down the embankment.

"Take off your boots and tie them into your bedroll. If they get soaked, they stretch, and when they dry, they shrink. They'd be mighty miserable for days." He sat down and pulled his boots off.

While Edmund yanked off his tight-fitting boots, Jase attached a short rope to Maggie's bit and handed the other end to Edmund. He attached another rope to Jasper's bit.

"Jase, I can't swim."

"Me, neither. We'll let the horses tow us across." Jase grasped Jasper's tail.

"If Maggie heads the wrong way, guide her with the rope or splash water in her face, and she will turn back." Jase urged Jasper into the water.

Edmund latched onto Maggie's tail as he encouraged her to go down into the river. The cold water swirled and gurgled about them. Edmund gasped for air as the cold penetrated his body. *Elizabeth faced worse. I can do this.* Edmund felt a powerful tug against him. He held Maggie's tail tighter and strained his neck to keep his head above the water. Ten long minutes later, they climbed onto dry ground and up to the top of the ravine.

"We'll camp here for a few hours. It's the heat of the day, and the horses need to rest," Jase directed.

They moved several yards toward a large rock outcropping. One section stuck out like a small roof, creating a patch of shade. Jase fixed a small amount of feed in the feed bags and slipped the straps over the animals' heads. After the horses were comfortable, Edmund gathered dry sagebrush, and Jase took a glass bottle from his saddlebags and removed a Lucifer match to start a small fire. Jase poured water from the canteen into a small coffee pot and added ground, roasted chicory root. Soon the coffee was ready, and they munched on the travelers' biscuits as they rested in the shade.

Jason stood and pulled out the Colt Navy pistol he had tucked into his belt. "Come on. You need some practice handling and shooting."

"No. I said I didn't want a gun, and I don't want to know how to shoot it."

"And what would you do if a rattlesnake bit me and I couldn't kill it? Or Jasper falls and I get killed? Who will put him out of his misery if he breaks a leg? What could you do to help me fend off a pack of hungry wolves? Even if you're only going to be here a month or two, if you stay at my ranch and ride with me, you need to be able to protect yourself, so I don't need to protect you. I got enough to do looking after myself."

"All right! All right! But I'm not ever going to use that against aperson."

"Okay. We'll use my cartridges. I load them myself. It's cheaper than buying them at the mercantile, but you're rich, and you can buy what you need after this time."

Edmund sighed, rolled his eyes, and said, "Fine," in a steely voice.

"This pistol has six chambers for bullets. Make sure you only put in five and have the hammer resting on the empty chamber. If you don't, you're likely to shoot yourself in the leg or somewhere else." Jason loaded the bullets into the pistol as he talked. "You got that?"

"Yes, I've got it. I don't want to shoot myself, obviously."

"Good." Jason ignored the sarcasm in Edmund's voice. "Now, for target practice. Do you see that barrel cactus?" Jason pointed to a small plant about twenty yards away. "There is a rock right behind it. If you hit the rock, we will see the dust or a chip fly off and know your aim is good."

"Fine."

"We won't worry about drawing the gun from a holster, since I doubt you'll wear one."

"You're right on that. By the way, why do you wear your holster on the right side with the gun handle...?"

"Butt. It is called a gun butt."

Edmund took a deep breath. "Okay, gun butt. Why do you cross your other hand over to draw the gun?"

"It is a faster draw crossover. Sometimes I wear two holsters and draw with both hands, but I prefer using my left hand."

"I'm left-handed, too."

"Yeah, I noticed." Jason turned his attention to their position facing the cactus. "Now, to stand…." The lesson went on for over a half-hour: stand, aim, wrist straight, forearm straight.

Edmund was relieved when Jason said, "Let's stop. You haven't hit the rock once. You're always too high or too wide. This is about all I can stand for today. Let's pack up and go."

"Good. I'm ready." Edmund handed the gun to Jason and wiped the sweat from his face with his sleeve.

Jason unloaded the chambers and pocketed the unspent shells.

"Here, this is your gun. Keep it in your bedroll. We'll clean the guns tonight after we make camp."

Edmund took the pistol and wrapped it in his blanket. He saw a fat lizard doing crazy pushups on a small flat rock. He laughed. Jason turned and looked at the lizard. "Ain't nothing but a horn toad trying to keep his belly from touching the hot surface. He'll crawl off soon." Suddenly, the lizard shot a red, blood-like liquid from its two eyes into the air. It streamed out twelve inches and landed near a large, black, fuzzy spider that had taken that moment to crawl out from under the rock. It had moved its long black legs over the edge and pulled itself into the view of the horned toad. Edmund jumped when he saw the fierce- looking spider, and the blood stream added to his surprise.

"The spider is a Tarantula, and the toad is just squirting at it to warn it off," Jason explained.

"Are they dangerous?"

"The spider eats beetles and stuff, and its bite isn't dangerous to humans. Same for the horn toad."

After they packed up and just before Jase mounted Jasper, he looked at Maggie. "Wait a minute. I see flies buzzing around her leg." He walked over to Maggie and shooed the flies off the foot she was stamping and trying to swish with her tail. "Look. She has an open sore. It must have happened while crossing the river. Flies will lay eggs in the wound, and they hatch into worms."

Jase took from his saddle bag a hard, white bar of calomel and cut off a small piece. He removed his boot and pounded it into a fine powder with the heel. Then, taking the powder in his hand, he blew it into the open sore on the horse's leg. "This will kill off any worms that may hatch in the sore and help it heal."

"That bar looks the same as what I use on some of my patients' wounds. It is mercurous chloride. I never thought of using it on a horse."

"We just call it calomel. The name is good enough for me without gussying it up fancy."

Edmund felt the sting of Jason's remark. *Does he think I'm trying to throw my education in his face?*

They rode for four hours and came to a riverbed with just a trickle of water. The horses picked their way down the bank, across the bottom consisting of scattered puddles, and up the opposite bank. Edmund saw more dry, dusty land. "When do you think, we will get to where the Taloes set up their sod house?"

"We're here. It's the only place hereabouts that fits the description."

"I don't see a sod house."

"Likely, the roof fell in overtime and is now under the surface. See how the land has two slight bumps in it? Bet that's where the soddies were. Do you want to dig around to see if we can find some wood frames for the windows?"

Edmund sat back on Maggie. *All this way, just to see this? It's nothing.* "No, I don't see a reason to know for sure. I thought we might see Malise's grave."

"Don't you see it?" Jase asked. "That bunch of rocks sitting out there on the flat land with no other rocks scattered about. I bet that marks the grave."

Jason and Edmund dismounted and hiked twenty feet back from the mounds of dirt. Three boulders were grouped together. On one rock were scratches that were illegible except for the letter M, which appeared to be the deepest.

Edmund stood quiet for a moment. "I think she was trying to follow Elizabeth and Garrett because of us, and she died. Her parents must have been devastated. I guess her mother couldn't stand it out here anymore, and so they moved back to Minnesota."

"Yeah, but we can't do nothing about it. We couldn't then, either. But now, we have a starting point. It was from here Garrett led the oxen to where they crossed the river. We can go in that direction, and maybe we'll figure out where they entered and where Elizabeth came out. Eli showed me where he found me, but I could have floated down the river for miles before getting hung up in the tree."

Does Jase feel any sympathy for this little girl or her family? Edmund stood staring at the rock with the fading name. He knew in a few years it would all be gone.

Jase took off his belt and crouched near the rock. With the buckle in his hand, he scraped over the grooves of the child's name, making the letters deeper.

Edmund smiled and took off his belt. After an hour and a half of work, Jason got to his feet and stated, "That should last another twenty or more years."

❋ ❋ ❋

They rode farther north. Each day, they started in the deep dark and watched the sunrise. They trotted at times to break the monotony of the steady swish of the horses' hooves moving through the sand and the hard clop on the rocky surface. Edmund found the sound was relaxing and was lulled into sleep in the saddle. He smiled when he saw it affected Jason the same way. He didn't like the bouncy trot, yet he knew it was needed to wake up the horses and riders. They camped at noon for three hours, and just before sundown, they made their final stop for the day. Jason always knew where water was available. They groomed the horses at the end of the day with small brushes and cleaned the packed-in dirt from the hooves with Jason's hoof pick. The two men lit a small campfire using dead brush from the yucca and the mesquite, drank their coffee, and had the biscuits as they cleaned their guns. During the day, they drank some of the cold flour. Edmund dreaded the evening meal, as it never varied, but he thought better of complaining to Jason.

As they rode, Jason pointed out the hackberry trees, the yucca, mesquite, juniper, tumbleweed, and sage. At times the land seemed white, and then it morphed into yellow, brown, and red. The earth and the foothills were made of soft, sandy rock. After Edmund wondered out loud what kind of rock the mountains were, Jason headed that way, and Edmund saw it was like the rocky foothills, composed of various colors of sandstone. The colors ran in straight bands around the mountains. One mountainside held drawings carved into it.

"This country is really quite beautiful, in its own way. It has a majestic feel. But what are these drawings? Who did them?"

"Reckon it was the Indians that drew them, but I don't know why the heathens did it. Don't care to know, either."

Edmund kept quiet.

The land went on and on. The heat went on and on.

Chapter Twenty – One

Abigail set down the two wooden buckets and unfastened them from the yoke. Dipping a gourd into a pail, she poured water at the base of each plant in the vegetable garden. She moved the buckets along with her as she progressed up the row. After two rows, she straightened up and surveyed the work to be done. Closing her eyes for a moment, she sighed. *I'd best go in and see to the bread rising, feed the chickens, and later finish here.*

She wiped her bare feet on the porch's rag rug. Glancing through the doorway, she could see her cousins were not in the house. After scrubbing her hands and punching down her bread dough, she re- covered it with a cloth and strode to the barn. She laughed as she remembered the trick she'd played on the chickens. Without discussing it with Uncle Lemuel, she hadn't fed the flock for two days. On the third day, she'd fed them insects from the garden. They gobbled them like sweet chocolate. Now, the chickens worked for her. She took a few seeds and laid them in a line to the vegetable plot. The chickens followed her to the garden. They ate the bugs as she dipped the gourd in the second water bucket to finish watering the plants.

A one-eyed hen pecked up a potato bug. Two larger chickens scurried over to the hen and chased her away. "Leave her alone," Abigail hissed. She kicked at the two hens. Squawking and fluttering their clipped wings, they scooted to a different row. Abigail plucked an insect off a sprout and set it by the good eye of the hen.

Tears filled her eyes and streamed down her face. She wiped them with her hand and left a dirty smear on her cheek.

Lord, it's so blasted hot, and I'm exhausted. I don't know what to do! Does Uncle Lemuel want me to move into his bedroom? She shuddered and stifled a sob. *I can't stand the thought of him touching me, of me giving him his wifely propers. Lord, I can't do it.* The insidious thought had crept into her brain to stay. For two days, she'd tried to think of other things. She'd tried praying it away, but it had swept in and taken over every moment of the working days and sleepless nights.

She picked up the buckets and yoke and trudged back to the barn. Entering through the single door cut into the double doors, she stood for a minute to adjust her eyes from the harsh glare of the sun. The smell of old, musty hay mixed in with manure and urine hit her in the face. She hung the yoke on a peg.

She froze. "Who's there?"

Holding her breath, she listened. Her stomach felt empty and queasy. "Is someone in the barn?" She listened to the silence. "I guess it's mice." She stacked up the two buckets.

"That's right. Just us two little mice frolicking in the barn. Come join us, Cousin." Silas and Otis burst into laughter as they stepped out of a stall and approached Abigail.

"You haven't mucked out the stalls yet. Uncle Lemuel will be mad if you don't get your chores done. And you were to help him with a fence out in the pasture." Abigail backed away from the men toward the door.

"We did help with the fence. A farmer, Raul, saw Pa in the field, and they began talking business. The fella wants to buy a mule. Fat chance."

Her voice shook. "Why?"

"Cuz Raul is a Mex, and no one around here likes them, and everyone knows no Mex has money enough to buy a good mule. They can only get one by stealing it."

"Oh." Abigail edged farther back.

"We come up to do the barn chores, but when we saw you, Otis and me thought we'd do you instead." Silas stepped forward and grabbed her by the arms. He swung her around to Otis, who wrapped one arm around her neck and put his other hand over her mouth.

"Here, stuff her apron in her mouth. She's a she-cat." Otis took his hand away from her face. Abigail inhaled in panic. Silas lifted her apron and stuck it deep into her mouth. Otis untied it in the back, and Silas shoved it deeper into her throat.

Abigail tried to claw at them, but each time they let go of one arm they tightened their hold on the other. They shoved and dragged her toward an empty stall. She stumbled forward. Her arm slid over the top of the wood wall. She felt slivers dig into her forearm through her sleeve. Silas grabbed both her arms. She threw her weight against him and tried to kick Otis. He pulled a cinch strap from a hook and bound her hands and forearms together. Silas threw her down on the dirty straw and sat on her legs.

The rafter birds fluttered and flew from the barn.

"Now, ain't this nice. Bet you ain't never been poked before."

"Tain't likely, Silas. What fella would be interested in an ugly woman?"

"Yeah, that's what I figure. I like being the first one to do it. You pull up her skirts and pull down her undergarment. I got to unbutton my pants and drawers."

Abigail struggled to scream. The apron choked her. The foul smell of the soiled hay added to her gagging and coughing reflex. She flailed her arms against Otis as he knelt on her shoulders and bent forward over her. He clawed her dress and petticoats up to her waist. His putrid breath hit her face as he laughed.

Silas pulled her pantaloons down past her ankles. "Hey, the bottom half of her ain't ugly. Betcha, you'll like me doing you better than you will when Pa gets you into his bed. He sure was rough on Ma."

Abigail felt his body come down on top of her. Their laughter flooded into her ears as searing pain penetrated her. Screams would not come, only tears and gagging. The world disappeared in a void of deep blackness. She couldn't make a sound or see. The pain ripped into her again and again and again. It stopped for a moment. Then it began with renewed intensity.

Silas and Otis's laughter and yells of ravishment drowned out the sound of the barn door banging open and Lemuel's footsteps pounding toward them on the barn floor.

"You boys get off her. Now! When I saw the birds come streaming out of here, I knew there was trouble." Lemuel wrenched Otis off of Abigail and pulled her dress down. He shoved Silas back. "You untie her and get her on her feet. I thought I learned you better. Well, by golly, you're going to learn."

The boys pulled Abigail up and yanked the apron from her mouth.

Screams tore from her throat.

"Abigail, quit yelling and git. Go pack your stuff. And you two, get over there." Lemuel pointed to a post. "Abigail, I said quit yelling. You ain't hurt that bad."

Abigail heard distant screaming. Her brain was lost in a mass of terror. Pain shot through her face and brain, once, twice.

"Girl, you hear me?" He slapped her again.

Blinking, weaving, gasping, she realized she had been screaming, and her uncle was yelling at her. His words had no meaning. Her head nodded as an involuntary reflex.

"Go to the tool shed and pack your stuff. I'm taking you to town at daylight tomorrow. You be ready. I'm sending you back home. You git."

Abigail stumbled toward the barn door. She looked back. Uncle Lemuel was taking off his leather belt as he marched toward his two sons. They backed against the wall and tried to pull a hay bale in front of them.

Their words made no sense to her. "Pa, we didn't do anything you ain't done yourself. All guys do it. It's our manliness. You know that."

"She's your cousin. It's against the Good Book."

"You were going to do it after you got married."

"She's a niece by marriage, not by blood. She needed someone to provide a place for her, and we needed her for cookin' and such. Who's going to do the work women do? Your ma did well enough, until you boys ran off to the gold fields, and she came down with the blue miseries that winter. You two came back smart as you please after I paid for Abigail to come out here to take on woman chores. Do you think I can have my propers after my sons have had her?"

Abigail got out the door and staggered to the house. She heard the whop, whop, whop of the leather belt and the screams of her cousins. Stumbling into the kitchen, she took the pig butcher knife and ran to the tool shed. After she barricaded the door behind her, she curled up on her cot as she clutched the pig cleaver to her body. Abigail rocked back and forth, whimpering.

Chapter Twenty – Two

Edmund sat in the porch shade, sipping cool water from a gourd as he leaned back against the roof post. The setting sun behind Jason's house turned the clouds pink and purple; the horses in the corral were swishing flies and drinking from the trough. Horned larks, killdeer, and pigeons sang and cooed. He let his body sag as the weariness eased its way out and left him relaxed and content. He surveyed the land stretched out before him--the same dry dust and dirt and sand, but now he saw a beauty he had not noticed before. The soil had different colors, from red to brown to yellow.

After Jason told him the names of the plants, he saw them differently. The tall and spiny yucca, the Whipple Cholla cactus, the prickly-pear cactus, the piñón pine, the juniper, the arrow weed, sagebrush, the beehive cactus, the ocotillo, the paintbrush, and his favorite, the larkspur. He knew there were many more plants he hadn't learned the names of that had variety and color, adding to his growing appreciation. He rubbed his chin and face; he had not shaved all week. Staring at his light brown hands, he noted the nails were cracked, torn, and filled with dirt, causing him to pull out his pen knife from his pocket. He cleaned and smoothed the nails as best he could. Now he looked more like Jason. Seeing Jason leave the barn and head toward him, he said, "I'm glad I spent this week with you at your ranch. I've enjoyed it. Thank you."

"I have to say, you've learned a lot. Your riding improved from a miserable awful to a fair capable. Your gun handling, however, is still the worst I've ever seen. Best you carry your pistol in your doctor's bag in case you need it. If folks hear about your shooting skills, they'll feel safer by not seeing you with a gun."

Edmund wondered if his brother was joking or giving advice.

Jason sat down on the porch next to him. "Sorry we couldn't find any trace of Elizabeth's grave or where you were found."

"It's all right. I saw the spot where Eli found you. I'm glad you kept the cradle. Garrett's craftsmanship is evident in the construction, despite the battering it took in the river." Edmund handed him the gourd.

Jason took a swallow and handed it back. "I think Maggie will make a good horse for you. She's steady and doesn't get rattled when you've given her mixed signals for what you want her to do."

"I feel secure when I'm up on her. I like her looks, too. Her bay coat is shiny and sets off the white blaze on her face and the one white stocking leg."

"Keep her fed right and groomed, and her coat will stay shiny. Takes work, but she'll do right by you."

"I'll buy her from Sam. I've decided to stay for a few months."

"If you decide to go back East, though, Sam might buy her back." Jason stretched his arms.

Edmund thought he saw a look of disappointment cross Jase's face. It threw him off balance. *Is Jase upset I am staying or that I might leave?* He stumbled for the words to cover his confusion.

"Sounds good."

"I'm going to get a harness that needs mending." Jason rose up.

"Wait, Jase. Do you hold it against me that I said you were a murderer when you killed Miranda?" "Nope."

"Then what's the matter? You never say more to me than what is necessary. We never sit and talk."

Jase watched a dust devil swirling by the corral. "Because you know things I ain't likely to ever know. I ain't gonna see a big city. I ain't likely gonna read many books, like you done. You talk like book talk. Oh, you try to fit in. You got some clothes like me before you came out here to the ranch, except for the boots-- they're still those low-cut city ones. Not much good out here."

"They are more comfortable for me than the high-cut Western ones. I tried some on in town."

"Yeah, our boots are made for riding, not walking. But that's not all. You try talking like me, but it ain't natural for you. I can't see you ever liking it out here. I think you belong back where you came from."

The words had been said. They sounded cold and hard coming from Jason, but Edmund knew they were the same words he had been thinking but denying. He could get used to the severe living conditions, but the attitude of the people was too harsh for him to accept.

"I think you are right. I do belong back East. I'd like to stay in Wild River for a while, though, if you don't mind."

Jase cleared his throat. "Don't care what you do. Suit yourself." With that, he moved off to the barn.

Edmund's eyes were on Jase's back as he walked away. *He doesn't care about having a brother. I felt alone in Connecticut after my parents died, but I had a dream of making a difference; I could heal. And now, I have a living connection to a real living, breathing brother-- a twin. I feel like I'm constantly holding my breath, waiting. Always waiting with dread. Will Jason kill someone else, or will he get killed? Will his life blood spill into the dirt and mean nothing? If I went home to Connecticut, I would wonder every day what was happening with him. Perhaps he would die, and I wouldn't even know of it until long after, if ever. I'm afraid the wondering day after day would be worse than staying here waiting for it to happen. I don't belong here, and I can't go back home.*

Edmund got up and approached Jason as he entered the tack room.

"I'd like to ask a question that's been on my mind for a while."

"What?"

"Folks don't like Mexicans much around here. I'm wondering why." Edmund studied Jason. "I'm not judging you or the other people in town. I'm just curious."

"Easy to answer. What happened at Sara Flats back in '58 is a good example of the feelings Mexicans and Americans have of each other."

"Never heard about it."

"Likely not. Likely not important back East. But out here, it sure was. Sara Flats is sixty miles from here. It's near the Apache Pass, where Cochise and his band lived." Jason picked up a worn harness and a leather punch and searched among short pieces of old leather straps. "Years ago, there was a company named the Jackass Mail Route. It ran a stage line of sorts, but it went belly up because it couldn't make enough money. The Butterfield Overland Mail Company took over the route and built stations every twenty miles between Tipton, Missouri, and San Francisco." Jason picked up a piece of leather and measured it against the harness. "A man by the name of Cooper was in charge of one of the construction crews. The crew was going to fortify a Jackass station at Sara Flats." Jason put down the harness and implements. "You let me read the journal, so I'll let you read about this for yourself in an old newspaper account." He went out of the barn and into his cabin. Edmund followed. Moments later, Jase came out and handed Edmund a yellow newspaper worn and torn at the creases.

Edmund unfolded it. "You've kept this a long time."

"One of the men in the story, Charlie Wilcox, was Eli's brother. Besides, we don't get much to read out here, so we save what we can. The whole issue is about the slaughter at Sara Flats. It's written by the man who lived it. I'm going to get the harness to fix while you read." Jason stepped off the porch.

Edmund sat down and read, "The True Account of the Slaughter at Sara Flats, New Mexico Territory, by Mervale Cooper, foreman of the construction crew for the Butterfield Overland Mail Company.

"My crew and I arrived at the old Jackass station at Sara Flats, New Mexico Territory. We aimed to make it a secure compound in case of Apache attacks, as their stronghold was not too distant, and they used Sara Springs, a half-mile away, as a rendezvous.

"We planned to build a corral for the animals and a storage room and ten-foot-high stone walls around the compound. It was late summer, and the station was to be operational by mid-September.

"The crew members were Charlie Wilcox (we called him Old Charlie, as he was the oldest member of the crew at the age of fifty-four), James Hawthorne, Lars Johansson, Bert Sims, Bonifacio Gomez, Jorge Flores, and his brother Pedro Flores.

"The day we arrived, Old Charlie and I dismounted and, taking rope, stakes, and mallets, paced off the dimensions of the compound around the old site. The rest of the crew rode off to get a load of rocks and boulders from the ravines and gulches. Before nightfall, we tethered the animals and set up camp. Shifts of two men stood guard till morning.

"Day followed day of the same routine: caring for the animals, hauling rocks and boulders, and building the compound. The animals soon had a corral inside the remnants of the old wall. After several days of grueling work, the walls of the storeroom and the wood rafters for the roof were up but not yet covered; also, the ten-foot- high walls surrounding the compound were nearly finished. Day and night, two of us were on guard duty, keeping an eye out for the Apaches.

"On September 6, 1858, Old Charlie slept at the main gate. I bedded down in the storeroom at the northeast corner of the building, and Hawthorne slept outside the doorway of the storeroom. Johansson took his turn on guard duty with Gomez. The starry, moonlit sky was quiet until the sounds of distress from the horses and mules in the corral awakened me. A soft whistle tickled the air. A moment later, the thud of blow upon blow followed by horrific screams of pain and terror filled the darkness. I jumped up, reaching for my revolvers under my saddle and for my rifle standing in the corner. I thought we were under attack by the Apaches. Before I could get to a weapon, the three Mexican members of our crew burst through the open doorway. Flores swung a broadax towards me. I punched and sent him staggering backward. In the moonlight I saw the ax in Gomez's hand as it hurled down on me. I threw up my arms. It hit my left hand and went down and struck my leg. In fear for my life, I didn't feel it at the time. I hit Gomez in the face. He sank to the ground. Flores came at me with a short-handled broadax. The blow cut the palm of my hand, and the next one hit my right arm so hard it became numb and useless. I grabbed the rifle with my left hand and swung it as a club; it knocked the ax from his hands. As I pointed the gun at the men, they backed out of the doorway. Exhausted, I couldn't hold onto the rifle. It fell to the floor with a thud, which drew the attackers back in for another charge. I grabbed one of my revolvers.

"I fired as Gomez entered the room. The Flores brothers caught him and dragged him out. I sank to my knees and listened. They took the horses from the corral and galloped off. Bleeding heavily, I bound up a long, deep wound in my leg. I made a tourniquet of my bandana and a stick to stop the bleeding in my right arm. Gathering up my weapons and staggering to the yard, I climbed on a stack of barrels to see over the wall and positioned myself with my rifle to stand guard. I feared the attackers would return. Apprehension was my companion as I continued to scan the barren land lit by moonlight.

"Throughout the night, I listened to the groans of Johansson and Hawthorne. At daylight, I crawled to Hawthorne. Two deep gashes in his head exposed a gray, pulsating matter covered with buzzing flies. He begged for water. I had none. I found Johansson, who had been on guard duty but watching for the wrong enemy. His brain protruded through his open skull. He was conscious and trying to sit up. I made my way to the gateway. I found Old Charlie, his body slumped over, his head crushed. Obviously dead.

"The three of us survivors needed water. The Mexicans had taken the water bags and canteens. The only water was Sara Springs, a half- mile away.

"The mules and donkeys were chained in the yard. I dragged myself to them and set them free. They ambled to the grass outside the compound and followed the smell of water to the spring. My wounds kept me from crawling to join them. For the rest of the day, I lay in the dirt and listened to my two friends cry for help.

"With darkness, coyotes began circling the compound, getting closer and closer to Wilcox's body. Soon I heard them outside the yard tearing Charlie's flesh, a sound I shall never forget. Johansson and Hawthorne pleaded and moaned louder. In the deep night, Hawthorne became quiet. I knew in my heart he was dead.

"In the morning, the ravens and buzzards circling overhead came closer. Some perched on the rafters of the unfinished roof. All day, Johansson and I lay in the heat. No relief. At dark, the wolves joined the coyotes. I listened to them snarl and fight each other over Charlie's remains. When one of the beasts slunk by the gate, I shot at it to keep it from entering the yard.

"The next day, the sun blazed forth again. No water. No relief. My tongue swelled. I panted and gasped for breath. Lars Johansson, his head nearly split in two, managed to get up from the ground. He staggered about, seeking water. I talked to him as best I could with my swollen lips and tongue. He whimpered but didn't speak. I don't know why he wasn't dead. The fourth night, I continued shooting at the coyotes and wolves when they crossed the gateway. It kept them out of the compound.

"I drifted off into a haze. I awakened in the morning to the sounds of the buzzards roosting on the rafters. I knew I was close to death, and they would soon feast on me. My vision faded in and out. My head was spinning, the pain indescribable.

"I heard footsteps enter the compound. I hoped it was our attackers or the Apaches coming to finish the job. A man named McDonald, who was going to the Rio Grande from Tucson, entered the compound. He had water! It was too late for Johansson, as he died later that day. A road crew, slated to open the stage depot, arrived and gave assistance. Two men left immediately for Fort Buchanan, 110 miles away, to bring back a doctor. One of the men who stayed behind got sick when he saw the maggots infesting my arm.

"Six days later, the army doctor arrived. Dr. Bernard Sidney dressed the wound in my leg and saved it. He bandaged the cuts on the palm of my hand. He amputated my right arm at the shoulder. A week later, I went by wagon to the fort, where I stayed for six weeks, until I was up and walking. My fallen comrades were buried near the stage station under heavy rocks to keep off the wolves. My right arm is buried there, too.

"A three-hundred-dollar reward is offered for the three murderers. I hope this account will help catch, try and convict the three men who committed this dastardly crime."

Edmund folded up the paper and joined Jason.

Jase glanced up from the two pieces of harness he was splicing together with a leather cord. He put down the awl he used to make the holes through which he wove the cord as he handed a worn saddlebag to Edmund. "I carved your initials in these, if you want them."

"The letters are fancy, like artwork. Thank you." Edmund studied the saddlebag and shifted his weight. "The crime described in the paper happened years ago. Why does it matter now?"

"Like I said, the Charlie Wilcox mentioned in the article was Eli's much younger brother. Charlie was born after Eli and Wilma left the Ozarks. They sat right there on the porch, talking about their folks and the people they knew back in the mountains. Eli smiled for weeks after that. When I read the newspaper account to him, he took the death hard, it being his only kin. He wasn't the same after that. Also, folks depend on the stage coach line. It brings us news, mail, and people like you out here. It helps settle the area and makes life easier for everyone. The men killed were on the lookout for an enemy from the outside, not from the inside. The murderers deceived and turned on the men they worked with side by side. As far as I know, those three were never caught. People don't forget. It rankles. And Mexican bandits come across the border and attack ranches and small settlements even now. I've often fought off Mexs trying to get at my whiskey."

"Surely, you can't blame an entire group of people for the acts of a few?"

Jason took the paper from Edmund. "Don't seem like a few to me. It's all of them. My earliest memory was of a drunken Mex barely staying on his horse wanting to buy whiskey from Eli. Pa said no, and the man took out a gun. He was so drunk he waved it around, not able to aim it. He rode off saying he'd be back with friends. Pa kept his rifle handy for days. I don't think he slept much, either." Jason tucked the paper into his pants pocket.

"Did the man come back?"

"No. But it was the first time I knew danger and saw Ma and Pa worried." Jason picked up the harness. "Look at what happened at the Alamo and at Goliad. The Mexs showed no mercy."

"My father, Michael Proft, told me about Goliad."

"Yeah, so you know that the Americans were holed up in a fort and fought against the Mexican Army. They surrendered after they heard about the Alamo and that Santa Anna was going to add reinforcements to fight the Americans. Three hundred men laid down their arms. They were marched out to an empty field, and everyone was murdered, even the sick and wounded. We don't forget."

"Some Mexicans fought with the Americans and died with them. My folks saw it. People are individuals. You can't paint an entire group of people with the same brush."

Jase pulled the leather harness hard to see if it was strong. "I can. They're the only ones I've met. You haven't lived out here long enough. The man I killed the day you came to town was a Mexican. No one bothered him when he started his ranch. Sure enough, one night I caught him stealing from the feed store. Because I didn't kill him then and there, I had to face him years later. If he had killed me, he'd have gone after Clement and likely killed him."

"The townspeople were there. They could have stopped him."

"They're shopkeepers. They don't use guns. They can't face down a man out to kill. Nope, it was up to me, whether you understand it or not. Shows you don't belong out here." Jason picked up his tools and marched back into the barn.

Chapter Twenty – Three

Abigail twisted the handkerchief into knots after using it to catch searing tears. Listening to the iron-rimmed wheels of the wagon as they ground over the dirt road in rhythm with the mule's hoof beats, she edged over to the far end of the wagon seat. The odor of Uncle Lemuel's sweat was repugnant and nauseating in the dry heat of the day. Her nostrils recognized the smell of Silas and Otis. Her tight throat forced down swallow after swallow of bile. She gripped the seat to keep from sliding closer to Lemuel as the wagon jolted over a small rock. Her mind jerked from his smell to his words.

"Abigail, you got it worked out in your mind what you're going to tell the doctor?"

"Yes, Uncle Lemuel. I think so."

"You ain't going to say anything to bring shame on your family, are you?" He slapped the reins against the mules' rumps to urge them on. "Giddy up there, Marigold, Obadiah."

"No, Uncle."

"You know I whupped your cousins good."

"Yes, I know." Abigail tried to keep her voice steady. She looked down at her hands. The gloves lay in her lap. It was too hot to wear them, and her uncle had seen her scars many times.

"I ain't sayin' what those boys did was right, but it was just boys being boys. I reckon they need to go out and find gals to marry. Their wives can take care of their manly needs. They're good boys, but being seventeen and nineteen, they need to get themselves rooted down with wives and children.

And it sure wouldn't be fittin' for me to marry you like I figured on doing, after you been with my sons. You understand?"

"Yes." A tear slid down her face. In her mind, she agonized, *Please, please stop talking and get to town. I never want to see you again. I want to get far away. Please, shut up.*

"I got a hen in the back of the wagon to pay the doctor, and I got twenty dollars to give you after we get to town. It ain't enough to buy a ticket all the way back to Ohio, but it's all I can spare. You're my niece by marriage, and I feel it's my duty to help you. I reckon you can get a job someplace on your journey home to earn the rest of the money. You can tell your folks when you get back to Ohio you didn't like living out at the ranch. Too lonely, say."

"Yes, I will." *What am I going to tell them? I'm so ashamed and humiliated, I don't want to go home. I want to crawl into a hole and die.*

"Don't reckon anything should come about after what the boys did, but we need to be sure. It's best you see the doctor right away and get things taken care of to be on the safe side. No sense takin' chances. You don't want to be carrying a bastard."

As they entered the main street of town, Abigail pulled on her gloves.

❊ ❊ ❊

"How do you like the glass window in your room, Doc? It opens and closes. It came in on the last freight shipment, and I installed it myself when you were visiting at your brother's. I left the leather curtain on it for privacy." The hotel clerk smiled in self-satisfaction at Edmund.

"Very nice. A great improvement."

"I figured a city man like you would appreciate it. Nothing is too good for a doctor, I always say-- yes, sir, I always say it."

"Thank you, Mr. Buttwill. I do appreciate it," Edmund interrupted. "I imagine having the saloon next door run by your brother is a comfort."

"Yes, sir, that it is, that it is. He owns the saloon and I the hotel. He uses my stove for cooking up the steak and eggs and coffee he sells. Our buildings connect, and it's real convenient. And…" He glanced over at the door. "Oh, yeah, I forgot. This lady wanted to see you." He pointed behind the doctor.

Edmund turned. "Miss Lester, it's nice to see you. I hope you're well." He went over to the side of the doorway where Abigail sat on a high-back chair.

"I'm fine. A bit of a problem with...with my arm." Struggling to keep her voice steady, she forced herself to smile. She cast an anxious glance at Mr. Buttwill and raised her voice a bit louder. "I've got this awful splinter deep in my arm, and I'm worried it may become infected."

"You are quite ashen. Mr. Buttwill, do you have a room where I can examine Miss Lester's arm?"

"Sure, use the storage room in the back. There are chairs there and a stove. Towels in there, too. If you need something else, let me know."

The doctor and Abigail nodded their thanks to Mr. Buttwill.

In the dusty room, Abigail rolled up her sleeve to expose a long sliver embedded in her forearm and a cluster of smaller slivers.

"How did this happen?" Edmund frowned.

"I was in Uncle's barn, and I tripped. My arm slid against the stall. The mules chew on the wood, and it's rough. It happened yesterday. Since my uncle was coming into town, and I'm not going to stay at his place much longer, I packed my things and decided to ride in, too." Abigail stared at her shoes. "He sent a chicken to pay you. It's at the stage depot with my trunk."

"I'll need to open the skin to get out the deeper splinters, and the longer one. I'll put carbolic acid on the wound to stop infection. It will burn like heck, but it shouldn't be painful for too long. I'll get my bag. Back in a minute." Edmund left the room.

Abigail heard his boots on the wood floor and going up the stairs. She paced the room, fighting back tears. *How am I going to tell him what I really need? Oh, Lord, what am I to do?* She heard his footsteps coming down the stairs, past the desk counter, down the hall to the door. She trembled.

While the doctor tended to her arm, Abigail rambled, telling him about her life at the ranch, her homesickness for Ohio, and her decision not to stay. She explained about not having enough money. She dreaded the moment when she had to tell him the real reason she'd come to see him. As he finished bandaging her arm, she blurted,

"There's something else. I don't know how to say it." Abigail felt the blush covering her face.

"Please, don't be embarrassed. I will be very professional and understanding. I'm familiar with problems ladies have a hard time discussing. " He walked over to his bag and turned his back to her. He cleaned the scalpel he'd used to remove the splinters from her arm. "I…I had a friend who had an older sister, about twelve years older.

She died when she was eighteen." *Will he know I am lying? I never had a friend whose sister died.* "She died because…because she never developed…ah, became a woman. She never had her monthly."

"Yes, it is called amenorrhea. It does happen sometimes."

"So, whenever I do not have my time regular, I get quite concerned. I was wondering if there was anything I could do to sort of…clean out my body, so to speak. If…if you know what I mean?' She choked on the last words as tears dropped into her lap. Her face burned a flaming red. The room felt stuffy and close.

She saw the doctor's back stiffen. *He knows! He knows!*

Edmund stopped cleaning his implements and stared at his bag. The silence in the room hung heavy in the heat. He turned to face Abigail. "Your cousins returned home from the gold fields, your uncle said. How are they?"

"Fine, fine." Abigail's voice shook, and the tears flowed. "I don't know why I'm crying." Sobs shook her body. She held her shredded handkerchief to her eyes.

Edmund pulled out his linen handkerchief and handed it to her.

"It's all right. I understand. We'll get this arm cared for right away, and then you can get a room here at the hotel. We'll tell Mr. Buttwill you'll need the room for a few days, as this is a serious wound, and you may feel under the weather for a bit. Once in your room, we will take care of other things. I've had women patients with this problem back East."

"Thank you. I can't say how ashamed I feel and…and awful."

"Don't. Everything will be fine in a few hours."

After registering her, Hotel Buttwill showed Abigail a room. Edmund and Abigail left the door open, and Mr. Buttwill sent for Abigail's things at the depot. The doctor said, "I need to get some things from my room. Excuse me."

Abigail sat on a chair and shivered. She twisted Edmund's handkerchief until it was in knots. Her thoughts raced like a steam locomotive. *Will he really help me? He blames me, I'm sure--men usually do. When this happened in Ohio to a neighbor girl, a man said, "A woman with her skirts up can outrun a man with his pants down." Maybe the doctor thinks that, too. He won't respect me anymore.* She held her knees as she rocked back and forth.

❋ ❋ ❋

Edmund paced in his room. He stopped and stared out the window. *People are walking and talking and going about their business as if nothing is wrong. A woman is suffering agony, alone in her room, and life goes on as always. I'm sure she was molested by one of her cousins, and the family is covering it up.* Edmund paced again. *I don't blame her, but when an unmarried woman gets pregnant, everyone else blames her. She's an outcast, and Abigail's disfigurement adds to it. Life would be horrible for her. She wouldn't be accepted by the town, maybe even by her own family. With the scarring on her face it will be hard to find a husband, and with an illegitimate child, it could be impossible. I think she is at her limit, so if she gets pregnant it might be more than she could bear.* He thought of the scullery maid, Colleen. He shook his head. He opened his suitcase and rummaged through several packets and glass bottles wrapped in a cloth. *Colleen wanted my help and ended up on the cobblestones below a cold attic window. All my professors at medical school were opposed to this, but the assault against Abigail was recent. She came to me for help. I can't turn her down, can I? Should I? Can I stop a possible life?*

Dr. Proft went down to the kitchen and heated water in a tea kettle, then carried it up the stairs. His thoughts tumbled like rocks in a churning stream.

❋ ❋ ❋

Doctor Proft returned to Abigail's room. He saw her shaking, almost to the point of fainting. His back stiffened. *I need to approach her with cold professionalism. If I am sympathetic or sound soft in my tone, I think she will collapse. She needs to think this is a usual occurrence for me and for other patients. Nothing out of the ordinary.*

"This is ipecac emetic. Take it, and drink a cup of the slippery bark elm tea I have in this tea kettle. The directions are on the packets. It's a laxative. If it doesn't work, you can use the castor oil in this bottle. Use the chamber pot in this room, and I'll bring the one from my room. You should be fine tomorrow, but you will feel weak. Do you think you can do this on your own, or do you want me to stay?"

"I can handle this by myself. Please, don't stay."

"Good. I'll stop by every few hours, but if you need me at any time, send Buttwill for me. Here's your trunk and portmanteau. I'll leave now." He went out the door as the men with her belongings entered.

"Thank you." Abigail tried to smile. Her hands shook as she took the bag from the clerk when he entered the room. The depot man brought in her trunk, and then the men left. She closed the door, and as she turned the key, her sobs erupted. *Every time he looks at me, he will think about this. He will hold it against me.* She collapsed on the bed and buried her face in the pillow.

Four times the doctor entered her room to take out the chamber pot and pitcher of wash water and replace them with fresh. He spoke only to ask if she needed anything, and she always replied with a single no. He never looked at her, keeping his back turned toward her. He stopped coming when he saw that the water and chamber pot were clean.

❈ ❈ ❈

Throughout the night she lay on the mattress and rocked back and forth, back and forth, whimpering softly like a puppy wanting its mother. She stopped with a start when she heard footsteps on the stairs or in the hallway going past her room. She sucked in her breath, fearful someone would hear her. After the sound of the steps drifted away, she listened to the noises coming from the street--a horse, now and again clopping, carrying its rider, or pulling the creaking wheels of a carriage taking its rider homeward. *I can't go home to Ohio. They will know what happened. One look at me, and they will know, or someone will come who will find out and spread the news.*

Someone always does. Things like this can never be a secret. I would be a burden to Jack and my parents. A shame, fodder for gossip, shame that will live as long as I do. Voices broke the silence and her thoughts as men left the saloon next door and talked or sang or cursed before the doors closed and were locked for the night. Minutes later, footsteps shuffled and stumbled in the hallway. Abigail held her breath as she heard the door to the next room open and close. The squeak of the bed in the next room as its occupant thrashed in his hot box came through the thin walls. His snoring took over the squeak and signaled he'd found relief in sleep. After each interruption, the black, hot stillness covered her like a shroud as she went back to her rocking and whimpering. The only break was the infrequent, cool breeze of the night.

Lord, I know it was my fault when I got burned. I knew even as a child. My parents told me so many, many times not to run in the house. I am guilty of disobeying, and the punishment of pain was so great I begged you to release me and let me die. You didn't. Why?

I lived, and I thought you were giving me another chance to be obedient and serving. Now, this horrible shame. People say women ask for this. They evoke this from men. How did I, Lord? How did I cause this? How can I live with it? I can't, Lord. I can't. I understand now how Aunt Martha could do what she did.

Abigail's eyes gazed up in the blackness to the ceiling. She knew it was flat, with the rafters showing in the floor above. Her eyes darted back and forth, searching the black, empty pit she was trapped in.

It will be light soon. Tomorrow, near midnight, when most people are asleep, I can climb the stairs in my bare feet. There must be an area where the rafters are exposed--maybe a storage room. I could tear strips from my clothing to tie together into a rope. There must be a way. There has to be. I cannot live like this.

She saw the streaks of light penetrate the darkness as the sun brought the beginning heat of the day. She closed her eyes and moved her arms over her face to block it out and with it the despair of another day. Soon the street was alive with sounds. Footsteps and voices in the hotel increased in number and intensity as the day blew into another hot blister.

❋ ❋ ❋

Edmund wandered aimlessly up and down the street. A few more boards had been nailed into a walk, with steps for the uneven elevations, but nothing else had changed while he'd been at his brother's place. The heat, the smells, the sounds of animals and buzzing flies, and the glare of the sun filled the street. His stiff muscles felt the taste of ranch life. Sadness weighed down his shoulders after seeing Abigail's eyes.

Each time he entered her room with fresh water, he pretended not to look at her to give her a sense of privacy, but his eyes found her in the mirror above the washstand. He saw pain, a body of great, hopeless pain. The spark, the eagerness, her enthusiasm, all were gone, replaced with despair.

She needs more than twenty dollars to get to Ohio. If she uses the money to buy a ticket, she could get stranded somewhere, and then what? What if there aren't any jobs for her? She should earn the money before she leaves town. But how? And under the present circumstances, does she even want to go home? She said before she thought she would be a burden once her brother married, and the couple moved into the farm house with the parents. She said she felt like an extra left foot. Her eyes are beyond sad, dejected, with no joy, no hope, even no life, just like the scullery maid in Connecticut. Lord, I don't want to lose another patient like that. What can I do?

Edmund studied each building as he went down the side of the street. He considered each establishment as a job opportunity. He frowned. *Nothing is suitable for Abigail, except possibly the mercantile and the hotel, but neither of them needs any extra help, and she wouldn't want to be seen by the customers.*

Clement and Hortensia stepped up onto the walkway.

Edmund lifted his hat. "Good day. I wonder if you know of a job suitable for a young lady."

"Who?" Hortensia asked.

"Miss Abigail Lester. She decided not to live at the ranch with her uncle and cousins and needs to earn money for her passage back to Ohio."

"The poor girl with the disfigurement? We heard about her," Clement said.

"Well, if you ask me, she made the right decision in not staying out at the ranch. Her relatives would not be the easiest people to live with," Hortensia added.

"Sia, they're fine. They mind their own business, and so should we. Lemuel Baxter is a hardworking man. He raises fine mules and asks a fair price," Clement scolded.

"Hard is right." Sia's face changed from sympathy and disapproval to a saucy smile. "Doctor, if she came to cook and clean for her kin, why couldn't she do it here in town? More people come all the time by stage and stay at the hotel. The food served in the saloon ain't fittin' for a coyote--you know that yourself. She could cook one or two meals a day for folks, and when she doesn't have meals to make for customers, she could take in washing. We womenfolk wash our sheets, blankets, and towels twice a year because it's hard work. But, with folks staying at the hotel, Mr. Buttwill might pay her to wash the linens whenever new guests come. It would make a name for him amongst traveling people," Hortensia offered.

"A splendid idea! I'll bring it up with the two Buttwills right away." Edmund tipped his hat and started off but turned back to say, "First, Hotel Buttwill will have to get sheets for the beds." He chuckled and strode back to the hotel.

Hortensia called out to him: "Doctor, come for supper tonight." He tipped his hat again.

"Appears like he's taken an interest in Miss Lester," Clement said.

"Wouldn't hurt any. Might help him stay around these parts if she decides to stay as well," replied Hortensia.

Clement snorted and said, "I think I married a schemer and a matchmaker."

"Don't be silly. I mind my own business. You know that."

Chapter Twenty – Four

Edmund headed straight to the hotel counter and said, "Mr. Buttwill, come with me. We need to see your brother."

Hotel Buttwill looked up from his work. "Why? What's wrong?"

"Nothing is wrong. Come." Edmund took Mr. Buttwill's arm and pulled him around the counter, to the back door, and over to the back of the saloon. "You go get your brother and bring him out here. We need to talk."

"What about, for land to Goshen?"

"Never mind. Hurry up."

Hiram went into the back door of the saloon and returned with Buster.

"Hey, Doc. What you got my little brother all fired up about? I got customers in there that will drink up my profit if I don't watch 'em."

"I'm trying to do you a favor. You are missing out on a great opportunity."

"We are? How so?" Buster, the saloon owner, crossed his arms and stared at the doctor with skepticism.

"Miss Abigail Lester is a splendid cook. You know if Lemuel Baxter liked her cooking, everybody else will."

"Yeah, so?" Hotel Buttwill said as Hiram shifted his weight from foot to foot.

"No offense, Mr. Buttwill, but your food is not edible, not even stomachable. If you had a good cook, you could charge more for the food, you would have more customers eating here, and the guests at the hotel would gladly pay to get good food."

"Didn't know she wanted to work in town," Hiram said.

"Yes, she does. It is too lonesome out at the Baxter ranch. She needs to earn some money. She will cook for you two for her board and room and some pay on the side. One thing, though. She does not want to serve the food, just cook it. You will need to take the orders and bring the meals to the customers." The doctor focused on Saloon Buttwill.

"That's easy enough."

"Great. Look. Connect the back of the hotel and saloon with a small porch, clean out your two storage rooms, and knock out the wall that separates them."

"Knock out a wall!" Hiram and Buster said together, though Buster's voice drowned out his brother's.

"Yes. That would make for a large kitchen area with the cook stove in it and room for a large table and shelves and all that women need in their kitchens. She can tell you more once I talk to her and get her to agree. Also, you need to convert that little room in the back for her. Then she won't have to go through the lobby every day."

"You mean you don't know if she will cook for us? Why you takin' up our time?"

"Believe me, she will do it. Will you agree?"

Hiram and Buster faced each other. "Sure." Their voices combined again.

"Great. I'll go talk to her. Oh, yes--somebody will need to fetch the water from the well and chop and deliver the wood. Maybe you can hire the boy Kenny to do it. And he could help her clean up the area. Women like clean kitchens, you know." Edmund gave them a wise look as if he were an authority on such matters before he turned and strode back inside the rear of the hotel. He turned, stuck his head out the door, and instructed, "Hiram, you need to furnish clean sheets for your guests. Abigail can wash them for extra pay. It will be good for your business. Oh, yes, and pillowcases, too." He left before the two men had a chance to comment. He took the stairs two steps at a time and knocked on Abigail's door.

❋ ❋ ❋

With her knees drawn up to her chest and her arms wrapped around them, Abigail rocked back and forth on the mattress. The blanket was tossed on the floor near her dress, chemise, pantaloons, stockings, and high-button shoes. Her only covering was her long cotton nightdress. Perspiration matted hair to her forehead as the rest fell in damp tangles down to her waist. Long streaks of tear stains traveled down her face and made smudges where they mingled with sweat and grime. A slight breeze entered through the open glass window, stirring the dust and grit of sand as it left more behind.

At midday, she heard the assured steps of the doctor approach her door. She knew his strong, sure walk. She held her breath. The knock came on her door. She feared he would want to see her, and he did. *Why? Why can't he leave me be? He knows my shame.*

"Please go away. I'm resting." Her voice came out weak and strained. Her throat felt tight and hard from swallowing down sob after sob after sob.

"Miss Lester, I need to speak with you."

"I'm fine, Doctor. I don't need you."

"But I need you, Miss Lester. If you don't open the door, I'll get Hiram Buttwill's keys and open it."

"All right. Wait a moment." Abigail swung her legs over the edge of the bed. She stood and fell back down. Her legs felt weak, and her head ached and seemed lightheaded. She came to her feet in slow determination and inched her way to the door as she held onto the bed frame. As she turned the key in the lock, she stepped back and said, "Please wait." She made her way back onto the bed and grasped the blanket from the floor to hold it in front of her. Bending her head and looking down, she said, "Come in."

Dr. Proft entered and, with the door still ajar, said, "Thank you. I have come to ask a huge favor of you."

"What favor can I possibly do for you?" Abigail raised her heavy head and looked at his smiling face. She pushed some of her sweat-matted hair off her forehead where it fell over her eyes.

"Cook."

She gave him a blank stare, trying to let the word settle into her brain and make sense. It didn't. "What?" She dropped down on the bed.

"The food at the saloon is indigestible. Unless I go every evening over to Hortensia and Clement's at supper time and get invited to sup with them, I won't have a palatable meal. Hiram and Buster will enlarge the cubbyhole they call a kitchen and get Kenny to help you clean it up, and you could cook one meal for the evening and serve the leftovers the next day for lunch. There are plenty of folks coming in on the stage, and there are men in town who don't have a wife cooking for them."

"No, really, I can't." Abigail turned her face away from him.

"Yes, you can. Buster will take the orders and serve the food. You just cook it. They will pay a dollar a week plus room and board. You can save the money to buy your ticket back home. They will fix up a small room for you near the kitchen, so you don't need to go through the lobby. And I'm sure they will hire Kenny to chop the wood and get the water and help with the cleaning. Please, please, say yes, for the sake of my constitution."

"I…I don't know. I…." Abigail's eyes searched the room for an answer. Her gaze came back to the doctor's pleading face. *If I don't agree to do it, he will not leave me be. I need him to leave me alone until I can follow Aunt Martha's way and finish my misery tonight.* Taking a deep, shaking breath, she said, "When would I have to start?"

"As soon as you are strong enough." Edmund sighed in satisfaction. "I'm going to Hortensia to see if she will make us lunch, and we can eat it here in your room. I'm sure you are feeling weak. A couple of decent meals in you will make all the difference. I'll be back as soon as I can." Edmund closed the door behind him before Abigail had a chance to speak.

Abigail heard his boots go down the stairs. *I wish he would leave me alone. I must pretend I'll do as he says, or he may guess my plan and try to stop me.* She rubbed her sweaty hands over her face and brushed the rest of her hair back. She got up off the bed and tottered to the washstand. After she washed her face in the water, she dipped a small linen towel into the cool liquid and laid it across the back of her neck. She took the washbasin and placed it on the floor next to the bed. At last, sitting on the bed, she washed and dressed. Abigail finished by placing a lace veil over her head. She faced him with a thin smile when he entered with a tray of food.

❋ ❋ ❋

Hiram knocked at the door to Abigail's room and pushed it open, as it was not closed. Abigail and Edmund looked up from where they sat on two chairs with a tray of eggs and steak placed on the bed.

"Doctor, this here is Benny Crawford. He came to fetch you to his pa's ranch. His pa got hurt."

The doctor addressed the gangly boy of about fourteen standing next to hotel Buttwill: "Is the ranch far from here?"

"Not far. We can get there in three or four hours by horseback," Benny answered.

"I'll get my bag and things I'll need for the trip. My horse is at the livery. Meet you there."

"Thanks, Doc." The boy ran from the hotel as Edmund took his leave of Abigail and hurried to his room.

※ ※ ※

Hours later, Abigail heard a knock at her door. "Miss Lester, ma'am. My name is Kenny. I'm supposed to help you clean up the kitchen. Can we start now?" Kenny held his hat as he stood outside Abigail's door.

"Tomorrow. Come tomorrow," Abigail called from her room.

Won't people leave me alone? Just through tonight,- -that's all I need.

"Cain't we start some, today? I need the money. I got the time now, too. My chores are finished at the livery. Please, ma'am?"

The door opened a crack. "Do you really need the money now?"

"Yes, ma'am. My pa and I don't get much work at the livery, not from paying folks. The more work I do, the more I get paid. Can we do some now? You just come with me and show me what you want done and how, and I'll do it."

"Talk to Doctor Proft. He knows what needs to be done." Abigail started to shut the door.

"I cain't, ma'am. He left for the Crawford place. He may not be back for days."

Abigail sighed. "Wait a minute." Abigail finished closing the door. *I know what it means to need money and not have an opportunity to earn it. If*

Doctor Proft won't be back for a few days, I can still do what I need to before he gets back. Maybe I can hold out for a day or two. Maybe!

❋ ❋ ❋

Edmund tied Maggie to the hitching post next to Benny Crawford's horse. Benny led the way into the frame ranch house.

"Ma, Pa, I got the doctor."

A woman parted the curtain serving as a door to the bedroom.

"I'm glad you came. Seth is in fierce pain."

"Benny said your husband was kicked by a steer?"

"Ain't ever seen the likes before. The steer got Seth good. It sent him flying into the corral fence post. He's in here."

Edmund entered the bedroom. Seth lay on the double bed, eyes closed, biting his lower lip.

"Heard you come in. Sure need help with the pain."

Edmund unbuttoned Seth's shirt and examined the discolored ribs and shoulder. He touched the area, and a torrent of swear words poured from Seth's lips. Edmund listened to his breathing.

"Mrs. Crawford, your husband has broken ribs and a dislocated shoulder. I need to tear strips from a cloth to make bandages. Do you have a sheet I can use?"

"We don't have any sheets. We got towels. Will they do?" Edmund studied the towels she picked up from a table. "Too short. Anything longer?"

"I got a bolt of yard goods I'm going to make into shirts for the men." She opened a wardrobe closet and pulled out red-and-blue cotton cloth.

"Fine. I'll bind up the ribs. I want your boy and you to hold on to his good arm and legs as I pull his shoulder into place and bind up the arm."

He turned to Seth. "Swallow this. It's laudanum. It'll help relieve the pain." The doctor poured the liquid into the spoon. "I'll leave these packets of willow bark for making tea to use for pain after the laudanum wears off."

An hour later, Seth Crawford slept, and Edmund packed his supplies.

"Doctor, thank you. What would we have done without you? We want to pay with our two finest-laying hens."

"One is sufficient. I can't take it with me. Do you mind bringing it to Wild River the next time you're in town?"

"Be right happy to."

"Do you know of anyone in the area I should see before I return to Wild River?"

"Mrs. Prudence Warns has been suffering from headaches for ages. Her place is a four-hour ride due north. It would be a blessing if you could call on her. Please, take supper with us and sleep in Benny's bed. He can bunk in the barn. You can leave in the morning."

"Thank you. I'm happy to accept your offer."

The meal of leftover baked beans made into porridge and fried salt pork with gravy alongside a slab of crusty Johnnycake made Benny's eyes widen, also his smile. Edmund was positive they were eating better than they would if he weren't there.

After sunset, flaming bits of rags floating in grease provided a glow of light. The smell of the burning grease mingled with the smell of the supper. They didn't need the light for long, as everyone retired after the evening darkness enclosed them in its arms.

At sunup, Edmund regretted spending the night. Benny's mattress was thin as dried horsehide. He was satisfied Seth would heal well and accepted a cup of coffee and a slab of bread with bacon grease. He departed after breakfast.

❋ ❋ ❋

Four hours later, Edmund saw the chimney smoke and located the Warns homestead. A woman, barefoot, directed five barefoot children in oversized, grubby clothes while she stirred laundry in a cauldron over a fire pit. When he came into view, she put down her clothes stick and picked up a rifle leaning against a washtub. The children stopped and stared at him with wide eyes and fingers in their mouths.

"Young'uns, back to your chores. Git." They scrambled back to their previous activities but kept turning and staring at the stranger.

"Need to forgive their bad manners, Mister. They don't get to see many people. You come to see my husband Charlie? I'll have one of the young'uns go to the back meadow and fetch him."

"No, I think I came to see you, if you are Mrs. Prudence Warns? Mrs. Crawford said you were having headaches."

"You the doctor I heered of?"

"Yes, I'm Doctor Proft, and I'll be glad to help if I can."

"Step right down off your horse. Jamison, come and get the doctor's horse and take it to the barn. Feed and water it." A boy of six, without a sign of fear for the big animal, led it to the barn.

After examining Mrs. Warn, Edmund prescribed two teaspoons of charcoal dissolved in water to be drunk at mealtimes. "If the headaches occur before bedtime, drink a cup of pennyroyal, catnip, or mint tea while soaking your feet in hot water. I'll leave dried samples with you." The doctor handed her brown paper packets.

"If the headaches continue, come to Wild River, and I'll give you a medicine I make of castor, gentian, and valerian root with laudanum, along with sulfur ether and alcohol."

"Much obliged. Money is scarce out here. We have tokens made by the general store in Wild River. We got them from a trade we did with our neighbors. The people at the general store take the tokens for goods. Would they do?" She counted out five pieces of metal stamped with the store's name.

"This will be fine. Thank you."

"Emma Hanson, a day's ride from here, is expecting. It would be a great relief to her if you would stop by and see her. She lost her first two."

Edmund's spirit groaned in silence, but he said, "Of course. Point me in the right direction."

An hour later, he rode toward the Hanson ranch. Mrs. Warns had supplied him with a glass of buttermilk for lunch and two cold potatoes for supper on the trail. She'd insisted he put axle grease on his chapped lips. The dust blew onto the grease and stuck. He tasted dirt and grease for hours. But he conceded to his mental grumblings, it did make his lips feel better. At twilight, he made a cold camp. He sat up, jumping at the sounds in the night. Benny's mattress had made sleep miserable, but this night was worse.

When daylight streaked over the horizon, Edmund saddled Maggie and headed off in what he hoped was the right direction. At noon, he saw barbwire fences along a rough road. He followed it and reined in at a lean-to with a canvas tent attached to it.

"Mrs. Hanson," he called.

A man came from the other side of the tent. "What you want here?" He held his rifle across his arms.

"I'm Doctor Proft. I heard Mrs. Hanson was with child and might need my services."

"Praise the Lord. You're what we been praying for. Step down." The man led the way behind the tent. "This here is Emma. She ain't due for a spell but is a might worried." Emma straightened up from adding wood to the cookstove set up on flat dirt and apart from the tent.

"Emma, this is Doctor Proft."

"Glory be."

"My sentiments exactly. Doctor, you can use the tent."

A half-hour later, Emma, and the doctor, emerged and joined her husband by the stove. Emma was blushing but smiling.

"Mr. Hanson, everything is fine. She should deliver in a month. If you can, you should bring her to Wild River in three weeks. She can finish her time there."

"We'll do it, Doc. Thank you."

"Doctor, will you look at John's teeth? They are hurting him fierce, but I know he won't say anything."

"Sit down on the stool, John. Open wide." Edmund touched the deep brown and black teeth. John howled. "Three teeth, two on the upper and one on the lower, need to come out. Your gums are swelling from the infection, and your teeth are rotten. I'll put a mixture of tincture of aconite, chloroform, alcohol, and morphine on this bit of cloth. It will ease the pain. Hold the cloth on both sides of this tooth." Edmund put John's fingers over the cloth on the tooth. "In ten minutes I'll pull it. We'll do the second and the third the same way. After the teeth are out, I'll put a fresh mixture on a cloth, and you can rub it on the gums to clean them out. It'll ease the pain. It'll be several weeks before you'll be able to chew much."

John's face got serious during the doctor's talk. His eyes widened in horror when the doctor approached him with pliers in his hand, but after the extraction he smiled, showing the areas of missing teeth.

"You can stay here tonight, Doc. We'd like the company."

"Thank you, but I'm eager to get back to Wild River." The doctor glanced at the sleeping areas and remembered Benny's mattress. *I might as well stay awake on the ground on my way home as try sleeping here.*

"Okay, if you're dead-set to do it. Go straight west, right into the setting sun. In the morning, keep it behind you. It will take the rest of today and to noon tomorrow. Please, take these two fresh-baked loaves of bread for your help. How's your bag of feed holding out?"

"Sam, at the livery, filled the bag with grain for Maggie. She has eaten most of it."

"Folks out here depend on a fit horse, so I'll put more oats in the moral so you can feed her proper tonight."

"What is a moral?"

"The feed bag, of course." Emma said matter-of-factly.

Chapter Twenty – Five

"Otis, you take the Colt pistol. Silas, you take the Winchester. One of you go east, and the other go west. Get as far as you can today and stay out all night if need be. Find that missing jenny." Lemuel handed each of his sons a weapon.

"Pa, that just leaves you with your single-shot rifle." Otis took the Colt and loaded it.

"Yeah, Pa. All this fuss over one mule. We got dozens. Likely, a pack of coyotes got her." Silas took the Winchester and put it into the saddle scabbard.

"She's my mule, and I want her back, or bring back the bones. Be here tomorrow to look after the stock. If you ain't found anything, I'll head out early and take a look around myself. I'll come back later in the day, and I expect them chores to be done."

The boys watched Lemuel leave the barn and go to the tool shed. Otis led his horse out of the stall as Silas picked up a bridle and slammed it against the wall.

"What's with you? We get out of chores," Otis said.

"We get out of chores so we can sit in a saddle for hours in the heat, scouring for a missing mule we don't need, and with Abigail gone we ain't got any decent food to take with us." Silas bridled his mount and jerked the animal around as he saddled it.

"You hurt that horse's mouth, and Pa will git after you good. Think of this as a way to get shuck of Pa for one night. Besides, if you do find the jenny before nightfall, you can come home, and Pa will be right pleased with you." Otis led his horse out from the barn and mounted. "See you, brother." He rode off.

Silas muttered, "Hell will freeze over before Pa will be pleased with anything I do. Besides, I know'd I ain't goin' find any mule." He mounted and rode in the opposite direction.

※ ※ ※

Edmund poured the remains of the coffee pot onto the campfire. The fire sizzled, spurted, and blackened. He found glowing embers and poured the last drops on them until they, too, were out. The smoke drifted up into the dark sky, leaving behind the smell of burnt cow chips and twisted dry grass.

The moonlight lit up the stand of trees by his campsite. He packed the coffee, the remains of the bread, the pot, and the cup in his doctor's bag and picked up a canteen. Edmund poured water into his Stetson, one of his concessions to Western attire. Easing over to Maggie, he held the water by her nose. She slurped a bit and withdrew her head. He checked the rope hobbling her front hooves to be sure she could take steps and eat grass. He packed her feed bag of grain and laid it next to his saddle, then patted his companion's neck and shoulders.

"You ready to call it a day? I sure am. The judge said he would spread the word that a doctor was available. We've been busy for days taking care of people. We'll set out early and should be back home in Wild River by noon if we aren't lost. Good night." Edmund gave Maggie a few more pats, lay down on a blanket, and used the saddle for his head. He realized what Elizabeth had meant in her journal when she'd written about how insignificant she'd felt on the prairie. He felt small and alone, as if he were the only person on Earth, but talking to Maggie helped. He had ridden the half-day without seeing another soul. *I'm following their directions to Wild River, but I wonder if I'm lost. Everything looks the same. Well, it's too late to change my mind about staying at the Hanson place now.* He stared at the sky as he replayed the day through his mind: sand, dirt, tumbleweeds, a few trees, more sand and tumbleweeds, wildflowers he didn't know the names of, and more tumbleweeds. At times he came across a dirt path; at least, he told himself it was a path. It consisted of ruts, small holes, broken-down grass, and it would always end near a tree or a creek bed. *The Hansons said to keep facing the sun in the afternoon, keep heading west. Hopefully, their directions are as good as the loaf of bread they paid me. Those three thick slices with the coffee made a good supper.*

The smoldering campfire smelled pleasant, considering what he'd used to make it. Still, it helped that the slight breeze was blowing the smoke away from him. The stars emerged like fireflies, and the moon, like a lamp burning in a sea of black, brought a sense of reassurance. Maggie's shadow blended into the dark trees. His mind plagued him with Jase's words, "Don't camp by yourself. Be sure someone is with you, so you can take turns on the lookout." They had camped together at night when he'd visited Jase's ranch. He wondered if Jase had stayed awake while he'd slept.

Edmund settled back but lay awake listening to the night sounds, some soft and gentle, others startling and sharp. He sat up and listened, reaching for his revolver. Straining to hear the direction of the sound that pierced the air, he realized a hawk, an owl, or another predator he couldn't identify had captured its dinner, and he had nothing to fear. He reclined against the saddle. His eyelids, heavy with sleep, fought his brain. The desire for slumber said, *It's foolish to stay awake. It's perfectly safe. Maggie would make noises if an animal got too close.* The side of caution told him, *Sit up and stay awake. Sleep tomorrow, back in town.* His mind went in circles. *It's foolish to stay awake. Sleep. Jason does it. You're new out here--better stay awake. Foolish. Sleep. Stay awake.*

He jerked. What? A fiery, brilliant explosion blasted inside his head. Pain pierced through it, sharp as a pitchfork. He felt his body hurtling down into a dark, deep crevasse. Then no pain, no light, no stars. Nothing.

❈ ❈ ❈

With the first streaks of dawn, Lemuel led his horse from the barn. He glanced at the house, barn, and corrals. Everything was quiet except for a few chickens clucking and the rooster beginning to crow. *Early dawn and late dusk are the best times, the still times. Those boys didn't come home last night. I bet they didn't Jind the jenny. Bet they won't today, either. I figure I know where the mule is, now that I thought on it all night, and I aim to check it out.*

Lemuel headed down the road and then turned north. Three hours later, he crossed a small creek that fed into Wild River. Urging his horse up the bank, he scanned the rock and sandy soil. Patches of grass and a few cottonwoods dotted the landscape. He neared the crest of a small, rocky hill, dismounted, and tied the reins to a mesquite bush. There, he withdrew his Mississippi Rifle from its scabbard. Getting down on his belly, he inched his way to the top of the hill. Removing his Stetson, he peered down at a small adobe house with a barn and brush-wood corral. In the corral was an old horse munching on some hay. Just past the corral was a field of dirt and sand half-plowed. A wood plow with an iron blade stood in a row of turned earth. A man in a sombrero adjusted the yoke collar on a brown, sleek mule as he led it toward the water trough.

Lemuel's eyes squinted and his jaw tightened as he clenched his teeth. *I figured it right. That's Jorge. He wanted to buy that mule but didn't have two hundred-fifty dollars, and now he has my mule. He's a thieving Mex.* He eased his rifle forward and pulled back the hammer with his thumb. Then he saw the repeating rifle propped up by the water trough. *If I don't get him with my shot, I won't have time to reload.* He heard someone bang a metal pan inside the house. *Best I get the boys, as I might need more firepower. Maybe I'll get Clement, too, to make this legal. I got this Mex dead to rights.*

❊ ❊ ❊

"Hey, *amigo*. You know someone who like to buy this fine *caballo*?"

Sam put down the pitchfork and came out the stable door. He eyed the man in a sombrero standing by a tired horse with a Mexican saddle. An unsaddled, well-groomed, sleek bay with a white blaze and one white stocking was at the end of the lead rope. It was obvious which horse was for sale. He walked over to the bay and ran his hands over its back and withers.

"You want to sell this horse?"

"*Si*. You know someone who wants to buy?"

"Yeah, I know someone. I saw him an hour ago. I'll send my boy to get him. You wait here."

"*Gracias, Señor*."

Sam strode back into the stable to find Kenny, cleaning one of the stalls. "Kenny, put down the shovel. I want you to locate Clement. Bring him here.

Be sure he brings his gun. Don't say anything to Jase if you see him. You hear me, boy?"

"Sure, Pa. What's wrong?" Kenny leaned the shovel against the wall and glanced out the door. "Say, Pa, ain't that the doctor's...?"

"Hush up. Do what I told you. You bring Clement with his gun. I'm going out there to talk to the Mex. Git."

❈ ❈ ❈

Lemuel, Silas, and Otis reined in at the sheriff's office. They dismounted and burst through the door.

Clement, putting on his holster and gun, saw them.

"Clement, I want you to arrest the Mex living at the old Miranda place. He stole a sorrel jenny from me. I want it back and him hung."

"I'll check into it later. I got to see Sam right away. He says a fellow is trying to sell the doc's horse. He reckons the man stole it. I want to get there before he takes off. I'll ride out to your place tomorrow if I can. This here is more important than a mule, as the doc could be hurt or dead."

"This can't wait, either."

"It has to. All of you, clear out. I got business to do."

The three Baxters left the office and mounted their mules. They watched the sheriff head for the livery stable.

"We going to wait, like the sheriff said?" Otis asked.

"No, we ain't. We'll get Jason Wilcox to help. He's good with a gun, and he'll be interested in helping when we tell him the fella who got my mule is living at the old Miranda place. Likely a gang of thieves. He'll want to clean them out. But, not a word about his brother's horse, ya hear? We don't want him coming into town to check it out when we need him at the Mirandas'."

"We're going to Jase's place?" Silas asked. His grinning mouth exposed his yellow and brown teeth.

"Yep. Anything wrong with that?" questioned Lemuel.

"No, Pa. I just think we three can handle one Mex."

"There may be more in the house. And one at least has a repeating rifle. Don't hurt none to get more firepower on our side."

The three headed their mounts toward the edge of town.

✽ ✽ ✽

Jason, Lemuel, Otis, and Silas dismounted and tethered the animals. They crouched behind rocks on the crest of the hillock and studied the one-room ranch house at the bottom. A mule stood in the corral, munching on wisps of hay.

"See, Jase, my jenny. The Mex is another Miranda, and he tried to buy a plow mule from me a few weeks ago, but he didn't have the money. There it is, in his corral, and you can see from the plowed field over there he's been using her. I never come out this way, as the land ain't much good, but I suspicioned it was him who took the mule when I didn't sell him one."

"Yep. You're right. But I don't see him. He could be in the barn or house. Could even be he's not at home."

"I'll find out." Lemuel scrambled up and yelled, "Hey, Miranda, come out. I aim to get my mule, you thief."

A voice shouted from inside the house, "I paid for the mule. I ain't a thief."

Silas yelled, "Liar!" He aimed his rifle and fired at the cabin. A moment later, a shot rang out from the house. Lemuel ducked.

"What you do that for, Silas? I was an open target, you fool."

"Silas, I planned on talking to Miranda," Jase said. "At least enough to convince him we'd take him to town to stand trial. We could decide after we had him if we really would take him to town or hang him here. He ain't gonna listen now." Jase crouched behind a boulder and considered Silas. "Why are you so gun-quick?"

Another shot chipped the rock near Otis's head. Before anyone could twitch, another bullet hit the dirt near Lemuel.

"There're two down there shooting. He's got help, the dirty thief." Silas cocked and shot his Winchester several times. Lemuel pulled the trigger on his Mississippi Rifle and reloaded. Otis and Jason joined in with rapid volleys from their pistols. Glass broke in one window, and splinters of the wood door cracked and flew. Clumps of adobe broke off the walls in the torrent of bullets.

Shots from the cabin zinged the dirt and rocks near the men. Rock dust flew into Otis's eyes. "Yow!" Tears pooled in his eyes, and he wiped them away with his shirt sleeve.

"Hey, we're too close together. We got to spread out!" Lemuel reloaded his ball and powder rifle. "You all right, boy?"

"Yeah, my eyes are watery is all."

Jase flattened his body and eased over to the side of the boulder to peer around the rock as the firing continued on the other side.

"Quit shooting. There's a woman in there. I saw her head by the window."

"Yeah, and she's firing at us. It makes her fair game," Silas snarled.

"I've never hurt a woman, and I'm not starting now. Let's try talking with Miranda. He might give himself up to save his wife."

"We ain't parleying, are we, Pa? We need to wipe them out." Silas cocked his rifle my mule. He knew this could happen." Otis, Silas, and Lemuel opened fire.

"I'm going down there and get him out." Jase belly-crawled back to the horses. A bullet brushed against his pant leg and hit the dirt by his knee. He sucked in air as his brain warned, *Crippled for life if that had hit.* Behind the crest of the hill, he mounted Jasper. Jase urged him into a full gallop.

"He'll shoot you!" Lemuel hollered.

"That's my lookout. I ain't shootin' at a woman." Jase raced down the hillside and swerved to the side corral. Bullets from the house hit the dirt near him. He heard the Baxters firing. Reaching the windowless side of the cabin, he felt a searing burn tear along his side. He gasped and fell off Jasper. He rolled to the back of the house, where he lay still for a moment, playing dead. Firing continued at the front of the building. Getting up, he drew his gun and kicked in the back door.

A man and woman turned from their crouched positions by the front window. Jase saw the fear in their faces. Before they could react, he shouted, "Put your rifles down, and no one will get hurt."

The two set their rifles on the floor. The man put his arms around his wife and shielded her from Jase.

"I've got them. Come on down!" Jase called out to the others.

"Stealing a mule out here is a big offense, but I expect you knew it."

"I did not steal. I have a bill of sale. It's in the jar on the shelf. Let me get it and show you."

"Okay, but don't try anything."

Miranda grabbed a jar from a shelf and took out a paper. His hands shook as he handed it to Jase.

The Baxters burst through the door. "Great, you got him. Hey, you're bleeding, Jase," Lemuel stated.

"Yeah, a graze. He's got this bill of sale." Jase handed it to Lemuel. Lemuel read the paper. "My signature all right, but it ain't my writing. And I never saw the hundred dollars. Hey, this is Silas's writing."

"Pa...."

"Si, he is the one who brought the mule here and the paper. He says you changed your mind. I gave him the hundred *dinero*," *Señor* Miranda interrupted.

"You sold him the mule and put my name on the sale? What did you do with the money? I ain't seen it. Speak up, boy."

"Yeah, Pa, but I wanted cash money, and you never give us any. Right, Otis? I didn't think you would miss the jenny. You've got a huge herd."

"I know every one of my stock. You wanted us to kill this man so I wouldn't find out it was you who stole the mule?"

"Pa, he's a Mex."

"And you're a thief. I wondered why you kept firing when Jase galloped down here after I told you and Otis to stop. You could've killed Jason. You get your things and leave the ranch. Keep the money. It's all you'll ever get from me."

"I figured the bullet that got me couldn't have come from the cabin, as there aren't any windows on the side. You didn't want me to talk to the Mirandas. I'll remember this." Jase glared at Silas.

"Yeah, well, I'll get even with you yet. Pa wouldn't have found out if it weren't for you. And you got other things to worry on, like your brother."

"What do you mean?"

"A guy came into town today trying to sell the doc's horse. Clement was going to the livery to arrest the guy when we were in town. Clem wouldn't come with us. Your brother's likely dead."

Jase glowered at the Baxters. "You knew about Edmund, Lemuel?"

"Clement likely got it settled. But I reckon we should have told you. I owe you for that and what my boy did in nearly getting you killed."

"As much as it galls me to say this, you leave these people alone. I don't mind killin' Mexs, but they got to do somethin' to show they deserve the killin'. I'll tend to you later, Silas. Now, I'm headin' for town." Jase stalked out the door to his horse.

Lemuel shoved Silas out of the house. He looked back at the man and woman. "The mule is yours, Miranda. Silas, stay out of my sight. You ain't my son no more. Otis, come with me. We're going home." Lemuel stomped out to his mount.

※ ※ ※

Two hours later, Jason burst through the jail door. Clement stood by the bars, talking to the man inside the cell.

"Jase, take it easy until we get this sorted out."

Jase picked up the keys from the desk, unlocked the cell, and entered. "I want to know what you were doing with my brother's horse."

"This man is Amato Soto. He said he bought the horse." Clement followed Jase and pulled back on his right arm to draw him to the cell door.

"*Si*. I buy it from him. I got a bill of sale." The man sat on the cell cot.

Clement handed Jason a piece of paper. Jason glared at it, crumpled it, and threw it on the floor. "It's a meaningless bunch of words." Jase pushed Clement against the bars, knocking him off balance, as he grabbed the prisoner by his shirt and threw him up against the wall. Jason doubled both hands into fists. Punching Soto twice in the face, he then plowed a fist into the man's stomach. Amato doubled over and slid to the floor. Jason drew back his foot and slammed it into his ribs.

"Take it easy, Jase. We have to find out where the doc is. Don't kill him." Clement regained his balance and again pulled Jason back. "Tell me where my brother is."

"Don't know. I bought the horse from a smiling, young *gringo*. He said he was cash poor and wanted to sell the horse. I say, 'How much?' He says, 'What you offer?' I say, 'Fifty *dinero*.' He says hundred. I say, 'I don't have hundred. I got sixty.' He says okay, and he gave me a bill of sale. I can't read English. I think it a good bill of sale."

"Where did you get sixty dollars?"

"I worked on ranch up north. I worked hard. I get paid eighty. I buy things for my *señora* and daughter. I have sixty left I used to buy horse. I'm going home to family." Amato struggled up and sat on the floor, leaning his back against the cot. "We live in Aqua Prieta. I think I'll sell horse for maybe seventy-five or hundred. It's good horse."

"Where did you buy it?"

"I met *gringo* on trail between Bitter Creek and Separation. He said his name is Smith."

"You're a liar." Jase kicked Soto in the side. He raised his boot again and, before Clem could stop him, stomped down with his heel on the man's right hand.

Amato screamed in pain.

Clement pulled Jase to the cell door. "Jase, get your horse, and search for the doc. We know Crawford's oldest boy came to get the doc and take him to Bitter Creek because a steer kicked his pa. Pick up his trail from there."

"Keep him in jail until I get back. If I don't find Edmund, I'll talk to him again." He grimaced in anger as he regarded the man on the floor and put his fists near Amato's eyes. "If you killed my brother, I'll beat you to death."

❈ ❈ ❈

Lemuel and Otis poured water into the corral trough. Mules stood head-to-tail in groups of two, swishing their tails to discourage the flies.

"Otis."

"Yeah, Pa?"

Lemuel put down his bucket. Otis kept working. "You've been following your brother all your life. You've looked up to him and done as he done. That is over. You got to take up being a man of your own." Otis stopped working but held onto the pail. "What you mean, Pa?" "You got to leave and go find yourself a wife. I don't want you to come back here until you're married. Don't want you to go to Wild River, where Abigail is. Might get folks talkin'. No, go farther away. Here's five dollars." Lemuel pulled the money from his denim pocket. "Whoo-ee! Thanks, Pa." Otis took the money and stared at it as a

broad smile filled his face.

"When you run out of money, you'll need to work for your meals. Take Lizzie. She's steady."

"Okay, Pa."

"I raised you boys the best I could. Don't you get a woman in the family way until after you're hitched. And don't go by appearances. You need a woman who's able to do the chores. She needs to be a helpmeet, like the Good Book says." Lemuel took the pail from Otis's hand. "Go, get your things and Lizzie. Best to set out while there's plenty of daylight."

"Okay, Pa." Otis stuffed the money in his pants pocket and dashed out of the corral. The gate swung closed after him.

"Otis."

Otis stopped and turned. "Yes, Pa?"

"Make sure she can cook before you ask her. And clean yourself up a bit before your courtin'."

"Sure will, Pa." Otis turned again and ran to the barn. "Sure will." "Son, stay out of trouble. I won't be there to help you," Lemuel called after him.

"Yeah, I will."

Lemuel watched the strong legs of his son as he ran. *He thinks he is off on a fun adventure. He doesn't realize the decisions he makes will affect the rest of his life. He's still a boy.* Water filled his eyes and spilled out. He took off his crumpled hat and wiped his face with a faded bandana. *The sun sure is bright today.* He replaced his hat.

Two mules plodded up to Lemuel and nudged his arms. He pulled old carrot pieces from his pocket and put them into the flat palms of his hands. The mules snatched the carrots and chewed. He held their heads close to him and took a deep breath of their scent. *Those boys don't appreciate how good they got it here. I was working by the time I was five. Every cent I earned hauling water, cutting and hauling wood, cleaning stalls, was every cent my pa took and drank or gambled away. My ma was a whore in the saloon and cared nothing about her " bastard kid." I slept in old barns, old wood boxes, under buildings. I hung around folks when they was fixin' to eat, hopin' they would give me the leftovers. To run away, I had to sneak out of town in the dead of night in a freight wagon while my pa was getting drunk, so he wouldn't know I was gone until he sobered up some in the morning. If he caught me, I don't think I' d be alive today. That's why I love you mules, horses, and burros. You take care of your young'uns, and you are true to what you are and work hard and are always dependable.*

You're better than people. People want to get things from a body and not give nothin' back. I gave my boys a good place to sleep, plenty of food, honest work so they could have something when I am gone. I read to them from the Good Book so they would know how to live right, and I didn't let them get near no saloon, no whisky, no cards, and no whores. Did the best I could. He wiped the moisture from his eyes and buried his face in a mule's mane as he again breathed in their comforting scent.

❈ ❈ ❈

"Hey, Otis, wait up."

Otis stopped his mount and turned in the saddle. He saw Silas cantering up the road. Silas slowed, and Otis nudged Lizzie forward. The mules walked together like old friends.

"I avoided our old man and got my things from the ranch. Where are you going?"

"Pa said I was to find me a wife, one who can cook." Otis straightened his shoulders and sat tall.

"A wife? Come with me. We'll get women when we want one at a brothel. I got money. We can go to saloons and have a good time. Likely, we can win more at poker. Come on. You don't want to work for the old man the rest of your life."

"The money from the Mirandas won't last long, especially if the two of us are living on it."

"I got more. Don't worry, little brother."

"More? Did you take money from Pa's cash box?"

"No. He'd kill me for sure. I sold a horse."

"A horse? We aren't missing any of our mares."

"Wasn't Pa's." Silas's glee sounded in his voice.

"Was it you who stole the horse from the doctor?"

Silas laughed hard. "Yep. The night before we got Jase and went to the Mirandas', I was checking the herd on the range, looking for the jenny, only I knew where it was. I saw the doctor put out his campfire, but I didn't know it was the doc until later. I waited until I figured he was asleep and bashed his head. Nearly broke my gun butt. Took his horse and things to sell over in Pridesville, but I met this Mex and sold him the horse. I writ words on a paper, so he thought it was legal. He must have gone to Wild River to sell the horse, thinking he'd make an easy profit. I didn't think he'd be stupid enough to sell it around these here parts. I figured, as he was heading to Mexico, he'd sell it there."

"If Jason ever finds out, you're a dead man."

"How's he gonna find out? No one will believe the Mex. Are you going to tell him?"

"Think I'm crazy? He'd like as not shoot me as you."

"So, I ain't got no worries. Come with me to Pridesville, and we'll live it up."

At the fork in the road, Otis sank deeper in the saddle. Lizzie stopped. Silas reined in, and the two mules waited, swatting flies with their tails. Otis reflected on life on the ranch. *I'm up before dawn, working until collapsing into bed at night, sometimes not getting to bed for a day or two when the foals are born.* He thought of the endless chores needing to be done. *And what if I can't find a wife? Pa won't let me back on the ranch. I'd have to work some place else as hard as on the ranch and have nothing but a few dollars at the end of the month for pay. Going with Silas would be different. We could travel, drink in the saloons, sleep with loose women, and win money at the poker tables.* Otis contemplated his brother. *We always got along. Silas leads, and I follow.* He stared at the horizon as his mind worked like a jenny hitched to a grindstone, going around and around. *Pa said, "You got to take up being a man of your own." I don't know if I can.* Otis's thoughts now raced through his brain. He sucked in air and grinned.

"No. I'm going to get a wife if I can. You're too much like Pa, except you don't have a ranch. If I followed you, I'd likely wind up with nothing. If I follow Pa, the ranch will be mine, and I won't have to share it with you." He thought he saw disappointment and resentment flash in Silas's eyes.

"When Pa has worked you to death, you'll be sorry."

"Could be. But I'm heading to Separation. It's farther east than Wild River, and bigger, too. Likely they'll have unmarried women."

"Your life, brother." Silas held out his hand. "Could be, we'll cross paths again."

Otis blinked. He'd never shaken hands with anyone like he was a man. He pumped Silas's hand. "Bye, big brother." Squaring his shoulders and turning his mount to the right, he heard Silas's start at a walk and then break into a trot as it veered to the left.

Chapter Twenty – Six

Jase reluctantly eased his horse to a walk. He had pushed the animal hard for two days and a night, stopping to rest for an hour or two whenever Jasper heaved with fatigue. Minutes later, Jason fought his horse sense and pushed Jasper on. The Crawfords tried talking him into resting but, when they saw it was to no avail, sent him on to the Warns' place. The Warns said Edmund had gone to the Hansons'. Five hours later, the Hansons gave Jase the same directions they'd given to Edmund.

He found signs a horse had traveled across the land, and other times he knew he was on another animal's trail to a stream. An exasperated sigh burst from his lungs. "This isn't smart, but I'm going to do it. Jasper, I've stood on your bare back in my stocking feet before. This is the same, only I'm not taking time to unsaddle you or remove my boots. I got to git as high as I can to see as much land as possible. Stand steady." Jase spoke in an even, commanding tone to his horse. He rose to his feet on Jasper's back to see as far as the land allowed. A few tumbleweeds blew across the dry soil. Jasper stood his ground. The land was flat, except for small hills to the side and huge mountains farther away. Clouds scudded by, casting huge, moving shadows. Dry heat slammed up from the earth as it pounded down from the sun.

Disappointed, Jase sat down in the saddle and urged his mount into a walk. A piece of paper blew up against the horse's flank. Jasper shied, and Jase steadied him. He bent down and grasped the paper. It was a folded packet labeled laudanum. Jase shot a look in the direction of the wind. Jasper responded to the tension in Jason's thighs and calves and trotted forward.

Jase searched for signs, and a mile later he spotted a clump of cottonwoods. His heart beat faster. A huddled form lay in the burning heat, several feet from the trees. Jase galloped forward. Nearing the body, he threw the reins down, grabbed a canteen, and dismounted before Jasper stopped. He stared at Edmund's face covered in dried blood. He closed his eyes and swallowed hard when he saw the top of his brother's head caked with dead flies and matted hair. "I'll kill the dirty Mex. I swear I will!"

Opening his eyes, he bent down, put the canteen to his brother's swollen lips, and let the water trickle. He gasped when the lips parted. He held up Edmund's head and poured in more. He saw the throat swallow. "Edmund, it's me, Jase."

Edmund didn't respond. Jase took off his bandana and soaked it with water. He wiped the blood from Edmund's eyes and forehead. The eyelashes were stuck on his brother's skin. Jase washed them until they loosened.

Edmund fluttered his lids, and they opened.

"Edmund, it's me, Jase. Can you hear me?" Edmund swallowed. "Yes." His voiced cracked.

Jase lifted Edmund's head and poured another trickle of water into his mouth. He swallowed and strained to utter, "I think a tree fell and crushed my head. I couldn't stand up. I couldn't see. I tried crawling. I wanted to find Maggie. I think I'm dying."

"I'm going to help you up and get you to the shade of the trees. Can you stand?"

"No, my head exploded. I think my brain is smashed. Can you see it?" Edmund's eyes closed, and his head fell back.

Jase sat Edmund up and put his arms around him to half-drag, half-carry him to the shade. Propping him up against a tree trunk, Jase picked up the doctor's empty bag, which had been tossed to the side. He found several small bottles, packets of medicine, and medical instruments and deposited them in the bag. He then brought his horse up to the trees. Giving Edmund another drink, he said, "Can you sit on my horse? We need to go back to town and get you help."

Edmund gave him vacant stare. Jase thought his brother's eyes looked dead.

"No. Mirror, in saddlebags."

"Your saddlebags are gone, but I did find a mirror. I put it in your doctor's bag." He found it and placed it in Edmund's hands.

"Help me hold it up to my eyes." Edmund stared into the mirror.

"A concussion for sure."

"I know that's bad."

"Could be worse. I can talk and see, although everything is double and hazy. I'm not paralyzed, but I know I can't stand or ride. You have a mirror?"

"Yeah."

"Get it and hold it with this one. I need to see the top of my head." Jason returned and held the two mirrors. Edmund studied his head. "Too much dried blood. Wash it off as best you can and cut the hair close to the scalp around the wound. Did an Indian scalp me?"

"No." Jase clenched his teeth and took out his knife. He gritted his teeth as he cut Edmund's hair. "But I know who hit you and stole your horse. Clement's got him in jail. I'll help hang him for a horse thief." Jase set aside the knife. "Did it hurt when I cut the hair?"

"No, too numb. But the inside of my head is a different story."

"Can you see the wound better?" Jase held the mirrors up and hoped his brother would say yes. The sight and smell made him nauseated, and he wanted to be done with it.

"I think it's a scalp wound, with a crack in the skull." Jase peered off into the distance. "What does that mean?"

"The skull should heal by itself in time, but the scalp has to be sewn back together. Get the needles from the flat leather case."

Jase located the case. "The needles are here, but I can't see any thread."

"Get long horse hairs from Jasper's mane or tail." Jase hurried to Jasper and returned with horsehair.

"Get the whiskey you carry in your saddlebag and pour it into a coffee cup. Place a needle and the horsehairs in the cup. Pour a bit of whiskey on the scalp, then look for a packet of sulfur and sprinkle it on. Put whiskey on your neck scarf and use it to cover the wound after it's stitched."

Jase followed Edmund's directions as he talked. "It's bound to burn. How will you stitch your scalp if you pass out from the pain?"

Wild River

"I'm hoping I do pass out, but whether I do or not, I can't stitch it. You'll have to."

"Not me. I can't stick you with a needle. I ain't a doctor." Jase stood and stepped back a few steps. "We'll get to town, and someone there can do it."

"I'll not make it to town. I want to die with my head sewn together. I've seen you repair harnesses. Sew my scalp the same way." "You're talking foolish!"

"No. I'm blacking out. You may as well get it done because I can't...."

Jase stepped closer to Edmund. "Hey, don't quit. Wake up." He saw it was useless. He stared at the needle and horsehair thread. He wiped the sweat from his forehead with the sleeve of his arm. "I wish I had never met you." He picked up the needle.

❋ ❋ ❋

"Edmund, you've got to wake up. We need to move. A storm is coming." Jase shook his brother roughly to rouse him.

Edmund moaned but did not open his eyes.

Jason finished packing the doctor's bag and his own saddlebags.

"I didn't finish any too soon, from the looks of the sky. We got to go, brother."

Jase brought Jasper close to Edmund. Jasper tossed his head and twitched his ears around in all directions, pawing the ground. Jase knew the horse was ready to spook and take off. He glanced at the sky, where heavy, foreboding clouds scudded up from the horizon, heading to their location like a locomotive. The clouds turned green.

"We ain't got much time. A tornado is comin'. We've got to move to the other side of this hill and lay flat. It's our only chance. You got to git up on Jasper." Jase held the doctor's two arms and pulled him to a sitting position. He bent Edmund's knees until his feet were on the ground. "Help me. Push on your feet. Stand up." Jase yanked on his arms, and Edmund stood and swayed as Jase held him. He positioned the doctor's hands on the saddle horn and pushed his left leg into the stirrup. Giving Edmund support, he shoved him up into the saddle.

"Hang on. We don't have too far to go. Steady, Jasper." Jase mounted behind Edmund and guided the horse down the side of the hill and away from the oncoming storm.

The sky roiled like a gray-green sea. The wind whipped the grass into froth. Branches cracked and hurtled through the air. Tumbleweeds blew, bounced, and flew like balls.

Jase stopped and dismounted. He pulled his brother down onto the ground. "Lay flat! Don't sit up." Jason whipped off the bandana plastered against Edmund's scalp and tied it around the doctor's nose and mouth. "I got to hold Jasper down. If he runs off, you'll die before we get to town. Do you hear me? Lie flat."

Edmund moaned. He sat up but fell back. "Take care of Abigail. She's afraid."

Jasper felt the strong pull on the reins. He snorted, his eyes wide in terror. Jase grabbed the bridle with one hand and pulled his shirt off over his head with the other hand. He slipped it over Jasper's head, covering his ears down to his mouth. "I don't know any Abigail. She's fine. Lie flat!" Jason shouted. He wrapped the reins around Jasper's front knees, pushed his weight down on Jasper's head as he pulled down on the bridle, and yanked up on the reins to make the front legs buckle. Jasper's head went down, and then he fell to his knees and rolled to his side. Jase lay over the neck and shoulders of the horse to keep it low against the earth.

Edmund tried to sit up.

"Lie flat!" shouted Jase, but his voice was lost in the roar of the green-black train.

The wind's blast filled their ears as dirt, leaves, and prairie debris pelted them. Without his shirt on, the sand stung Jase's skin like tiny bees.

❈ ❈ ❈

Clement ran out the office door and stepped onto the boardwalk. The sky told him why the town's alarm was ringing. People scurried into stores and headed for cellars. Men turned the horses tied at hitching rails loose. The animals galloped down the street in a melee of fear. Sabilla and John Platt threw the goods they had on the boardwalk into the store and closed the shutters on the store windows.

Clement saw Abigail trying to catch a chicken running in the street. Hanging onto his hat, Clem reached for her arm. "Leave it be and come with me."

"But it's a good-laying hen."

He pulled her a few steps. She looked up at the sky and raced with him to his house at the end of the street. They dodged a tumbling, empty crate and three boards not nailed down in the boardwalk.

"Sia, where are you?"

He heard the wood door of the root cellar bang.

"Over here, hurry!" His wife opened the door as Clement arrived. Clement held the door for Abigail to go down the steep steps. He followed and barred the door. Hortensia lit a lantern.

"I see you were ready," Clement said.

"I came down here when I saw how dark and green it was getting. I knew you would come. Are you all right, Abigail?"

"Yes, but what is happening?"

"Dear, haven't you ever been in a tornado?"

"Tornado! I've heard of them but haven't been in any."

"This is our third since Clem and I came here forty years ago. Folks here don't usually build a root cellar. The soil is too sandy. We were fortunate to find this good section of land with clay. We both came from Minnesota, where everyone has a root cellar. We built ours first and lived in it for a year. A good thing we did, right, Clem?"

"Yep, that first year with the root cellar was when our first tornado hit. I wonder if that darn old river doesn't attract them."

"That's silly, Clem. Don't you believe it, Abigail. Wild River is a good place to live."

They jumped when something heavy slammed down on the wood doors.

"What was that?" Abigail asked.

"Don't know, but this tornado is hitting hard. Help me get the sacks and bushel baskets out away from the wall, and we'll slide in under the shelves."

The three yanked and threw things away from the wall to clear a place to crawl under the low shelves.

"Lie flat as you can!" Hortensia shouted above the sound of a train rolling through the air.

The wind's fury slammed down.

❈ ❈ ❈

Amato sat up on the jail cot chained to the wall. Staring out the window, he saw the sky and the horses careening by, and he heard the frantic shouts as people ran for safety. He scurried under the bunk and covered his head with his hands. The sound of cracking, splintering, crashing wood from the roof ripped from the building drowned out the sound of the wind, but only for a moment. The glass in the front office shattered. The shards flew and rained down in clinking, slicing daggers. The front wall collapsed. The cell bars twisted and pulled up from the floor with a groan.

An eternity later, it was gone. Rain fell in torrents. The wall, with the cot attached, stood alone. Ignoring the pain in his ribs from Jase's beating, he braced his back against the wall and kicked debris away from his sanctuary under the cot to crawl out. There, he stood on rubble and in the open.

Tossed articles of clothing, furniture, and tools littered the street; the windows were blown out, but the buildings remained, except for the jail. He looked toward the livery. Horses ran to the barn from the fields to escape the torrential rain. He stumbled out of the chaos. A part of the desk lay jumbled next to a flattened wall. He grabbed his gun belt from the debris with his left hand as his swollen right hand hung by his side. It was numb and useless since Jason had stomped on it.

He ran to the livery and found his horse trembling in the corral. He took the halter rope and looped it. Tying it to both sides of the halter, he made reins and galloped his *caballo* in the direction of Pridesville.

❈ ❈ ❈

Clement eased his way out from under the shelf and pulled himself up to his knees. Hortensia crawled out, got to her feet, and helped Clement up. "Doggone these old legs," muttered Clement.

Abigail rose. "Is it over?"

"I'm gonna see." Clement clambered up the steps and removed the bar from the door. He pushed. It didn't budge. "I think something is blocking it. Hortensia, grab the bar and push against the door, and Abigail, see if you can get up here and push with me."

They strained, pushed, and grunted, but it didn't open. They stepped back and gasped from the exertion.

"Hey, Clement, Hortensia, you down in there?"

"That's Sam's voice. Yeah, we're here, Sam! Can you get us out?" Clement said.

"John Platt and I will pull this tree off the door. You'll be out in a jiffy."

"Oh, Clem, our shade tree. Our dear friend is gone."

The door opened, and rain pelted in. Clem climbed out and helped the women scramble up. Abigail perched on the thick tree branch that had blocked the door. The rain soaked through her clothing. Her wet hair fell across her face. She brushed it away and stared at the mess. The house, elevated on a slight hill, gave her a vantage point from which to look down at the town.

Her eyes widened at the devastation of windows broken; pieces of buildings hanging, dangling by a nail; roofs gone; horses, chickens and dogs running wild. Behind the general store, a milk cow mooed as it struggled to get up. Abigail and Hortensia watched Sabilla, carrying a rifle, walk up to the animal and shoot it in the head. Abigail sucked in her breath.

Hortensia turned and said, as she surveyed the damage, "Things don't look too bad." She tucked wet hair back behind her ears. "And our tree still stands. Just the one limb blew off."

"Yeah, I think we got off lucky this time," Clement agreed.

"Abigail, are you all right?" Hortensia asked.

Abigail turned from staring at the dead cow to look at Hortensia. Her eyes felt dead, just as dead as the poor beast in the field. "I feel defeated, flattened, like the jail."

"Fellas, we better see if the prisoner got killed," Clement said.

"Sia, you know what to do. You organize the women to start cleaning up the small stuff. Get back to the owners what you can identify. The men and I will head out to the ranches and homesteads to check on folks. Appears it went west to east."

Hortensia noticed Abigail's eyes. She held her arm and pulled her along. "Come, the rain is letting up. We'll each take a bushel basket and scout around town for anything salvageable, so the owners can claim what's theirs." Hortensia laughed and said, "We'll likely find some of your kitchen in with the horseshoes at the livery."

Abigail struggled forward and hugged the basket Hortensia shoved into her hands.

Chapter Twenty – Seven

Amato Soto rode his horse around the edge of Pridesville. He came to a cantina as dusk edged the horizon. Dismounting and tying his horse in the back of the building, he entered and sat in a corner. As darkness descended, more men entered, and a three-piece band began to play. He got up and ambled toward the men at the bar, listening to them talking. Entering into the conversation, he described the young *gringo* with the smile. A drunk said the man might be the one playing poker the past two nights at the *gringo* saloon.

Amato left the bar by the back and shuffled to the saloon. Light glowed from kerosene lamps through the glass windows, onto the boardwalk and the street. He went to the alley by the building and leaned against a wall in the dark, cradling his swollen right hand, trying to ease the throbbing. Sharp pain stabbed his body if he took a deep breath. Panting short bursts of air, he listened to the laughing, cursing men and the player piano playing the same two songs over and over, "Buffalo Gals," and "Lilly Dale."

He stood in the dark throughout the night. Dawn eased over the horizon. Most of the people in the saloon had left, but not the man he waited for. *Has he been in the saloon? Has he left town? Has he ever been in town?* The questions swarmed in his brain like mad hornets. He jumped when the doors opened, and he saw the man he wanted standing in the light of the doorway. The gun in his left hand felt awkward. He left the dark shadows of the alley. He stepped off the boardwalk and into the street.

"Hey, *gringo* who calls himself Smith, I'm taking you to the sheriff. I'm telling everyone you're a horse thief."

The man stared into the gray light of dawn. "Who's talking crazy? I ain't a horse thief."

"You sold me a horse you stole. You go to jail. I have a gun." Amato raised his left hand. He pointed the pistol at the man with the grin. His hand trembled.

"No one is taking me to jail." The man pointed behind Amato.

"Hey, sheriff, just in time."

Amato turned. An old man approached the leather goods store and stood with a key in his hand. "I ain't the sheriff."

A blast slammed between Amato's shoulder blades. His knees buckled. He fell on his face. Rolling over, he tried to sit up but lay back, gasping and gurgling blood from his mouth. The *gringo* walked up to him with his gun in hand. He put it back into his belt. "Dumb Mex." He sauntered away, sneering.

The old man ran to Amato and bent down to hear the dying man utter, "Eskarne…."

❋ ❋ ❋

Jase reined in Jasper in front of the hotel. He slid off and helped Edmund down. He shouted, "Hotel Buttwill, get out here and help me."

Hiram Buttwill came out. "Well, well! What happened? Was it the tornado? Did it get you? My stars, my stars!"

"Shut up and help me bring him to his room. Soto near killed him and stole his horse."

The men struggled to hold Edmund upright and help him up the stairs. There they eased him onto the bed.

Jase took off his brother's shoes and suit coat. "I saw the jail. Where is the prisoner?"

"He escaped. He got his horse and didn't even saddle him. Kenny saw him ride toward Pridesville," Hotel Buttwill responded.

"Did Clem go after him?"

"No, he and volunteers rode out to the ranches and places where people might be hurt from the tornado. Ain't seen him since."

"Go get Hortensia and see if she will look after my brother. I'm heading out after the prisoner."

Mr. Buttwill left, and Jase removed Edmund's bloodstained shirt. Edmund opened his eyes and focused on his brother.

"Jase, don't go. You said the man had what he thought was a bill of sale. He could be telling the truth."

"Well, he ain't. It's obvious. I'll get him, and maybe I'll even bring him back for trial. You'll need to say you saw him before he hit you. We'll get him hung for sure."

"I didn't see who hit me, and I won't lie. Wait for Clement. Let him arrest the man. You'll kill him if you go. I don't want you killing anyone. I'd rather die first."

Jase could hear in Edmund's voice the strain to speak.

"That's your city ways again. You don't get it yet. He was caught red-handed with your horse and no bill of sale. We don't need any more proof than that. Not out here. Whatever justice we git, we have to git for ourselves. No one else does it for us." Jase studied his brother's quiet face. He had slipped into another deep sleep.

Jase seized the pitcher of water from the stand but found it was empty. He heard footsteps in the hall and looked through the open door.

Abigail stopped in the doorway. The hand holding her veil pulled it down and then fell to her side. She stared at the still form on the bed and the bloody head and shirt. "Is he dead?" Her voice was a whisper. Jason blinked twice when he saw her face. He swallowed hard.

"You're the lady related to Lemuel Baxter, aren't you?"

Abigail gazed at Jason. Her eyes stared without expression. Her mind tried to comprehend what he was saying. She closed her eyes and nodded.

"My brother is hurt. I don't want to leave him until Hortensia gets here. Fill this with water and come right back. Then stay and help Hortensia." Jason held the water pitcher toward her.

She eyed it for a moment before her trembling hands took it. She looked at him, then at Edmund. "Is he going to die?"

"Don't know. Go! Get the water!" Jason shouted the command. Abigail jumped and ran down the stairs to the well.

※ ※ ※

After Hortensia arrived and told Jason he was just in the way, he dashed down the stairs and headed for the jail and then the livery.

Hortensia sorted through the things in the doctor's bag, trying to figure out what could help Edmund. Abigail entered with the water and set the pitcher down on the stand.

"Oh, I'm glad you are here. Have you ever taken care of sick folks?" Hortensia saw Abigail's pale face and shaking hands.

"No. But I've been sick, for a long time."

"Yes, I dare say you know what it is all about. Well, it is up to us for now. We need to do what we can to keep him from catching a killing fever. And hopefully, the crack in the skull won't mean he'll be addled if he does live. I sure don't know. It would be a crying shame if he is. Jason said he didn't know if he saw some of the brain matter or if it was pus and dirt. If he did see the brain, that means bad news for sure."

"Don't say that. He has to get better. He has to. I hate this place so much. I hate it!" Abigail spat out the words.

Hortensia's focus went from Edmund to Abigail and back to Edmund. Abigail's anger registered as shock on Hortensia's face.

"Life happens all over. Doesn't matter where you are, there is life. It never stays good all the time, but it doesn't stay bad all the time. Now, let's put our heads together and see what we can do to keep him with us."

❈ ❈ ❈

Hortensia got up from the straight-back chair as Abigail entered the doctor's room with clean towels and soap.

"Thank you, dear."

"How is he?"

"I think he is better. He isn't restless and dreaming like he was. His eyes open at times. Could you bring some chicken broth? I think he needs some nourishment."

"Yes, I'll make it right away."

"Don't hurry. You look worn out. You stayed with him all night and worked all day. I'll stay tonight."

"No. No, I want to do it. He has done so much for me that it is the least I can do. I am so glad I didn't…ah, didn't leave, and that I'm here to help him."

Hortensia's hand reached over to Abigail's face, brushed a strand of perspiration-matted hair from her forehead, and tucked it under her scarf. "You will make a wonderful wife for some lucky man."

Abigail blanched. "No one would marry me, not with this face."

"You are making more of it than you should. Remember, a way to a man's heart is through his stomach." Hortensia smiled at Abigail.

Abigail thought of her mother and all the times she had said the same thing.

Chapter Twenty – Eight

Jase, waging a battle within, restrained his urge to push Jasper longer and faster. He clenched his teeth and bit the inside of his mouth every hour to ease his frustration when he slowed his horse to a walk or when he dismounted in the shade and gave Jasper water and rest. When he remounted, he put the animal back into a walk, but it wasn't long before he urged his horse into a lope...then without realizing it, they were into a gallop. Jase would wake to Jasper's stress when flecks of foam would fly from his mouth, or his labored breathing huffed in rhythm to his hoof beats.

Hours later, weary, they both entered Pridesville. Jasper plodded with his head down. Jase dismounted at the livery stable and paid two bits to the livery man for a good wash-down and grain feeding for his horse. He glanced around at the stalls and recognized Edmund's saddle and saddlebags. "Where did you get the saddle?"

"Fella brought it in with his own horse and saddle. He wants to sell it."

"A Mexican?"

"No, a man named Smith. Talk to the sheriff if you want it." Jase strode into the sheriff's office, which was bigger than Clement's. He found the man sitting at the desk with his feet up.

"My name is Jase Wilcox, from Wild River ways. My brother was bushwhacked, and his horse and belongings were stolen. The saddlebags are at the livery."

"I know the ones you're talking about. They got DEP carved on them. A fella calling himself Smith left them there. He's wanted for backshooting a man, Amato Soto, who said Smith was a horse thief and had sold him a stolen horse. We also want him for cheating at cards. We found pasteboards in the street where he stood when he shot Amato."

"My brother is Doctor Edmund Proft. Did Smith admit to being a thief?"

"No, but I got a wanted poster on him for two hundred dollars for the killing. I found the ranch name where Soto worked and wired the owner to see what he knew. He wired back that the guy was a hard-working cowhand and hadn't caused any trouble. Not likely he'd be involved in anything crooked. I also found the worn picture of a woman in his pocket. Somebody drew a nice, pretty lady."

Jase took the picture from the sheriff's hand. It had been drawn in pencil and had several smudges but still captured a face of gentle sweetness.

"Can you describe Soto?"

"A regular fella, only his right hand was busted up. The leather shop owner witnessed the killing and said Amato tried to hold his gun with his left hand, but he could tell it was awkward for him. He wouldn't have a chance in a fair fight, I reckon. Still, Smith tricked him into turning his back and shot him."

"Are you going to try, Smith?"

"Yep, we will if we catch him. We don't hold with back-shooting. Think it's the same as murder. He lit out of town. I should notify Soto's next of kin, but I don't know where he lived."

"I do. I talked with him in Wild River." Jase studied the drawing. "I'll take the body to his village, if it's all right."

"I've heard of you. You've a reputation, mostly as good, fair, honest, but a bit too hot-tempered. I figure no one will mind. The body is at the undertaker's."

"It'll be a four-day trip. I'll take his body and horse, plus my brother's possessions."

"Good. Don't envy you a ride in the heat with the body." The sheriff held out his hand, and Jason accepted it.

Jase gathered up Amoto's belongings and headed out of the office, staring at the dark yet animated eyes captured in the picture.

❋ ❋ ❋

Jase led Amato's horse carrying his master's body into the Mexican town of Aqua Prieta. He rode past an adobe church, a mercantile store, a cantina, a feed store, a basket-weaving shop, a pottery shop, and a few houses clustered around the town well. Several adobe houses were scattered along the sides of the road into and out of the town. Aware that people were stopping whatever they were doing and staring at him with a body wrapped in blankets lying over a horse, he squared his shoulders and sat taller.

A man approached Jase's horse and stopped it. He narrowed his eyes and, holding his head high, said, "I am the mayor. What do you want here?"

"Tell me where this man lived. I want to give his body to his family."

The mayor pulled back the blanket and lifted the head. His eyes lost the anger as he said, "First house on the right side of the road as you leave the square."

"Does his family speak English?"

"Yes, *gringo*." Contempt dripped from his voice. "We live close to the border, so it's necessary for us to learn your lingo." He turned and joined a group of people staring at Jase.

Jase headed the horses out of town. He saw the adobe house, where a woman using a hoe worked in a vegetable garden. A young girl sat in the shade, playing with a cornhusk doll and bits of cloth she used as doll clothes. The woman straightened up when she saw Jase and the horses. She left the hoe, came silently to the horse Jase led, and lifted the blanket. She pressed her head against the body.

Jase sat on his horse and listened to her sobs. When she stepped back, he asked, "Where do you want him?"

"The churchyard, *por favor*."

Jase turned the horses around and guided them back to the church.

The woman picked up the girl and followed behind the animals.

※ ※ ※

Jase watched the funeral from a distance. After the simple ceremony, he trailed the woman and child back to their home as he brought the horses.

At the doorway to the shed used for stabling the animals, he said, "My name is Jason Wilcox. I'm from Wild River."

"My name is Eskarne Soto. This is my daughter, Dometa. Thank you for bringing my husband home."

"His saddlebags and saddle are in Wild River. I didn't have time to stop for them."

"Why did he die?"

"He bought a stolen horse, which is now back with the owner. The man who stole the horse has the money your husband paid for it. He's the one who killed Amato."

"Thank you. You and your horse are tired. You can sleep in the stable lean-to."

"I'm partly responsible for your husband's death. You'll not want me to stay here when you hear what I need to tell you."

He saw her intent study of his face.

"Come, sit on the bench by the doorway, and we'll have supper. You can tell me about it. We will see."

"This is a picture of you found in your husband's pocket. It's a fine picture."

"Yes, my Amato drew this himself. He liked to draw. He wanted to become an artist, but there was no way. He did what he could. I will save this and give it to our daughter when she's older to help her know her father."

❋ ❋ ❋

Jase rolled up his bedroll and tied it behind his saddle. He raked out the lean-to. Using the last of the straw, he scattered a thin layer on the dirt floor, wondering whether *Señora* Soto could afford more. He had noticed people coming to Eskarne's one-room adobe house, bringing condolence gifts. Women had brought food; three men had brought a sack of grain.

Last night, they'd sat on the bench and talked until the stars were brilliant. Dometa had fallen asleep in her mother's lap. His face burned with shame as he remembered their conversation. He'd told the *señora* his part in accusing her husband and beating him. She'd closed her eyes, and tears had fallen when he'd recounted his stomping on her husband's hand and breaking it. He'd related what he knew concerning Soto being shot in the back, sensing her anger as her body had stiffened. After he'd told her every detail, they'd sat in silence. He'd decided to saddle Jasper and leave, and then she'd spoken.

"You did not shoot him. It was wrong to beat him, but you made up for it by bringing him home. You can stay the night if you want." With that, she'd gotten up, carried Dometa inside, and closed the door.

He lay awake all night. He went over her words a thousand times as he tossed about on the hay. A thought swirled in his brain: *She loved her husband, and her life will be much more difficult, yet she can forgive me. Would I be able to forgive if Edmund dies?*

He put the rake away when he saw the visitors leave. He washed his hands at the outside washstand and wiped them on his pants. Walking along the side of the hut, he noticed a deep, narrow trench dug in the hard earth with a loom on one side. He remembered seeing women sitting on the edge of the hole with their legs hanging down into it, reaching across to the loom on the other side as they wove their cloth. He realized for the first time the hard work it would be to dig the trench in the rocky soil and the craftsmanship necessary to make the loom. With that, he rounded the corner of the house, took a deep breath, then walked to the open door and removed his hat. Clearing his throat, Jase said, "I've come to say thank you for the supper and the lean-to for the night. I've seen to your horse and cleaned up the stall."

Eskarne stood from her chair by the table. He saw tear streaks on her face and twisted his Stetson. "I'll be leaving now."

A voice behind him said, "Move. I wish to enter and pay my respects to the *Señora*."

He did not like the commanding tone of the man's voice yet felt he needed to say, "Sorry." Jase stepped aside as a short Mexican man entered the dwelling.

"Eskarne, I heard of Amato's death. I am sorry. He was a fine man." The man removed his sombrero.

"Thank you, Iago."

"You will need a husband. Your roof leaks, and you do not have money to feed your daughter. You do not even have money to buy wool for the blankets. I have money. I have admired you for a long time since we were children. I will marry you and be a father to Dometa."

"*Gracias*, Iago. I will think on it. Please, give me a few days, out of respect for Amato."

"Of course. I will talk to you next week." He turned and glared at Jason.

"Iago, this is *Señor* Jason Wilcox. He brought Amato home to us."

"I spoke with him when he first rode in. Good day, Eskarne."

"*Buenos dias.*"

Iago continued to give Jason a hard look as he strutted out the door. Eskarne collapsed in the chair, tears streaming from her eyes. Dometa crawled up in her lap, patting her mother's face. Jase stood in the doorway, wondering, *Should I leave? Should I talk to her? I don't like seeing her cry. This is partly my fault*. Sighing, he thought, *I can't leave like this.*

"*Señora*, I can fix your roof before I leave. And I can sell your husband's saddle and saddlebags in Wild River and bring you the money. It will give you more time."

Eskarne hugged Dometa and gave Jase a smile. "*Gracias, Señor* Wilcox. It would help." "Please, call me Jase."

"*Si,* Jase. You should call me Eskarne, too, for you are now a friend."

"Thank you-ah, I mean *gracias*, Eskarne. I'll get to the roof right away."

"I will make coffee and breakfast. We can eat outside as we did last night."

"*Gracias.*" Jase put his hat on and strode to the back of the adobe hut. Grateful he could do something useful, Jase felt his body relax as he eased into the work.

❈ ❈ ❈

At twilight, the cantina's kerosene lamps burned in the deepening darkness. Village men drifted in and ordered tequila, and the men without wives to cook dinner ordered food prepared by the proprietor's wife. The menu of one item would change from tostada, tamale, enchilada, quesadilla, or frijoles, depending on her whims.

Iago entered and approached the plank bar. The cantina's owner, Ferruco, greeted him and asked what he wanted.

"Tequila and tostada, *por favor*." As Ferruco went to get the food and drink, Iago turned to two men standing at the bar and to the three men sitting at a table playing cards.

"What does that *gringo* want in our village?"

"He brought Amato back. You know that. You were in the square and at the funeral," said one of the men at the table.

"*Si*, Eloy. But, what does he want now? He is not one of us. Why does he stay at the Widow Erskarne's place? It is not right. He should leave. What does he really want?"

"Perhaps to help her. He has been fixing her roof. He sleeps in the lean-to with the horse. I have seen him myself go there at night and come out in the morning. He is doing a kind act," Eloy said.

"Kind act? What *gringos* do you know who try to help us? No, I say he wants something."

"What could he want? We are poor, and Erskare is poor," Jorge said as he leaned against the bar.

"He wants something. He is not a kind *gringo*. There are none. Do you know his name? I know it," growled Iago.

"What is it?" several voices asked.

"It is Jason Wilcox."

The three men got up from the table and joined Iago and the two men at the bar. Ferruco put down a platter of frijoles just as Iago said Jason's name.

"Wilcox. What is he doing here?"

"*Si*. That is what I have been saying. We know he hates all of us. He killed Miguel Miranda in a gunfight just a month ago. His parents told us when they came to sell their vegetables. They said their son was arrested and went to prison for such a small thing as stealing a sack of grain to feed his horse, and then he gets out and is shot down in the street by this Jason Wilcox, the same man who arrested him."

"*Si*," said Ferruco, "but they said it was a fair fight."

"Fair fight! How can it be fair, with Miguel just coming out of prison and not handling a gun for years? He was not a good shooter. He was a small rancher. That is not a fair fight. It is murder!" Iago pounded his fist on the bar.

"Wilcox was arrested," said Jorge. "His parents said so."

"*Si*. And a few days later, he is free. Was there a trial? No! That is not justice." Iago pounded his fist on the bar again. The pan of frijoles and another of tostadas jumped and clattered against the bar.

"What should we do?" Jorge asked as he twisted an empty glass in his nervous fingers.

"I say we watch Wilcox to see what he does. If he goes after anyone in our village, we will know it. If he leaves for the border, we will know and follow him."

"Follow him? Why?" asked Jorge.

"We will stop him and find out what he wants here. It is one thing to deliver Amato, but it is another to hang around at Eskarne's house. It is our duty." Iago lifted his tequila glass.

❊ ❊ ❊

Sipping on hot chicory coffee, Jason gazed into the modest house Eskarne called home. Simple furniture, a small fireplace and hearth with an adobe brick oven at the side for baking bread, and a washstand and shelving built into the wall comprised the main section. A blanket curtain was pulled back in the corner. A clean, made bed with a trundle bed under it filled the space. In one corner of the living area, bright-colored blankets were folded and stacked. Three colorful blankets were hung on the wall. They added a refreshing contrast to the sand-brown adobe brick. The colors were brilliant reds, blues, and yellows, with designs of the moon, lightning, and the sun. He stood when Eskarne came out carrying Dometa and a ball of yarn. Eskarne smiled and gestured with her head to indicate the place next to him, so he slid over on the bench, and she sat down. The little girl's wide brown eyes stared at Jason.

"Jason is the kind man who brought your papa home. Don't be afraid."

Sadness flooded Jason when he heard "'kind." *I'm anything but kind.* Embarrassment drove him to ask, "Did you make the blankets in your house? They are beautiful."

"Yes, I make them the old way, as in the time of my ancestors."

"I didn't know there was an old way. They are lovelier than the ones I've seen in Wild River, yet there are similarities."

Eskarne looked down at Dometa. "Do you want Mama to tell you a story?"

Dometa smiled at her mother. "*Si.* A happy story for *Señor* Jason and me. He looks sad."

Jason turned his face to the side and glanced down to hide his eyes.

"Back in the long days of before, Spider Man loved Spider Woman. He made the first loom for her so she could build a web. The long cross poles, he fashioned of sky and earth cords; the warp sticks were made of sunrays; he formed the batten from a sun halo; and the comb was white shell. The wise Spider Man knew his wife would need four spindles. He honored the North, where zigzag lightning lives, by fashioning a zigzag stick of jade. He made another spindle with a coil of turquoise to represent the South and flash lightning. The West is sheet lightning, so he made the stick of abalone whorl, and to honor the East, where rain streams live, he carved a coil of white shell."

Dometa played with the yarn and giggled.

"Spider Man and Spider Woman were not selfish. They decided to share their secret of web-making with the people. They chose the month of October as the month of black spiders. Then, their children come out of their nests in the world below to teach us how to weave by covering the ground with their webs before returning to the underworld. Before we touch the spindle to do our weaving, we honor the black spiders and Spider Man and Spider Woman. We utter a prayer and offer a sacrifice of precious stone, or eagle feather, or corn pollen. We do this to have good weaving."

Dometa laughed and clapped her hands. Jase grinned. "I've never heard that story."

"It comes down from my great-great-grandmother. She was a Hopi Indian captured by a Navajo raiding party. She married a Navajo and taught the women in the village the Hopi tradition of weaving. The Hopi used only a striped design, but the Navajo people added other shapes to the design to represent the seasons, times of day, and weather. My great-grandmother was Navajo. I learned from her."

"Did you make the blanket hanging on the wall?"

"Yes."

"How did you get the brilliant red?"

"Many years ago, my grandfather brought a cloth from Spain called *bayeta*. I unraveled it and used the red thread. Today, *bayeta* is too expensive, so I make a red dye from a plant, just as I extract the other colors, so the ones I use now are not as bright. But I honor my ancestors' traditions. I make the soft cloth as they did before the Long Walk." "The Long Walk? I've never heard of that."

"Your people call it differently. The *gringo*, your…." Eskarne turned her head and looked away. "Your Colonel Kit Carson led the soldiers in rounding up the Navajo and marching them to Bosque Redondo, a reservation near Fort Sumner, in the place you call New Mexico. Over eight thousand marched for hundreds of miles. Many died on the forced march, and hundreds more died on the reservation. The land was flat and treeless. There was no fuel. The vegetables would not grow, as the land was poor. The water was bad, other tribes raided their settlements, and they did not like the food the army gave them.

Starvation and disease took many lives. It was a hard time for my people. The people were there for four years, and then your General William Sherman was able to convince the Navaho leader Baboncito to accept a treaty, which included the sacred land of the Navaho, Canyon de Chelly. In 1867, the ones who survived were allowed back to their homeland to live on a reservation.

"We are thankful the reservation is on the land of our ancestors and the Canyon de Chelly is part of it. It is sacred to my people, as it is where Spider Woman lives. Those who returned were poor and needed to make cloth quickly. Today, the women make a faster coarse cloth, so it is not fashioned the same as before the Long Walk. I take more time and follow the old traditions with the soft cloth."

"Where do you find the wool?" Jason squirmed. He realized Kit Carson was not a hero to Eskarne.

"I buy the wool from Iago. He raises churro sheep. They survive well in the desert area. Marrying him will give me the wool I need."

"I heard you talking to him. Your voice sounded…reluctant."

"I do not favor him as a husband, but I must do what I can to survive. Dometa and I need to eat. He's stern, but he's honest. He's a widower and lonely."

Tension stiffened Jason's back as Eskarne spoke of marrying Iago. "I have a brother in Wild River. He has friends back East, in a place called Connecticut. If you want, I'll give him a blanket, and he can mail it to one of his friends and perhaps sell it. Other folks in the East might see it and want blankets, too. With money coming in, you could wait longer in deciding, but it will take a few months. His town is a thousand miles from here. It could be a long wait. I can sell your husband's saddle in Wild River. The money should hold you until we know if the blankets sell."

Jase relaxed as he saw relief seep into Eskarne's eyes. *The most beautiful eyes I've ever seen... and a raven's wing can't compare to the gleam in her black hair.*

"*Gracias.* Again, you are kind." She put her hand on Jason's arm. Her smile flashed her white teeth.

❋ ❋ ❋

Jason tied his bedroll to the back of his saddle. The roll was thicker than usual, as he had one of Eskarne's blankets rolled up inside to keep it clean. He mounted Jasper, and Eskarne handed him a canteen of water that he attached to the saddle.

Eskarne spotted Iago and five other men riding down the road at a trot. She picked up Dometa and held her. "Good-bye, *Señor* Jason." Dometa waved her small fingers and smiled at him.

Jason returned the smile. "Good-bye to you, too, little one with a big smile." He addressed Eskarne. "I will sell your husband's saddle and saddle bags and bring you the money as soon as I can. Can you survive till I return? Can you keep from marrying Iago?"

"I will try. It would not be a bad thing to marry him, but I do not wish it. I can wait for a few weeks, perhaps longer with my hope. Good- bye, friend."

Jason touched his hat in parting and started down the road toward the border.

As soon as Jason was out of sight, Eskarne ran into her home and found Amoto's pistol. She carried Dometa as she hurried to the village.

❋ ❋ ❋

Jason sat in the saddle with ease as Jasper lopped down the hard-packed dirt road. Sparse, dry bull muhly grass stretched out on both sides of the trail for miles ahead. An occasional cluster of cottonwood trees broke the line of sight. A mile from the town, a coulee appeared. Jase eased Jasper to the edge, and as the horse stopped to pick his way down to the bottom, men with bandanas covering their faces and rifles in their hands rode up from a bend in the ravine. Jase instinctively signaled Jasper to back away from the edge of the narrow coulee to flat, sure footing. The men surrounded him.

He tensed and resisted reaching for his guns. With rifles aimed at him, he knew he would not have time to draw and get off a shot. He eyed each man and recognized Iago from his sombrero. He saw the nervous, twitching fingers of another man with his rifle aimed at Jason's midsection. He figured that man would shoot in fear without thinking. He was the most dangerous of the lot. Three other men, he could tell, were not used to riding, as they had difficulty controlling their mounts. The horses turned and stepped about with restlessness. Jason knew the men did not realize they were giving the horses mixed signals with their posture and reins.

"What you *hombres* want?"

"What do you want with the widow Eskarne Soto? Why did you stay at her place?" Iago's demanding voice sounded over the confusion of the horses and the riders' unsuccessful attempts at controlling them. "Wanted to help her out, that's all," Jason responded with a quiet voice.

"Jason Wilcox, the hater of Mexicans and Indians, wanting to help a woman part Hopi, Navaho, and Mexican? You lie."

As Iago talked and the men tried to still their horses, Jason plotted his next move. A signal to Jasper to plunge ahead would cause the horses further stress and keep the riders from shooting. If they did shoot, they would likely hit someone else. While Jasper created chaos, Jason would grab his guns and lean partway out of the saddle as he fired to drop the man with the nervous fingers first, then Iago second, followed by as many waylayers as he could before one might get lucky and shoot him. Just as Iago uttered the word "lie," Jason tightened his knees, and Jasper responded by charging ahead to the edge of the coulee, pushing back two horses until their rear legs were over the edge. The horses slid down in a panic, taking their riders with them. Two shots rang out as the rifles tilted upward. Jason had his guns in his hands while the other three horses backed off. Men yelled as they hung on, sliding to the bottom of the ravine and urging their frightened horses back up the clay side. The three other horses were whirling around in circles and bumping into each other, which panicked them further. Before he fired, Jason heard the hard beat of hooves. He glanced around to see if more men were coming to the aid of the others. An approaching rider galloped wildly across the rocky terrain.

Within moments, Eskarne's horse was careening into the pack of standing horses, as she could not rein it to a stop. Jason reached out, grabbed the bit, and pulled back on it before the animal ran over the ravine's edge.

"Eskarne! What are you doing? Are you crazy? You could have been killed!"

Jason put his pistols in his gun belt and held the horse's reins as it danced in the dust.

"I saw these men leave town just before you, and I knew they were up to no good. They never ride out on horses. Their business is in town. And three of these men do not own horses. They borrowed them.

"I took Dometa to the cantina, and Vina is caring for her. I borrowed her husband Ferruco's horse because I knew you would need help."

"I can handle it."

"*Si*. You could kill them all. And then, what would their families do?" Eskarne faced the men. "Why are you after *Señor* Wilcox? He has done nothing to you! And take off those silly bandanas. I know each of you."

The men took down their masks and placed the rifles in their scabbards.

"Iago said Wilcox is an evil man, and we must protect you," Jorge answered.

Eskarne's fierce glare fell on Iago. A long moment of silence lingered in the tension-filled air before she spoke. "You are jealous. You want to marry me, and you are afraid if *Señor* Wilcox helps me I will not need you."

Iago stiffened and looked away.

"I tell you this now, in front of your friends. I will not marry you, whether I get help or not. It is not *Señor* Wilcox's doing. It is yours that has made up my mind. I shall never marry you. Blame no one but yourself." Eskarne took the reins from Jason. "You can go on your way now in peace. These fine, brave men will aid me in my return to town on this wild beast. No one will come after you." She eyed the men. "*Si?*"

"*Si*," they all responded sheepishly.

Jason smiled, touched his hat, and edged Jasper down and out of the coulee. He did not look back, but he heard the horses' hooves as they trotted back in the direction of the town.

"Jasper, that's one sure little spitfire."

Chapter Twenty – Nine

Jason bounded down the hotel stairs, carrying a package. "I'll mail this blanket at the stage depot. Thanks, Edmund, for the letter and address of your friend in Stamford, Connecticut."

Edmund held the railing as he descended the hotel stairs step by step. "I'm glad to help." At the bottom of the staircase, he watched Jason go out the hotel door, then leaned against the desk counter as he made his way to the back hall off the lobby. Opening a door, he stepped into the storage room converted into a kitchen. Abigail was scrubbing a cast-iron Dutch oven. She looked up when he entered and beamed. He noticed she didn't raise her headscarf from her shoulders to hide her face.

"Good to see you up. Please, sit here." Abigail carried a straight-back chair over for him.

He eased himself onto it, keeping his neck stiff. Bending his head brought dizziness and pain. "I've been in my room for two weeks, and I'm bored. I thought I would come down for a visit, seeing as you and Hortensia have attended to me every few hours. That is, if I am not in the way."

"I'd love your company. I'm glad you feel up to it. Here, have a cup of coffee." Abigail poured a cup and handed it to him.

"This is a lot better than Saloon Buttwill's. He says you've brought the hotel and the saloon more business. The word's out on your good cooking. I know I've enjoyed it immensely these past few days. I want to thank you for caring for me. Hotel Buttwill said you sat up the first two nights at my side."

"I'm glad I was able to do whatever I could. Hortensia and Sabilla were the biggest help."

"That may be, but I'm very glad you were present. You were the one I would have chosen."

Abigail felt her face burn. She searched for something to say. "I appreciate your convincing them to hire me. I've been busy every day, with the people coming through on the stage. Whether or not they stay at the hotel, they want to eat. The townspeople enjoy it, too. People have been kind."

"I hope the work hasn't been too hard for you. You're stuck in this hot kitchen in the summer heat. I don't want you to get sick."

"Don't worry. I do the stove work in the early morning, beginning at four or five. It's finished by nine. During the day, I clean the kitchen and the tables, including the ones in the saloon, before it opens at noon."

"Are you responsible for ridding the tables of flies?"

"That was easy. I put out bowls containing powdered black pepper, brown sugar, and cream. The flies disappear." Her face was radiant. "The two Buttwills are discussing adding a room on to the saloon for the ladies to eat, where liquor is not served. They'll have their own door through the hotel. And the Buttwills pay Kenny two and a half cents a week to chop the wood and carry in the water I need for the day. A big help." Abigail brushed a strand of hair from her eyes with the back of her wet hand.

"I bet Kenny is happy to add to his penny collection." Edmund chuckled.

"Yes, and he told me a Mexican couple, the Mirandas, grow vegetables. They've been taking them across the border to Mexico to sell, but Kenny set it up for them to come by the kitchen so I can buy what I want. It's good for everyone. Here, have a dish of apple roly-poly."

"Thank you. I'll pay for it."

"I should say not! It's my treat. I'm glad you're getting better."

"Yes, I think I'll be able to see patients today, as I'm thinking clearly now. Next week, I'll be up to riding out to treat people. But, I'm not camping out. I've learned my lesson."

"What a relief. Hortensia will be glad to hear it, too. I'll tell her when I see her. Sabilla comes every day to check on you, too. We visit for a bit. We're going to set up a laundry area, and once a month we'll wash linens for the townsfolk and the hotel guests, to earn money." Abigail dropped her voice to a whisper. "We might get Hotel Buttwill to change the blankets on the beds more than twice a year, maybe even use sheets and pillowcases. That would be nice for the guests."

"Will you use the money to buy your ticket home?" Edmund lifted the fork of poly to his mouth and slid it in.

"I was thinking of leaving." Abigail thought *Leaving forever* as the picture of the rafter beam flashed through her mind. I've...I've decided to save what I earn. I'll stay here, where I can support myself. I don't want to go home and try to find work. I think I might be useful here and the work takes my mind off the...the unpleasant things." She thought a glint of relief flashed in Edmund's eyes. She watched him lick his lips as he savored his poly. Abigail scrubbed hard on the Dutch oven as a smile settled on her face. "Oh, my bread!" She opened the oven door and, using a rag, pulled out two loaf pans. She turned the pans upside-down over the ashbin under the stove. The two brown loaves disappeared. "They will cool slowly, now." Her smile deepened.

"Are you going this Sunday to the service?"

"No, I'd be too uncomfortable. People would stare."

"I don't think people will stare once they become accustomed to you. They'll see your personality, not one side of your face. Folks will notice your lustrous brown hair with flecks of gold in the sunlight. And no one has lovelier eyes than you do. No one."

"I don't know what to say. No one has ever said "

"I think you should forget the scarf. Let your hair and eyes shine."

"Hey, Doc, Mr. Hanson wants to see you in the lobby." Hotel Buttwill stuck his head in the door. "His wife needs you."

"Be right there. Thanks for the roly-poly. Let's count on going together on Sunday. All right?"

"Yes." Abigail felt her face flush.

Edmund left, and she hummed, "Kiss Me Quick and Go," as she picked up a cast-iron spoon.

Lord, maybe you let me live not as a punishment for disobedience, but to be here now, living happily as I am. Thank you, God. Could it be, you took some bad things you didn't want to happen, and turned them into blessings?

✳ ✳ ✳

Jase left the Overland Stage Depot after mailing Eskarne's blanket and marched down to the livery stable. "Hey, Sam."

"Yeah." Sam came to the corral gate, leading a sorrel by the halter.

"You got Soto's saddle?"

"Sure. Right there, hanging over one of the stall walls. You want it?"

"How much can you sell it for? The widow needs the money."

"Not much, for sure. It's worn and beat- up. Maybe five dollars."

"She needs more. How about my saddle? What can you get for it?"

"Yours? You don't want to sell that. It's worn, but you got that fancy scrollwork carved in it. You keep it in good shape, and you need it."

"I'll use Soto's. It's good enough. What can you get for mine?"

"At least twenty, maybe more. I can display it in the hotel lobby, and folks coming in on the stage will see it. Might sell faster that way. You sure you want to do this?"

"Get the money to me as soon as you can, so I can take it to Soto's widow and little girl. And sell his saddlebags, too." Jase turned and strode up the street.

Sam watched Jason's back as he departed. He shook his head and said out loud to himself, "I'd never believe it, except I heard it from his own mouth. Lord, be." Sam grinned as he guided the sorrel through the gate to the stall.

※ ※ ※

"Cousin."

Abigail stiffened. She turned and stared out the open back door. Otis stood in the doorway, his hat in his hand. Abigail's hand shook as she laid the spoon on the worktable. She picked up a butcher knife.

"Why are you here, Otis?" She approached the doorway. "You're not coming in."

"I heard you were working as a cook. I got me a wife. Had to go all the way to Lester's Peak. She's fifteen. Her name is Sally. Her folks had a passel of young'uns. She's used to hard work, and she can cook. I love the way she laughs, and her eyes are filled with devilment." Otis leaned forward and looked around. He whispered,

"She back talks. I don't know what Pa will say if she does it to him, and I know she will. Pa might take the strap to her." Otis edged closer to Abigail. She backed up another step. "Sally's my wife. Do you think I should stand between her and Pa and protect her?"

Abigail noted the worry etched on Otis's face. "Yes, I do. If he goes after *your* wife, you need to protect her. Protect her from all danger as best you can. Cleave to your wife."

"Is that what 'cleave' means? I've never known."

"I think it does, and not to go after other women. Would you take a strap to her if she talks back to you?"

"Heck no. I'd be afraid. She's little, but she's strong. She can chop a cord of wood in no time. She'd likely hit me back and break my jaw.

She can back talk me all she wants. I'll tell Pa she can run the house, and he can run the ranch. I reckon that's fair. Don't you?"

"Great, Otis. My best wishes to your bride. I hope she likes it at the ranch." Abigail tried to close the door.

"Wait, that ain't why I'm here." "Why, then?"

"I was bragging to Sally about what Silas and me done to you, and she said I had to come in and apologize. She says it was wrong to take a woman when she don't want it. So, I come to do what Sally said. I apologize."

"Thank you. Good-bye." Abigail's hand with the knife shook as she tried to close the door again.

Otis stuck his foot in and grabbed the door. "I gots to tell you, we met Silas at the edge of town. He's camped by the trees at the north end, out of sight. He doesn't want folks to know he's around. He heard he didn't kill the doc when he stole his horse."

"That was Silas?" Abigail interrupted.

"Yeah. And later, he killed that Mex over in Pridesville, the one Jason beat up. Silas prowls around town at night, searching for the doctor. He aims to kill him and leave without anyone suspecting he was in town. He's coming in right before sundown, hoping to spot him alone."

"Why? Edmund--I mean, Dr. Proft--didn't see who hit him."

"Silas knows that, but he blames Jase for Pa kicking him off the ranch, and he wants to get even."

"Why did Uncle send Silas away?" Abigail interrupted again.

"It's a long story. He thinks he cain't likely get Jase, but he figures he can kill the doctor real easy. My Sally and I want kids, so we don't want the doctor killed. I figured you could warn him, and Jase, too."

"Yes, I will. And…." Abigail swallowed hard as she closed the door. Just before she snapped it shut, she said, "Thank you, Otis."

❋ ❋ ❋

Abigail raced to the hotel lobby. "Mr. Buttwill, is Dr. Proft in his room?"

Buttwill stared at her face as her scarf lay on her shoulders. "Ah… no. John Hanson brought his wife to town. She's in labor. They're at Clement and Hortensia's."

Abigail hurried out the hotel door and down the boardwalk, oblivious to the stares of people as she flew by. She saw Clement, Hortensia, Jase, and Edmund standing at the door of Clement's house.

"Good work there, brother. The baby didn't want to come proper-like," Jase said.

"Yep, the ma and baby owe their lives to you, Doc," Clement said as he offered his hand.

Edmund shook his hand and glowed. "It's a good feeling to deliver babies."

Abigail ran to the gathering.

"Abigail, what's wrong?" Hortensia asked.

She panted and held her side. Taking a deep breath, she gripped Edmund's arm and blurted, "Silas Baxter is out to kill you to get even for something Jase did. Otis told me."

"Where is he?" Jase's voice carried an iron edge.

"He's camped nearby, but I don't know where." *Can he tell I'm lying? Edmund might not want him to know, but Jase started the trouble somehow. He should handle it.* She glared at Jase. "He's hiding. He's coming in at sundown. I wanted to warn Edmund to stay out of sight. Silas might give up and go away."

"Jase, let Clem handle this." Edmund eyed his brother.

"Yeah, Jase. I can handle it," Clement seconded.

Jase glanced at Clem. "You can't face Silas. He's younger and faster. I'll get him. Pass the word around town. The first person who sees Silas should tell him he can clear out and not come back, or I'll meet him in the street. His choice. But this is between him and me. He's to leave Edmund out of it." Jase clamped his teeth together, turned, and strode off toward the livery.

"He's a hothead." Clem shook his head. "He's right, though. Silas is better than me. Most everyone is."

"Clem, I'll stop Jase. I don't know how, but I must. I'll worry about Silas later. You can find me at the hotel." Edmund trudged back into Clem's house to gather his belongings.

"Thanks, Miss Lester, for coming and letting us know. Hortensia, you staying and helping Mrs. Hanson?"

"No, dear. She has plenty of that. I see Sabilla and Clara in front of the general store. I'll hop over there and tell them about the baby." Hortensia headed toward the store as Clem turned and hastened toward his office.

Abigail watched Hortensia and the women have a brief exchange of words, and then they scattered in different directions. She felt the tears run down her face. She stood alone. Feeling helpless, she walked to the hotel, letting her scarf flutter around her shoulders.

❈ ❈ ❈

Hortensia went down the street, but instead of staying on the boardwalk, she darted between the buildings, searching among the piled boxes, crates, a grazing cow, chickens pecking in the dirt, and then the next alleyway.

Sabilla, behind the sheriff's office and then the general store, spotted Hortensia and rushed over to her. "Have you seen anything?"

"No. You?'

"No," Hortensia sighed. "Some ladies down at the other end of the street said they would send for us if they found him. Maybe we should try scouting around the livery stable?"

"Yeah, let's," Sabilla agreed.

Abigail ran from the backdoor of the kitchen area of the saloon.

"Hortensia!"

The two ladies stopped as Abigail hastened toward them. "You have to get Clement to stop Silas."

"We are working on it, dear. Come and help us search."

"You don't understand. Silas is dangerous. He attacked the doctor and took his horse. Then he went to Pridesville and killed the Mexican man who was accused as the doctor's attacker. He'll kill Dr. Proft, anyone, everyone." Her voice held a ragged sob.

"Dear, you go back to the hotel and calm down. We will take care of things here. Maybe Silas will come to the kitchen if he knows you're there. I'm going to get Clement and tell him to keep a look-see at the back of the hotel. We've got to find him fast, before someone gits killt."

Chapter Thirty

Edmund marched to the hotel. "Buttwill, round up your brother while I locate John at the general store. We need to meet at Sam's place."

Hotel Buttwill asked, "What for?"

"Do it!" Edmund took quick steps to the general store, and within minutes, the four men met at the livery, where Clement joined them.

"What's up? This is peculiar. Mighty peculiar if you ask me. I say, what you want us here for, Doctor?" Hotel Buttwill asked.

"Hiram, close your mouth, and let the doctor speak," Buster Buttwill admonished him.

The men's voices all echoed the thought: "What do you want of us, Doctor?"

"We need to band together and find Silas. I realize now that I can't stop Jason from killing Silas or getting killed unless we arrest Silas. If we all have guns and confront him, he will give up, and Clement, you can arrest him and hold him until we get this figured out, so no one gets killed."

"I ain't got a jail. Where would I put him?"

"Yeah, Doc. Besides that, just because we all have guns when we find Silas, it don't mean he will give up. He's just as likely to shoot his way out, killing most if not all of us. I don't put that past him at all-- I sure don't," Buster said with worry.

"Doctor Proft, I'm all for stopping the killings, but I'm not handy with a gun. Neither are these men, except for Clement, and like he's said, he is slowing up. Silas knows all this. He won't be taking any risk at all shooting his way clear and still going after you if you did get away, which I doubt," John Platt reasoned.

Clement put his gnarled hand on the doctor's shoulder. "Look, I'm going to do my best to find Silas, and if I can get a drop on him with my rifle, maybe he'll give up and I'll find a place to lock him up. But durned if I know where that would be. These men are right, though, Doc. They ain't no hands with a gun. Silas sees them totin' fire arms, and he'd know for sure he had the upper hand. No, the best thing is for me to get to Silas before he gets to Jason or t'other way around."

"I can't just do nothing. I have to act. Life is hard enough without everyone shooting each other."

"Doc, you just delay your brother as long as you can. Give us a chance to find Silas. That would help us a mighty lot," Clement said.

"I'll try."

The men left the barn as Edmund watched them. *How can I stop Jase?*

※ ※ ※

Word spread like wildfire through the town. The air felt laden with tension. Abigail dropped and spilled everything she touched; she jumped at the slightest sound and kept looking out the back door of the kitchen. Saloon Buttwill cursed out two customers for missing the spittoon and hitting the dirt floor. Hotel Buttwill prattled nonstop like a steam engine chugging. Jase cleaned his gun at the gunsmith's. Kenny scoured the areas behind buildings to find Silas. Edmund set his doctor's bag on a chair in the hotel lobby and paced the floor. Hortensia and Sabilla peered behind the shops and down the alleys, chatting with ladies they met. They would nod and disperse in various directions. Clem sat in his office, sullen and silent, until Hortensia yanked him out of his chair and up to the back of the hotel. At dusk, Kenny scurried into the hotel. "Doc, I found Silas and gave him Jase's message. He said he wasn't backing down from anyone."

"Don't tell Jase."

"I already did. He told me to. Jase is coming up the street from the livery. Silas said he is going to come from the other end of town. Might hide behind a building. Wouldn't put it past him. Jase didn't want me to tell you, but I told Clement, and he said to pass it on to you."

"Where's Clement?"

"Don't know. His missus pulled him out of his office and up the street. Reckon they went home. She's mighty skeered old Clem will get killt by Silas."

Edmund stared out the hotel window. He glared at his bag. "Thanks, Kenny. Go home right away." Kenny bolted out the door.

Edmund opened his bag and took out his pistol. He hadn't touched it since he had spent a week with Jase at the ranch. It felt awkward and heavy in his hand. He moved to the doorway and stared up the street.

Horses, men, women, children, and a few dogs walked in the heat of the late afternoon. Edmund stepped out the doorway and onto the boardwalk, carrying the Colt .45, pointing it to the ground. A few people glanced his way and picked up their pace to pass by him as their voices lowered. An unseen message shot through the air like a lightning bolt, and the boardwalk became deserted.

Edmund scrutinized the street all the way from the hotel to the stable at the far end. A few horses stood, tied at hitching posts, as dust devils swirled around them. The sun's heat beat down and blasted up from the hard-packed dirt. Edmund felt flattened by the two forces.

His stomach churned, sweat poured down his back, and his legs shook with tremors. His eyes searched the dusty haze for Silas. *If I can stop him, maybe I can keep Jase out of this.*

A wind gust blew the sign hanging from short chains above the harness shop. Edmund heard the creak and turned. Jase appeared on the boardwalk below the sign. He walked toward the other end of town.

"Jase, stop!" Edmund shouted.

"I got something to do. We'll talk later."

"No! Let Clement deal with Silas."

"He can't, and you know it."

"Then I'll deal with him. It concerns him and me, not you," Edmund called back.

"You can't, and you know it."

Edmund raised his gun. He aimed it at Jase's left side. "I'm not going to let you do this."

Jase stepped off the boardwalk and into the street. He marched toward Edmund.

"I mean it, Jase. I want your gun." Edmund stepped off the boardwalk. He took two steps into the street and stopped.

Jason halted and squinted into the sun.

Edmund watched his brother's expression change from a look of disbelief to a hard and determined grimace. He noticed Jase's jaw muscles tense and his eyes focus on the Colt .45 in his two hands as he held it straight out from his chest, pointing at Jase.

"Edmund, don't come any farther. Stay there." Jase sidestepped, drew his gun, and fired.

※ ※ ※

Edmund staggered back as he felt Jase's bullet graze his leg just above the ankle. His finger jerked. Noise erupted from his Colt. He stared at it, looked up, and met Jase's eyes. Shaking his head, he dropped his gun and kicked it. "Jase, I'm sorry " The rest of the words caught in his throat as he blinked in disbelief.

Jase closed his eyes and went down on his knees, twisting to the side, where he lay in the street, his gun in his hand.

People streamed from shops. They gathered around Jason. "Is he dead?"

"Yeah, I think so. His own brother, too."

"I don't believe it."

Edmund ran through the crowd, tearing his way to Jase's side. Kneeling beside the body, he felt for a pulse in the neck. He turned Jason onto his back. Blood soaked his shirt and pooled on the ground; more blood seeped from his lips.

Edmund closed his eyes as tears wet his lashes.

"Brother," Jase whispered.

Edmund opened his eyes. "It was an accident. I didn't mean it. I didn't want to kill you." His voice pleaded in anguish as his tight throat choked. "Oh, God, I'm sorry."

"Heck, I know it. You can't hit what you aim at." Jase sucked in air as pain flashed across his face. "Promise me you'll remember I knew it was an accident. Promise."

"I promise."

"This dying is getting to hurt fierce. I kinda wish it wasn't in the dirt, in front of folks, but I reckon it's all I deserve." Jase started to take a breath, but it escaped from his mouth as his eyes closed.

Edmund stared at his brother. Sobs shook his shoulders as his hands lay still on his knees.

❋ ❋ ❋

Clement, Sabilla, and Hortensia jumped with a start when shots blasted the air.

"We missed him. He got by us. Likely, the doctor is dead. Can't see him winning no fight with Silas." Sabilla shook her head.

"I'll go see what happened. T'ain't likely if Jase and Silas were the ones to meet up that Silas is a problem anymore. I'll check it out while you and the ladies keep looking for the scoundrel." Clement scrambled off to the main street.

Half a minute later, he came around the corner of the hotel, then stopped and stared at the scene. "Lord Almighty!"

Clement shuffled up to Edmund, took him by the arm, and pulled him up. "Carry Jase to the doc's room in the hotel," Clement instructed the men in the crowd.

Edmund stared as Saloon Buttwill and others lifted Jase, his head dangling, and plodded to the hotel. Buttwill kicked a headless, writhing rattlesnake out of the way.

"Come on, Doctor. You got work to do. You got to do what you can to make things easier for him." Clement pushed Edmund forward.

At the hotel, Edmund grasped his bag by the door and followed the men up the stairs. They laid Jase on the bed, wiped Jase's blood from their hands, onto their clothes. Jase's shirt was soaked. Short, gasping sounds wheezed from his chest.

"Get out! Everyone!" Edmund pushed the men out the door.

Hotel Buttwill stood in the doorway. "Doc, let us know if we can do anything."

"Get out!" Edmund shouted again, slamming the door.

※ ※ ※

"Wait. That couldn't be Silas shooting. There he is, leaving the back of the livery corral and heading for the outhouse. You go get Sam with his shotgun and Clem. Bring them here. I'll watch Silas."

"Hortensia, not by the privy. That don't seem right, you know what I mean."

"Sabilla, we ain't got time for niceties. We got to take care of this mess the men can't get right. Get Sam and Clement now!" Hortensia marched toward the outhouse. By the corral she stooped and picked up a plank of wood that lay where the tornado had flung it.

Sabilla raced off to find Sam, who she hoped would be near his livery, but she steeled herself to run all the way to the center of the town where the gunshot had been heard. "Men, instead of taking care of their business, run off to see the excitement like little boys."

※ ※ ※

Edmund slumped on the chair. His hair, matted to his face, dripped with sweat. His bloody hands lay in his lap. He didn't notice his clothes splattered with deep crimson stains. Jase's shirt lay on the floor. The stench of blood hung heavy in the stifling air. He heard several gunshots coming from some place below. *I don't care who got killed. I'm not running out there to help. These people are beyond civilized help. They can kill each other, for all I care. I have to go home to sanity in Stamford.*

He scrutinized his brother's pale face. He reached over and felt Jase's ice-cold hands, pulled a blanket over him. *How did I get sucked into this madness?*

A voice, husky and low, said, "Brother."

"Yes, Jase."

"Am I gonna cross the river?"

Edmund guessed his brother's meaning. "I don't know. The bullet broke ribs and a piece of bone, and it was wedged against your lungs. It will take time, but I think you will heal. This is the first time I took out a bullet. It's new territory for me."

"Why is my mouth sore?"

"You bit the inside of your cheek when you fell." *If I told Jase he was dying, he'd have accepted it as if I were talking about the wind. Life and death are simple facts to him.*

"I was your first patient in town and now your first bullet wound. I'm getting tired of being first. I wouldn't mind being second or third."

"I'll remember. Jase, I didn't mean to shoot. It was an accident."

"I understand. Remember your promise. Don't worry."

"Why did you move left? I aimed to your left. I thought you would stand still like you did when you went against Miranda."

"I had to get a clear shot at the rattler." "What rattler?"

"The one slithering out from under the loose boards when you stepped off the boardwalk. You made it angry, and it was coming up behind you. I figured you were wearing those low-cut city boots and could get bit. I saw I hit it before I went down. Next time, aim for me, and you'll miss."

"There won't be a next time. I've decided I don't belong here. I thought I could stay, but it's impossible. I'm going back to Stamford as soon as you're well."

"Now, you're talkin' sense. In ten or twenty years, it will be your time to live here. I have to go against Silas as soon as I am able, or he'll be a threat hanging over my head." Jase held up his hand. "I like knowing I've got a brother."

Edmund took his hand. "Me, too." He cleared his throat. "I'm going out in the hall. Get some sleep."

He closed the door behind him and staggered halfway down the steps to the lobby. His legs gave out and he sat down. He put his head in his hands.

The bell above the hotel door jingled. Clem led a mob into the lobby. "Is he dead?"

"No."

"Good, Doc," Clement said.

Edmund got to his feet up as the crowd pushed past him to his room.

"Come on, Doc. You got to hear this!" Clement called back.

Edmund eased his way through the crowd around the bed. Jase tried to get his elbow under him to push himself up to a sitting position but fell back instead. "Clem, what do you and these folks want? Has anyone seen Silas?"

"Good news we got for you, Jase." Clem and Hortensia stood beside the bed as the crowd continued to fill the room. "Hortensia organized the ladies to fan out over the town, searching for Silas. They figured he wouldn't suspect womenfolk spying on him. And sure enough, Hortensia saw him go into the town privy by the stables right after your brother shot you. He likely figured you were dead. Hortensia got a wood plank and barred the door. She alerted Sam, and he stood watch with his shotgun. She came lickety-split for me and my shotgun. Well " Clem laughed and slapped his thigh. "When Silas couldn't get out the privy, he tried shooting his way out. He had a hole in the door by the time his ammunition ran out. When he saw Sam and me with our shotguns on him, he gave up right smart, and we locked him up pronto."

"Where? The tornado leveled the jail!" Jason wheezed.

"The safest place in the whole town. Our storm cellar. There is no way out except the door, and we locked that good, and dragged the branch onto it again. He ain't goin' nowhere unless he digs himself out, and that would take weeks. And he ain't got that long." Clement beamed in satisfaction.

"Why?"

"Cuz I wired the Sheriff in Pridesville. He wired back he'd come and pick up Silas tomorrow and bring the reward money."

"Why did you wire Pridesville? What's he wanted for?" Jason wheezed.

"Didn't you hear? He stole the doc's horse and killed Soto. We agreed you'd get the reward money, two hundred dollars."

Jason's pale face seemed to blanch whiter. "He killed Amato and attacked Edmund?"

"Yep."

"Are you sure?"

Abigail, standing at the back of the crowd, pulled her scarf over her face and inched forward. "May I say something, please?"

People moved aside, murmuring, "Make room for Miss Lester. That's the cook. Make way."

She advanced to Jason's bedside and stood next to the doctor.

"Otis came to the back of the hotel. Told me Silas confessed that he was the one to attack the doctor and later shot the man you thought stole the doctor's horse. I believe Otis. I think he might testify against Silas at the trial, but Clement doesn't think he will need to, as the Pridesville sheriff says he has enough witnesses to convict him." Her voice cracked.

Jason stared at her.

She turned her head, so the scarred side of her face was away from him.

"Thank you for telling me. I know it must be hard to speak ill of your cousin."

"Yes, of course." Abigail edged her way to the back of the crowd.

"I think *Señora* Soto should get the money. I'll take it to her as soon as I can travel. I've been curious as to how she and her daughter are doing anyway. Thanks, Clem. I'm beholden to you, Hortensia, and everyone in Wild River." Jase held his hand out to Clem. "If something happens and I can't go, I know you'll get it to her."

Clem shook his hand. "Sounds good to us, don't it, folks?" Heads nodded, and in murmurs, the group agreed. Hortensia smiled.

"It ain't all, Jase. We, the town, want you to be sheriff."

Jase examined the faces of the men and women. "You're the sheriff, Clem."

"I can't do the job. I'm gonna get myself killed, and who will look after Hortensia?"

"But, what will you do? How will you live?"

"Hortensia and I got it all worked out. We'll go to your ranch, tend to the stock, and make whisky and beer. We can build up the herd a mite. Sam said Kenny could come and help at the ranch. He can do what my old bones can't. We'll show him ranch work, and he's real good with the animals. He can still chop wood and haul water for Miss Lester. He'll make enough money to live on."

"But Sam needs Kenny's help at the livery."

"Don't worry, Jase. He says he thinks *Señor* Miranda will come in from his place and help him, to earn extra cash money."

Anxiety roiled up in Edmund. "Clem, I'm not sure this idea is good for Jason."

"Hey, brother, I decide for myself. You don't need to look out for me. You're high tailing it back to Connecticut." Jason's wheezing cough forced him to quit speaking.

Before Edmund could respond, Hortensia moved forward and perched on the edge of Jason's bed. She picked up Jase's hand and held it in hers. "He's right, Jase. You've got to admit, you think you are a one-man show. Eli and Wilma taught you the best they could so you could look out for yourself, but times are changing. More people are coming out West now, with the war over, and the town needs able leaders, ones who can use their minds to solve the problems, not just their fists or guns. We watched you grow up, and we know you are as capable as the next fella." Hortensia rubbed Jason's hand and squeezed it. "We want you to exercise your good sense. Clement and I figure you should have help. No single-handed gunfights. You have to promise to not use your fists or gun unless you ain't got no other choice. Anything you hear about that needs a sheriff, you have to talk about it with Sam or Saloon Buttwill first, leastways until you get on to this new way of doing things We know if you give your word to stop and think before you do something drastic like, you'll keep it." Hortensia patted Jase's hand and gazed into his intent and misting eyes. "If we ladies can corral Silas and get him locked up without firing a shot, can't see no reason you can't use your smarts, too."

Hortensia grinned.

Clement pounded his right fist into his left hand. "And you got to ask the judge for books on the law, which you got to read. If you give us your word, we know you will keep it."

Clement pulled Sam and Saloon Buttwill toward the front of the crowd. "Right?"

"Right. This town is beginning to grow, and we're going to work together," Sam spoke up.

Several voices agreed.

Jason cleared his throat. "I'm to be the sheriff by committee?" His voice didn't hide his skepticism and disapproval.

"Yep. Hortensia and the womenfolk showed us we need to use our brains and work together," Clement answered.

"I'll try it, for a while, but I ain't sure it will work. With you and Hortensia living at my ranch, am I going to be living at your place?"

"Nope. Hortensia, you tell him. You're good at explaining things." Clem placed his hand on Hortensia's shoulder.

"The ladies and I are going to fix up the back room behind the jail once the town rebuilds it, make it into presentable sleeping quarters. The menfolk are building a bed frame, and the ladies are going to provide a goose-down mattress and pillow. We'll supply it with a sheet and blanket, and Hotel Buttwill is going to donate a heat stove for winter."

"What are you doing with your house?" Jase tried again to prop himself up on his elbow but failed, dropping backward onto the bed.

"Doc...." Clem turned to Edmund. "We ain't left you out. The house is yours as long as you want it. You can use the front room as your office."

"But I've decided to go home. I can't live here. I nearly killed my own brother. I just can't live this life."

Several voices murmured dissent, and a few said a loud, "No."

"Edmund, we're counting on you. More people are moving here. We need a doctor. You have to stay." Hortensia got up from sitting on the bed and took hold of Edmund's arm to stare into his eyes. "You have to stay, or none of these other plans will mean anything." She surveyed the crowd for approval.

Voices chimed in with, "We need you, Doctor."

"You have to stay."

"What will we do without you?"

Edmund heard the imploring tone. Hortensia reminded him of the day long ago when he was fourteen and his mother had held his hand and assured him of his parents' love and his importance to them. The silence that filled the room as people waited for his answer intensified the buzzing of flies and the oppressive heat. He scrutinized the men's and women's faces. His eyes rested on a face at the back of the crowd, by the door. Abigail stood with her scarf hanging loose about her shoulders. He saw her eyes, dark and wet, her lower lip trembling. He saw her lips mouth the words, "Please, stay." Colleen's face flashed into his thoughts, and he remembered the desperation in her eyes. It was the same desperation in Abigail's.

Edmund studied Hortensia, then Jase as he shook his head. "If Jase can promise to work with others, I guess I could stay and try for a month or two. But I can't promise more than that." A cheer exploded from the crowd; hard slaps pounded on his back from the men as the women applauded. He glanced at Abigail. The radiance he saw in her flooded him with comfort he'd never felt before. He beamed back at her.

The crowd looked at Abigail and cheered, "Hurray for Miss Lester!"

Epilogue

Edmund put down the ink pen and blotted the letter. He read:
"Dear Elizabeth,
"Your son Ethan did not die with Garrett. He is Jason Ethan Wilcox and has just completed one year as sheriff of Wild River, New Mexico Territory. He has met a wonderful woman, Eskarne. You might find it humorous to see how shy he becomes around her and the difficulty he had in working up the courage to ask her to marry him. He is a good husband and stepfather to her charming girl, Dometa. Jason repaired the cradle Garrett made, and someday it may rock his own child.

"I, your son Edmund, whom you sheltered from the cold with your body, was found by a wonderful couple and raised in Connecticut. I became a doctor and, after both of my second parents died, came to Wild River, where I found my brother.

"I thank you for the journal you wrote. It has been a connection, even a lifeline, for Brother Jason and me. I shall put this letter in the back of the journal you began and will begin a new journal for my children to read someday.

"Your grateful son, "Edmund Proft."

Edmund folded the paper and tucked it into the back of Elizabeth's journal, behind the paper Cecilia had written. He stood and placed it on the bookcase with his medical books. He sat down again and opened a new, leather-bound book of blank pages hand-stitched together by Abigail. He wrote on the inside cover: "This journal is written by Dr. Edmund Proft, son of Elizabeth and Garrett of Wild River, raised by Cecilia and Michael Proft of Connecticut, and married to Abigail Lester of Ohio."

On the first blank page, he recorded, "Abigail and I have a beautiful baby girl named Elizabeth, who was born in Wild River, New Mexico Territories, this day of...."

Printed by Libri Plureos GmbH in Hamburg, Germany